***Notorious Neal Sheridan was not at all what Colleen had expected.***

Which made him dangerous.

She'd met more ladies' men than she could count. But they all had one thing in common. They knew how hunky they were.

Neal didn't seem to have any idea just how broad his shoulders were. Or how his smile made a woman tingle inside. And take last night when they'd kissed. He'd kissed her like a starving man being offered a banquet.

Given his reputation, that didn't make sense.

It all had to be part of his deviousness, Colleen decided. Neal hadn't gotten his rep by being only as good as most men at seduction. He had to be *better* than most. Better than them *all*. *That* was how he disarmed even the most determined of women.

Of course, notorious Neal had not yet *begun* to contend with Colleen....

were sacred icons. This was all an act. A damn good one, she

Dear Reader,

At long last, summertime has arrived! Romance is in full bloom this month with first-time fathers, fun-filled adventure—and scandalous love.

In commemoration of Father's Day, award-winning Cheryl Reavis delivers this month's THAT'S MY BABY! *Little Darlin'* is a warm, uplifting tale about a cynical sergeant who suddenly takes on the unexpected roles of husband—and father!—when he discovers an abandoned tyke who couldn't possibly be his...or could she?

In these next three books, love defies all odds. First, a mysterious loner drifts back into town in *A Hero's Homecoming* by Laurie Paige—book four in the unforgettable MONTANA MAVERICKS: RETURN TO WHITEHORN series. Then fate passionately unites star-crossed lovers in *The Cougar*— Lindsay McKenna's dramatic finish to her mesmerizing COWBOYS OF THE SOUTHWEST series. And a reticent rancher vows to melt his pregnant bride's wounded heart in *For the Love of Sam* by Jackie Merritt—book one in THE BENNING LEGACY, a new crossline series with Silhouette Desire.

And you won't want to miss the thrilling conclusion to Andrea Edwards's engaging duet, DOUBLE WEDDING. When a small-town country vet switches places with his jet-setting twin, he discovers that appearances can be *very* deceiving in *Who Will She Wed?* Finally this month, *Baby of Mine* by Jane Toombs is an intense, emotional story about a devoted mother who will do *anything* to retrieve her beloved baby girl, including marry a handsome—dangerous!—stranger!

I hope you enjoy these books, and each and every story to come!

Sincerely,

Tara Gavin
Senior Editor & Editorial Coordinator

---

Please address questions and book requests to:
Silhouette Reader Service
U.S.: 3010 Walden Ave., P.O. Box 1325, Buffalo, NY 14269
Canadian: P.O. Box 609, Fort Erie, Ont. L2A 5X3

# ANDREA EDWARDS

## WHO WILL SHE WED?

SPECIAL EDITION®

Published by Silhouette Books
America's Publisher of Contemporary Romance

Thanks to Maria
for lending us her two,
and to Vera for her Bum Steer.

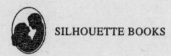 SILHOUETTE BOOKS

ISBN 0-373-24181-X

WHO WILL SHE WED?

**Books by Andrea Edwards**

---

## ANDREA EDWARDS

is the pseudonym of Anne and Ed Kolaczyk, a husband-and-wife writing team who have been telling their stories for more than fifteen years. Anne is a former elementary school teacher, while Ed is a refugee from corporate America. After many years in the Chicago area, they now live in a small town in northern Indiana where they are avid students of local history, family legends and ethnic myths. Recently they have both been bitten by the gardening bug, but only time will tell how serious the affliction is. Their four children are grown; the youngest attends college, while the eldest is a college professor. Remaining at home with Anne and Ed are two dogs, four cats and one bird—not the same ones that first walked through their stories but carrying on the same tradition of chaotic rule of the household nonetheless.

# WORLDWIDE NEWS

## THE VET OR THE STUD?

By M. C. Cooper

There's a lot of "love" in the air for the tour sponsored by Love Pet Foods. Colleen Cassidy, who plays sexy vet Sassy on TV, has two gorgeous studs after her! Neal Sheridan—a sinfully seductive real-life vet—has been seen using some serious rescue moves on Colleen. But Colleen's old flame isn't about to let her go so easily! Brick...

# Prologue

"So, that's the animal hospital," Dr. Nicholas Sheridan told the fourteen little Snappy Campers as he led them to the puppy poster in the waiting area. "Anybody have any questions?"

Fourteen little heads shook in unison as Nick and the camp counselors watched.

"Are you sure?" he pressed, knowing it was risky. Little kids could ask the weirdest things, but he was feeling reckless.

It was only four days before he was due to leave for vacation and nothing had threatened his plans yet. It was the closest thing he'd had to a miracle lately. Every time he'd even thought of taking time off in the past, something would happen. He'd sprain his ankle. His father would be taken ill. There'd be an outbreak of parvovirus, and he'd have to stay to help. This time would be different. He'd planned for every contingency. Nothing was going to keep him and his brother from their week in San Francisco.

Off to the side, one timid little hand had come up. "When I grow up, I wanna be just like Dr. Neal," the little girl said.

"You mean Dr. Nick, don't you?" the camp counselor corrected.

But the little girl—a green paper turtle pinned to her shirt said she was Bethany—shook her head, swinging her braids into her neighbor's face. "No. Dr. Neal." She was adamant. "When I grow up, I wanna be just like him." And she pointed to the puppy poster.

The poster—put out by Love Pet Foods—showed Nick's twin brother, Neal, sitting on the grass with a slew of puppies around him. Across the top, in large letters, it read Love Is All You Need. In smaller letters across the bottom, it told the time and network of Neal's veterinary medicine television show.

"When I grow up," Bethany said, louder, "I'm gonna have my own TV show and wear cool clothes and drive fast cars and never ever get married."

A chorus of "Me, too," filled the air, and Nick fought to keep a smile from his face. It sounded like a good life to Nick, too, but the look on the counselor's face said she didn't agree.

"Oh, no, no, no." The woman shook her head, her voice turning sad. "You don't really want that. Dr. Neal leads a terrible life. He travels all the time. He hardly ever gets to see his family here in Three Oaks. And he can't even play on a softball team because he'd miss the games."

Poor, poor Dr. Neal, Nick thought. Suffering the lonely life of a new girlfriend every week. Traveling the world instead of the back roads of southwestern Michigan. Eating at the best restaurants instead of at the VFW's Wednesday night spaghetti dinner.

The counselor's voice changed to a more cheerful pitch as she gathered the campers around her. "Now, let's say our thank-yous and let Dr. Nick get back to his patients."

After a disjointed round of thanks, the kids trooped out with the junior counselor. The other one stopped by Nick, her smile embarrassed and apologetic. "I'm so sorry about that," she said. "Bethany didn't mean to remind you. She had no idea what she was talking about."

Nick smiled. Funny how in July everyone in town found it necessary to apologize to him for every innocent remark about marriage. Or cars. Or deer. One of the reasons he was looking forward to leaving for a while. "It was nothing," he assured her. "But personally, I think you overrated softball."

She half laughed, as if not sure what he meant but certain he was trying to be brave, then hurried out after her charges.

"Poor baby," Nick's office manager said with a snicker. "To be rated after the great Dr. Neal. What a blow."

Nick gave Neal's poster a quick glance. "What blow? I agree with them. Who wouldn't want to be Neal?"

Sara gave him a look. "You don't," she said in that same impatient voice she used with her teenage kids. "You wouldn't be happy any place else. This is home. You love it here."

No, she was wrong. It was people you loved, and that kept you in certain places.

He'd learned that on a fifth grade field trip to the Museum of Science and Industry. He'd gone to the dollhouse exhibit with Donna instead of the rocket display with his friends because the teacher wouldn't let her go by herself. Soon dollhouses and rockets hadn't mattered, but Donna had. Her laughter, her smile, her hopes and dreams. They'd shared those dreams through all the long years of schooling and finally had been making them all come true. Then, two years ago this month, a deer darting across a road had put a halt to it all.

For long, long months, he had felt he was slowly dying himself, then realized he wasn't dead, but no longer really alive, either. He was stuck in a limbo of painful memories with no way out. All that was left was to go on.

"Who's in the lineup for today?" he asked.

Sara was pulling files out of a cabinet and didn't even give him a glance. "Your schedule's on your computer, you know."

This was a game they played every day. "Great, now if only I was as smart as Neal, I could access it."

She reached over with a loud sigh and pushed a paper across

the counter toward him, then followed it with an envelope. "We got a new Colleen Cassidy poster in the mail. If you don't want it, I'll offer it to Jeremy in exchange for a clean room."

Nick pulled the poster of the young woman out of the envelope. Love Foods' other spokesperson was sitting on a bale of hay, surrounded by a dozen kittens, with a slogan across the top that said There's Nothing Like Love. The time and network of her sitcom were at the bottom.

"I've never seen a vet dressed like that." Sara leaned over the counter to gaze at the poster with him. "Or should I say, undressed?"

Nick grinned but didn't take his eyes off the photo. The woman's cut off jeans were very cut off, and her cotton blouse was open way past demure. Soft red hair, smooth creamy skin and eyes as blue as the summer sky. And just as full of promise and laughter.

She was the food for dreams of silky summer nights—if one dreamed anymore.

"I don't think people watch 'Animal Life' to learn veterinary techniques." He folded the poster and, after a moment's hesitation, handed it to her. "Make Jeremy's day."

Two cars pulled into the parking lot right after one another, and the phone began to ring. Good. He liked it busy. He picked up his schedule and went to his office.

"Party time! Party time!" a parrot screeched when he entered the room. "Oops, my mistake."

"Shut up, Baron," Nick said.

He tossed his schedule onto his desk and steeled himself against the memories that lurked in the room. The desk plate Donna had ordered for him when he'd gotten his DVM. Her needlepoint animal designs on his office walls. Even the squeaking of his chair reminded him of her and how she laughed over it, teasing that he was turning into a creaky old man. She'd been gone two years now, but she still was everywhere.

Last year, he'd redone the labels in his supply cabinet, replacing her hand-lettered ones with typed ones, but it hadn't changed anything. Even where she wasn't, she was.

He leaned forward, covering his face with his hands. Man, but he needed this vacation. He really needed to go someplace Donna had never been. Someplace he wouldn't see her every place he turned. Someplace he could get a good night's sleep.

"Nick," someone called from the front desk. "Your brother's on line two."

Nick grabbed the line. "Hey, bro, what's happening?"

"Bad news," Neal replied.

Nick leaned back in his chair with a smile. "Don't tell me. You've dated all the English-speaking women in the world and now you're wondering whether to wait for more to come of age or learn a new language."

"Cute, Nick. Almost clever."

"Thank you."

"Actually, I have to cancel out on our outing," Neal said.

Nick's smile faded. "That is bad news." He tried not to let his disappointment into his voice. "I was looking forward to it."

"So was I. But I have to go on a marketing tour. My sponsor is busing me all over Illinois, Iowa and Missouri."

Nick closed his eyes and imagined being in one new town after another. "Sounds like fun."

"Yeah, right."

"I mean it," Nick said, opening his eyes. "It may not be Paris or New York, but they're all new places. Places you've never seen before. It sounds like fun."

"Only because you've never done it."

"It's got to be better than Three Oaks in July." Nick didn't have to mention why. Neal had been best man at Nick's wedding, just as he'd been one of Donna's pallbearers.

"Three Oaks may have a few ghosts," Neal replied. "But at least it's home."

Nick frowned. He'd always thought his brother had had it made. When their parents had divorced—before Nick and Neal had started first grade—Neal had been the one who got to go east with their small-town-hating mother. Nick was the one who stayed in Three Oaks with their small-town-loving father.

Now it sounded like Neal felt he'd missed out on things. Boy, just went to show that his brother wasn't so smart, after all. He had glamour, excitement, fame, and he wanted Three—

Nick felt his pulse quicken. Would he really want to?

"You know—" Neal was ahead of him.

"Do you really think we..." Nick went on.

"...the tour—"

"...the town—"

They both stopped.

"What about my patients?" Nick asked.

"I am a licensed vet, you know, and so is your partner." Neal paused. "But you hate public speaking."

"Not like I used to," Nick admitted. "But what if they decide to establish that State Animal Welfare Committee this month? You know my name's on their list."

"And it's been on their list for three years now. Nothing's going to happen in the next six weeks." Neal hesitated. "I don't know who my traveling partners are supposed to be. Could be singing cows, for all I know."

As long as they weren't ghosts. "I work with a local rescue group, and we have a big fund-raiser coming up. Think you can handle that?"

"What kind of question is that?" Neal asked. "I've handled more fund-raisers in a week than you have in your whole life."

Nick stewed for a moment, tapping a pen against the arm of his chair. "You know," he said, "we'd be doing the area a favor. We could use some rain." Whenever Neal played he was Nick, it seemed to rain cats and dogs.

"And there must be hundreds of animals awaiting rescue across the midwest."

"I've stopped having to rescue everything in sight," Nick said, then turned so he couldn't see the parrot in the corner.

Well, that had been last month. He hadn't taken in any strays since then.

"So what do you think?" Neal asked. "You game?"

Nick was silent. He'd have to shave his beard, but with a little luck, he wouldn't be too pale. And he'd miss the rescue society's dinner dance, but going to those things alone was a major pain, anyway.

Who would it hurt if they switched? Neal seemed to need the six weeks here in Three Oaks, and Nick had been vowing that he would get away this time, come rain or shine.

And what a getaway it would be—six weeks of the good life. He'd be in a world where relationships didn't last longer than fifteen minutes. Where ghosts wouldn't follow him day in and day out. Where he could sleep through the night undisturbed.

"Let's do it," Nick said.

# Chapter One

"I can't stand it, Colleen." Lance Reece glanced anxiously in the mirror on the back of the visor, his fingers playing with his blond razor cut. "Just look at it. It's too damn short."

But Colleen Cassidy was looking at the people milling about on the estate's driveway. Piranha waiting for a kill. Lions waiting for the Christians. Reporters waiting for a scandal.

And all she had for protection was Mr. Whiny, here. She turned toward Lance, the pouting star of a new teen soap opera, still preening in the mirror, and almost laughed. What was she thinking? She'd never needed a male's protection before and didn't now.

"You look fine," she told him. "Stop worrying. Just go into that party thinking that you look great, and everyone'll agree with you."

"That's easy for you to say," he whined. "You've already got your own show."

Yeah, she had her own show. "Animal Life." The hottest

sitcom on TV these days. And her character of Sassy Mirabel, the lusty veterinarian, was the talk of the town. But it could all cave in on her at any minute, and she'd be back auditioning for cheap movies and late-night commercials. Has-been roles like Aunt Jess had had to fight for that stole the remnants of your pride in exchange for barely enough to live on. Just one false move, just one piece of bad publicity, and that's where she'd be.

For a split second, nerves gnawed at her stomach and she felt exposed, left open for everyone to see. To see and to mock. Like the kids at school had, when they'd found out her stories of a mommy and daddy and a dog named Tommy had all been a lie.

But then she smashed those worries into the dust. She was a lot smarter at thirty-two than she'd been at six. Nothing was going to happen to her success. She'd make sure of it.

"We're holding up progress here." Colleen tipped her head toward the line of expensive cars behind them. "Let's get out and look happy."

Grumbling beneath his breath, Lance threw himself out of the car. Colleen went around to join him, putting her arm through his. "Big smile, sweetheart," she said softly. "It's show time."

As they wove their way through the careful display of vivid—and scentless—flowers lining the front walk, photographers swarmed around them. She smiled and acted cozy with pretty-boy Lance.

"Hello, all." She gave everyone a big smile and a wave.

The photogs got right down to business.

"Stand over there, will you, Colleen?"

"Give Lance that look. Yeah, that one."

"Big smile."

"Turn a little."

Colleen turned. They always wanted the full body profile, and she was more than happy to oblige.

When she'd started to blossom in junior high, she'd been ready to slug any and all of the boys who'd teased her, but

Aunt Jess—Mom had been long gone by that time—had just laughed. "Men like big breasts and tight buns," she'd said. "Show them the outside and they forget there's an inside." And she'd been right.

"Colleen. Lance. Great to see you." Trevor Madison was at the door, ready to usher them into his museumlike house. Somehow he managed to sound pleasantly surprised by their presence even though this was his party and, as their agent, he had demanded their presence. "Good turnout, huh?"

But Colleen wasn't interested in a critique of the party. It would be an exact copy of every other one she'd attended here. Instead, she looked at Lance. "Time to circulate, honey."

"Okay." Without questioning her, Lance wandered past the life-size ice sculpture and was swallowed up in a crowd of starlets.

Colleen pulled Trevor aside so they were half hidden by a potted palm. "Did you see that article in *Worldwide News?*" she asked, her voice barely audible.

Trevor looked puzzled. "Yeah, got a real kick out of it."

She batted away an errant frond that was brushing her ear. "It's a lie, you know."

"When has *Worldwide* told the truth?"

"What if someone believes it?" she persisted. "It could ruin me."

Trevor looked truly puzzled. "How?"

"I have a reputation to uphold," she said. "My show is built on that, and if people believe that I—"

"Colleen, darling. How have you been? I haven't seen you for ages."

Cold fear clutched at Colleen's heart, but she knew not to let it show. She turned slowly and pasted a bright smile on her face. "Cooper, great to see you. How have you been?"

"Hanging on, honey. Hanging on."

Colleen wished she could run to the far ends of the earth, or at least to Aunt Jess's back porch where anything she imagined could come true. But running was not an option.

Mary Catherine Cooper was a senior reporter for *Worldwide*

*News* and could make or break a Hollywood career with just a word. She'd done it too many times to count. It was a game to her now.

"Your new friend is very cute." The smirk Cooper called a smile twisted her lips.

"Yes," Colleen replied. "Lance Reece. He plays the bad little rich boy on 'Central High.'" Colleen struggled to cover all the items Trevor schooled his clients in. Mention the actor's name, mention the show and finish up with something nice. "He's a real gentleman."

"What a pity." Cooper's smile stretched to greater proportions. "Doesn't that make him rather boring for someone of your...interests?"

Colleen forced a throaty laugh. She had played to tougher houses. "Yeah, but gentlemen do have their pluses." Colleen paused and gave Cooper a look. "You know, they're so very obedient."

The reporter threw her head back and laughed uproariously. So loudly that people around them turned their heads to smile along with her. Colleen waited.

"It's good to see that you haven't lost your touch," Cooper said after a moment. "We were starting to worry about you."

"Worry about Colleen?" Trevor asked.

"Well, a certain someone has been saying that—"

"And you believed that?" Trevor scoffed with a wave of his hand. "If you want the real story, you need to stay close to Colleen."

Colleen stopped breathing as she turned her gaze toward Trevor. She was trembling in her Fabrizio sandals, and he was encouraging this barracuda to stick around?

"We've got something great planned," Trevor said. "Colleen here—or should we say Sassy Mirabel?—is going on a goodwill tour of the Midwest this summer. With none other than—" he paused "—Dr. Neal Sheridan."

Neal Sheridan? Colleen stared at her agent, her stomach contracting into a rock-hard ball of terror. Not Neal Sheridan. Anyone but him.

But even as Colleen was trying to jump start her heart, Cooper was laughing. "America's hottest veterinarian and its most studly one," the woman barked. "God, what a pair! Let's hope our Colleen can withstand his charms."

"Why would I want to withstand his charms?" Colleen used the wide-eyed, innocent look she had perfected, then added a sly smile. "He sounds like the perfect playmate to me."

Cooper barked out another laugh. "Maybe," she said. "But I think he's broken more hearts than even you have."

Colleen waved aside the warning. That was the least of her worries. "Believe me," she said. "My heart is perfectly safe."

"Famous last words," Cooper said.

The smirk on the woman's face irked Colleen. If there was one thing in this life she was sure of, it was that she was never falling in love. She wasn't letting somebody have that kind of control over her.

"Can you honestly imagine me in love?" Colleen asked. "Dancing in the streets of Paris? Throwing coins in a fountain in Rome? Or walking off into the fog at Casablanca? I'm in it for fun, not for forever."

But she couldn't deny Neal Sheridan worried her. Handsome. Smart. And studly. The man who supposedly could read a woman's heart by looking in her eyes.

And love was not the worst secret a woman's heart could hold.

Nick stared at the platter of pancakes the waitress had just left. It had been ages since he'd had breakfast out. He'd have to jog an extra couple of miles to work this off. He poured syrup over it all and cut off a piece.

"It's funny seeing you without your beard," Neal said. "Like looking at myself. I'd forgotten how strange that was."

Nick rubbed his hand over his jawline. "My chin's not even all that pale either. Either I had the world's scraggliest beard or it wasn't really ten years since I grew it."

"Doesn't seem that long, does it?"

"Seems forever," Nick said with a short laugh that died hard.

Forever and just yesterday. He saw Donna frowning at him as she ran her hands over his new beard, then gingerly rubbing her cheek against it. He'd offered to shave if she didn't like it, but she'd said it made him look distinguished. Wise, she had added.

"I'd better give you my hotel key before I forget." Neal's voice was brisk, as if he knew Nick's thoughts had wandered off. "My clothes are all there. I just brought my personal stuff."

Nick put his fork down and took the key from Neal's hand. He was actually doing this. In the twenty hours since Neal had called him, Nick had come up with dozens of reasons he should back out. He'd even started dialing Neal's phone number one time, but then he heard again in his mind the wistfulness in Neal's voice, and he hung up. This was insane, though. Sure, they'd switched places as kids, but they weren't kids anymore.

"John Hockaday, my personal manager, will meet you at the hotel tonight at nine. Or should I say he'll meet Neal at the hotel?" Neal corrected with a grin. "He'll be going along on the bus, and so will the sponsor's tour manager. Between the two of them, your days will be planned down to the second."

"Sounds easy enough." Nick put the key in his pocket.

He just had to remember why he was doing this. Neal needed a taste of real life, needed to see that it was crabgrass on the other side of the fence, not Kentucky bluegrass. Nick did wish they'd picked a different restaurant to exchange car keys and stuff, though. This one just off the toll road in Portage was where they'd exchanged lives since they could drive. It made him feel sixteen again. And Neal's perpetual runner-up.

The waitress came by with more coffee, but after she'd filled their cups, she didn't move. She stood there, staring at

Nick. "You know, you look just like that animal doctor that's on TV all the time," she finally said.

There was a tremor of excitement in her voice and a hopeful glint in her eye. Nick felt something stir inside him. Perhaps her excitement was contagious. Or perhaps he hated to disappoint her. He smiled—he couldn't help it—and stepped right into his brother's life. "That's me. Neal Sheridan."

The woman put down the coffeepot and took his hand. Her touch was gentle, almost reverent. "Oh, wow." But when she let go of him and turned to pick up the pot, she frowned at Neal. "You look like him, too." Her voice was confused.

"I'm his stand-in." Neal took a bite of his toast.

"Really? Cool," she said. "Wait till I tell the girls."

Nick laughed as she walked away. It had been a surprising rush, a thrill. And so very easy. But best of all, no memories had been stirred up by it.

"This is gonna be fun," he said and dug into his breakfast with new enthusiasm. "I think I might like being famous."

"Hope so." Neal took a swallow of coffee. "How about your practice? Any cases I need to be aware of?"

Nick shook his head as he ate. "I left a stack of files on my desk for you to review. Nothing's in a critical stage. The Millers' cat is being treated for a urinary tract infection. The Kerrigans' dog is due to whelp in two weeks. Routine stuff. If there's anything you aren't sure of, you can refer it to Jim. He only works part-time, but he's pretty flexible about his hours."

"What about your office staff?" Neal asked. "You hired somebody new."

Nick frowned. "No, I haven't."

"Yes, you did. A Lisa. She answered the phone when I called."

"Oh, that was just a friend of mine. Lisa Hughes. She's head of the local Hoofed Animal Rescue Society. I give them space at the office to keep their records, get mail and messages. That kind of thing. Lisa helps out on phones when we get busy."

Nick paused, slowing his eating. Should he tell Neal how moody Lisa had been lately? No, they never briefed the other in more than the essentials. The other stuff, all the odds and ends of a person's life, was the challenge to be met as you went along. Besides, Lisa was over it, anyway. He finished up his eggs and pushed the plate aside.

They walked out together into early morning air already heavy with heat. Nick's pickup was parked next to Neal's rental car, and it took less than a moment to get their suitcases and exchange car keys. But Nick didn't move to get in the car. His earlier rush at playing Neal had faded, and doubts washed over him once again.

"Sara pretty much runs the clinic and my calendar," Nick said. "Today's my day off from appointments—Jim handles them—but I go in to take care of paperwork." He should have finished all that paperwork before he left this morning. What if Neal couldn't figure out those state health forms?

"If you have any problems, let Hockaday take care of them for you," Neal said. "Are Dad and Grams around?"

Nick nodded. "Where's Mom? She still in Paris?"

"Until September," Neal said and put his suitcase behind the pickup's front seat.

"Good thing. She was always the hardest to fool."

Neal stared at him, waiting, so Nick tossed his duffel bag into the back seat of Neal's car. What if Neal flirted with all the women in town? They could all be expecting engagement rings by the time he got back. Or not speaking to him.

"Hey, you've never said if you have a current girlfriend," Nick said. "Or is that a stupid question for the king of hearts?"

Neal shook his head. "Nope, feel free to woo all the ladies from Chicago to Des Moines."

The idea was startling. That wasn't what this trip was all about. "I just want to get away for a while. Relax a bit, that's all."

Neal frowned. "Donna wouldn't expect you to become a monk."

"And who said I am?" Nick snapped. All right, so he hadn't dated since Donna had died. And had had no desire to. In fact, the only female who had stirred his interest at all was Colleen Cassidy, on that silly poster. But he wasn't planning on being a monk.

"If you're going to be me, you've got to be me," Neal pointed out. "Unless you want to concede my victory right here and now."

"No way." Nick felt a rush of annoyance, fueled as much by Neal's monk remark as by his brother's overconfidence. Neal always went undetected in these switches. Neal never got caught, and Nick always did. He was always too dull, too safe, too predictable, and everyone knew. Well, not this time. He would out-Neal Neal if he had to, but he was going to last longer. It was a contest all of a sudden, not just a brotherly gesture. It was a chance to prove he was as good as Neal, better even.

"Your run of luck has ended," Nick said. "You are going to be detected as soon as you hit town, while I'm going to pass as Neal Sheridan for the full six weeks."

"Yeah, right." Neal got into the pickup, then leaned out the open window. "Hey, bro, one more thing."

Nick paused, halfway into the car. "What?"

"Remember. Love is nothing but a pet food."


"I can't imagine spending six whole weeks with Neal Sheridan," Teri, the wardrobe assistant, said, a definite purr in her voice.

"That's just it," Colleen said. "If I'm going to spend six weeks with him, I ought to know a little bit about him. Just so I won't sound stupid when we talk."

"Talk?" The woman started to laugh. "One look at him and talking is the last thing on any woman's mind."

"She's not really planning on talking." Erma, the beautician, drew her words out in marked contrast to the rapid clip-clipping of her scissors as she trimmed Colleen's hair. "That's why she doesn't care which negligee you pack. She's not going to have one on long enough for either of them to notice the color.''

Colleen tried not to scream. Love Pet Foods had sent a hairdresser and a wardrobe assistant to her apartment to help her get ready for the tour. She was delighted to see them for the information about Neal Sheridan they might possess. Unfortunately, they couldn't seem to move beyond a discussion of his looks.

''Actually, I don't sleep in negligees,'' Colleen told them. ''I sleep in flannel. Or a T-shirt and running shorts when it's hot.''

Dead silence greeted her words. Absolute dead silence. If this was a stage play, they'd be reaching for her with the hook.

Erma snickered, then started to laugh. ''You sure got us,'' she said. ''Almost believed you for a minute.''

''I knew she was joking,'' Teri said assuredly. ''Sassy Mirabel does not wear a T-shirt to bed.''

''Sassy Mirabel doesn't wear a T-shirt a lot of places.''

*But I'm not her,* Colleen wanted to point out. Just like she wasn't Tanya the lusty space explorer or Lucinda the busty warrior queen or Lola the kindhearted bar girl, the roles that had led to Sassy.

But then again, wasn't she? She'd worked for years to cultivate that persona.

Erma moved around Colleen's chair. ''Next you'll be trying to make us think you wear long johns,'' the woman said.

''And white gloves,'' Teri added. ''Can you imagine 'Animal Life' if Sassy wore white gloves and heels?''

''No one would watch the show.''

''There'd be no show,'' Teri said.

Colleen closed her eyes. So she wasn't worrying over nothing. Her continued success did depend on her continued notoriety. And that depended on getting the best of *Worldwide News* and Neal Sheridan.

Teri closed one suitcase with a sharp snap. ''Wouldn't it be cool if Neal Sheridan's twin brother came to see him? Can you imagine *two* of them?''

In her worst nightmares, Colleen thought. "He's not a television star, too, is he?"

"No, he's just a vet. Has a practice in the Midwest someplace. Some small town in Michigan," Erma told her. "I think his name is Nick. Dr. Neal mentions him on his show a lot. Don't you watch?"

"Uh, that's my aerobics night," Colleen said, even as her thoughts were racing off in another direction.

Of course. How could she have forgotten? Lisa had told her ages ago about knowing Neal Sheridan because she was friends with his brother. If anyone could give Colleen a hint on how to handle Neal, it would be Lisa.

It seemed lifetimes ago that Colleen and Lisa had met, more than the twenty-five years it really was. When Colleen had been seven and still Jennifer Anne Tutweiler, she'd gone with Aunt Jess to an audition. Aunt Jess hadn't gotten a part, but Colleen had—she'd been hired as an extra for a western. Lisa's dad had been training the horses for the film, and even though Lisa was a few years older, the two girls became fast friends. It was the first time Colleen had had someone she could be herself with. It was the first time she'd really seen a dad up close, too, but that was neither here nor there. The important thing was that she and Lisa had stayed friends even after Lisa had moved to Michigan, about twenty years ago. And as soon as Teri and Erma left, Colleen dialed Lisa's number.

"Colleen!" Lisa cried. "You are just the person I need to talk to. You've got to tell me how to seduce a guy."

"I what?" Colleen carried her phone to the balcony and sat on a chair in the sun. Los Angeles was spread out below her, but she barely glanced at the spectacular view. She knew what it was—lots of glitter frantically covering up the secrets. "What in the world are you talking about?"

There was a long silence, then Lisa sighed. "Look, Colleen, I want this guy to bed me. I need your expert advice."

Colleen didn't know what to say, caught by surprise by Lisa's request. Lisa had always been the one person who never seemed to notice that part of Colleen's life. Indecision tore through her, and she was tempted to blurt out the truth. Just for once, she wished someone saw the real her. She wished there was someone she could be totally open and honest with. But it wasn't lack of trust that kept her silent. She and Lisa had been friends for twenty-five years. Colleen would trust her with her life. But how would Lisa feel about such a confidence this late in the game?

Besides, when it really came down to it, Colleen told herself, she was the expert. She made her living at being seductive, so who was more qualified to give Lisa advice?

"Are you trying to snag him?" Colleen asked.

"No," Lisa said. After a moment, she went on. "I like him, but I don't love him. He's a friend. A decent, caring friend."

"Decent and caring?" Lisa was so naive at times, it was scary. "Such a creature doesn't exist."

"He does, too," Lisa insisted. "He's dependable and honest and—"

"And what—married?" Colleen put her feet on the balcony railing, the metal warm from the sun. "Don't tell me you fell for the my-wife-doesn't-understand-me line?"

"He's a widower, if you have to know, but that has nothing to do with this."

"I see. It was his I'm-so-lonely line."

"I didn't fall for anything," Lisa insisted hotly. "If you must know, I want to have a baby. I've wanted one for ages and I want him to be the father."

Colleen was shocked, stunned into silence as she sat up, her feet hitting the balcony floor. This wasn't what she had expected at all. But then surprise gave way to another emotion— envy, of all things. What would it be like to feel so secure in your life that you wanted to bring a baby into it? A baby of your very own to hold and love and protect. She felt the emptiness of the apartment behind her and the emptiness of her life in the city below her.

No, no, she scolded herself. It wasn't emptiness—it was privacy. It was the way she wanted it. The last thing in the

world she wanted or needed was someone here when she came
home at night, someone whose happiness she was responsible
for. Lisa would make a good mother. The only mothering Colleen had ever done was to the fictional Tommy, and he hadn't
lasted very long.

Nope. Nobody was leaning on her, ever. No way. Never.

"So are you going to help me?" Lisa asked.

"I can't," Colleen said. "You'll never seduce a decent guy.
He'd be too concerned about the ramifications of making love
to do anything. You should use a sperm bank."

"There aren't any ramifications," Lisa argued. "I don't expect him to hang around or pay child support or anything. I
chose him for his bloodlines. He's from good stock. Hardy
stock."

"You've been breeding horses too long. You make it sound
like the same thing."

"Come on, Colleen. You're my only hope."

Colleen sighed. "Okay, okay. First of all, you need to act
sexy." She tried to think. She'd been doing it so long, it was
second nature to her. "Wear flimsy, sexy dresses. Sway when
you walk. Lick your lips real slowly. And your hair. It's still
kind of long, isn't it? Pin it up, then shake it loose when he's
watching."

"Haven't you forgotten batting my eyelashes at him?" Lisa
sounded sarcastic.

"Hey, you want to make it with this guy or don't you?"

"Sorry."

"Okay." Colleen was silent. It was hard to condense years
of seductive behavior into a short telephone conversation.
"What you really need is a book. One of those How To Drive
Your Guy Wild with Desire in Seven Days or Less things."

"Oh, Lordy," Lisa moaned. "Nick would laugh me out of
the room."

"Nick? This is about your vet friend, Nick?" Colleen slid
open the door to the apartment. "I need to know all about his
brother. What's he like?"

"Neal?" Lisa's voice had changed, and it wasn't breathless

with love. "Scum of the earth. No integrity. Insensitive. Not a shred of decency in his body."

Colleen laughed and stepped into her living room, then closed the sliding door behind her. "Sounds like the guy you should be after. He's got the bloodlines and probably wouldn't worry about any ramifications."

"Are you crazy?" Lisa cried. "I'd sooner die childless than go to bed with Neal Sheridan. I'd adopt a nest of baby tarantulas before I'd let that obnoxious jerk near me. Just thinking about it is enough to give me nightmares for the rest of my life."

Sounded like Lisa knew him, all right. "Can he really see into a woman's soul by looking in her eyes?"

"I wouldn't put it past him. You can't trust him an inch."

Colleen relaxed. Obnoxious. Insensitive. Untrustworthy. There was no need to worry. Neal Sheridan was no different than all the other guys she'd known. She'd been handling them for years, and she could handle him, too.

"I'm spending the next six weeks touring the Midwest with him," she told Lisa.

"Oh, you poor thing. You need all the luck in the world."

No, all she needed was a pair of sunglasses so he couldn't look into her eyes.

## Chapter Two

"Oh, this is so cool," the girl gushed.

Nick smiled and finished signing the napkin before giving it to the teenage girl. He was getting used to the idea that people would want his—Neal's—autograph, but wanting it on the napkin he used after eating barbecue ribs was beyond him.

The girl sighed and held the paper to her heart. "Mandy'll never believe it."

"No problem," Nick said. "Always glad to meet my fans."

With a silly grin and a flush to her cheeks, the girl disappeared through the line waiting at Mimi's Cheesecake Booth. Nick felt himself smiling as he turned and wove his way through the crowd in the other direction. It was a gorgeous evening in Grant Park. There was a faint hint of dampness from the morning rains and the nearby lake, but it was invigorating.

He'd spent the evening here at the Taste of Chicago, wandering the paths of the park and sampling tidbits from the best of Chicago's restaurants. Everywhere he went women smiled at him, kids ran up to ask for his autograph, and men shook his hand. A woman brought her dog to meet him, explaining seriously that Bootsie loved his show on flea control.

It was the most fun he'd had in ages. And best of all, no memories lurked amid the egg rolls. He felt free.

And he'd be free for the next six weeks. He could hear the words *July* and *marriage* and *deer* without an apology following. He could walk into any room without ghosts surrounding him. And best of all, he'd be able to sleep. It was wonderful. By the time he went home, the memories would have no power over him. He should have gotten away sooner.

Nick left the park, his step brisk and his heart light as he crossed Michigan Avenue. It was amazing how alive he felt, even here, surrounded by tall buildings with the elevated train roaring overhead and the stench of exhaust in the air. Horns beeped and cabbies screamed expletives at the people darting across the street to the park. On the corner, a man played the saxophone, the sweet, sad sounds blending perfectly with the symphony that was the city.

There was so much energy in the air, so much life, it was impossible not to be affected by it. He tossed some dollars into the man's empty saxophone case and received a jaunty musical salute in return. He laughed, unable not to. This was so different from Three Oaks, the two towns might not even be on the same planet.

He caught sight of a bank clock as he crossed Wabash and quickened his steps. He didn't want to be late for his meeting with Neal's—his—manager.

A few minutes later, a solemn uniformed doorman ushered him into the hotel's ornate lobby. The Captain's Cove Inn it was not. Marble and crystal were everywhere—no pressboard paneling or plaster sea gulls here. The thick plush of the carpet muffled his steps as he hurried past the registration desk and looked around.

A balding man in his late twenties was coming toward him. Great. Must be John Hockaday. But then a worry fluttered in Nick's stomach. How would Neal greet his manager?

"What happened to you?" the man asked. "You're out of breath."

Nick relaxed. He'd forgotten the first rule of masquerading—let the other person take the lead. "I didn't want to be late."

John looked baffled. "But you're always late."

Damn. Nick should have known that.

John went on. "In fact, I was figuring you for another ten or fifteen minutes."

Nick met the man's eyes with a sudden sour certainty in his stomach. He'd blown it. Hockaday was going to call his bluff and hand him a one-way ticket home. Goodbye excitement and hello same old, same old. Neal would lord it over him the rest of his natural life.

"You ready to meet everybody?"

Yes! Nick gave himself a mental high five. He'd done it. He'd fooled someone who knew Neal well, someone he saw often. He was going to pull this off.

But he kept his cool as he started walking toward the elegant bar. "So who all's going with us?"

John fell into step beside him. "You get my message?"

Nick frowned at the man, his steps slowing as apprehension crept in. Had he been celebrating too soon? "Which message? Is there a problem?"

"A problem?" John's lips twisted into a smile. "No, most men wouldn't consider this a problem."

The man seemed to be laughing, and Nick's uneasiness flared up again. Something told him to worry. Something told him to ask more questions. But he was Neal now. Neal the confident. Neal the assured. Not Nick the worrier. Neal wouldn't ask.

So he strode confidently into the bar, falling slightly behind so John could lead the way. They wove around the tables toward a group of a dozen or so men and women in the back, conversation hushing as they went by. Whispers trailed in their wake.

Nick smiled at the awestruck faces of the customers. His

confidence was coming back. He had to stop fearing exposure at every turn. No one would suspect he wasn't Neal. There was no reason for them to.

By the time they reached the table, Nick was on top of the world. He had everything under control. He could be Neal— there was nothing to it. This was a world that didn't expect depth, that didn't probe and search for other than the obvious. It was a world of make-believe, so why would it care that he was playing make-believe, too?

As he reached the table, he felt a presence beside him. A fan wanting an autograph, perhaps. He turned.

And his heart fell to the floor. It was Colleen Cassidy.

"Well, as I live and breathe, if it isn't Dr. Neal Sheridan," she said, her voice as soft as the kiss of morning dew on the grass.

Up close, she was a thousand times more beautiful than in that poster. A million times. Her skin looked as smooth as fresh milk. Her hair was the color of red-hot steel. Her lips looked soft and moist and ever so tempting. And if she would take off those sunglasses—

She did. But before he saw more than a flash of green, she slid her arms around his neck and pressed her mouth to his.

Her touch was like a bolt of lightning. A flash of bright light, a trembling of the floor beneath his feet, then searing heat. He couldn't breathe or think or do anything but feel. The press of her full breasts awoke strange responses in him. Mostly of the caveman variety.

His arms went around her, pulling her closer. Tighter. The fiery touch of her body spread over the length of him, but never had walking through fire felt so wonderful. His mouth moved against hers, drinking in all the warmth and magic of her.

Then she pulled away, slipping her sunglasses on as cameras continued to flash around them. She took a step back and smiled at the crowd, then once more at him.

"Well, Dr. Sheridan," she said with a teasing lilt to her

voice. "Every one of those delicious little rumors about you had better be true."

"It's great to see so many of you here on this sunny Fourth of July morning," Jim Becker said. The sound system sent a scratchy replica of his voice over the several hundred people gathered in front of the small stage in the McCormick Place parking lot. "Though we're saving a lot of our fireworks for when we come back here for the opening of the International Animal Care convention in just six short weeks."

Colleen kept smiling at the Love Pet Foods vice president, even though the man had no idea what he was talking about. Six short weeks? It was a contradiction in terms. The next six weeks could not be short, by any stretch of the imagination. She risked a quick glance at Neal, who was on the other side of the podium. He seemed engrossed in the speech, but suddenly his gaze shifted and his eyes met hers.

Or tried to. Thank goodness for sunglasses and the bright morning sun.

But even if he couldn't see her eyes, she could sure see his. Dark pools of mystery that called to her soul. He was a strange one. Not at all what she expected, which made him even more dangerous.

She'd met more hunks and ladies' men in the last few years than she could count. But they all had one thing in common— they knew how hunky they were.

Neal, on the other hand, didn't seem to have any idea just how broad his shoulders were or how his smile could make a lady feel all tingly inside. Which was crazy. He had to know.

Take last night, when she'd kissed him. He'd kissed her back with the hunger of a man who'd never been kissed like that before—or hadn't been in ages. Like a starving man given food for the first time in weeks. But given his reputation, that didn't make sense.

It had to be part of his deviousness. Lisa had said he wasn't to be trusted, and she must know. He hadn't gotten his reputation by being only as good as most men at seduction. No, he had to be better than most. Better than them all. And this apparent unawareness of his charms was just one of the ways he disarmed even the most determined of women.

Of course, he hadn't run into her before.

"So you all come out and see us again." Mr. Becker was getting to the end of his talk. "It'll be another chance to get samples of our products and meet your favorite Love stars."

With a wave to the crowd, he stepped from the podium, glancing at Colleen and then at Neal for either of them to say a few words. Neal started forward, only to glance her way. She waved him on.

Lordy, she hoped he wasn't into this whole gentlemanly act, too. The only thing worse than a man trying to pretend he was decent was one who actually was. But then, Lisa had the only decent man alive, so at least Colleen had been spared that trial.

Neal stepped to the microphone amid frantic squeals from the teenybopper crowd. "It's great to see such a crowd out here," he said. "Means you're all just as excited about this tour as I am."

Right, Colleen thought, but kept her smile bright. The free stuff they were giving away had nothing to do with it.

"And it means that you care about the well-being of your pets," Neal was going on. "You're interested in getting the best for them—nutritionally and medically."

Sure, Doc. All those teenyboppers in skintight tube tops were fainting every time he spoke because they were so worried about little Fluffy at home.

Neal wasn't done. "If you have any questions about your pet that I can answer for you, I want you all to feel free to ask me."

If Colleen didn't know better, she'd think they plucked this guy right off the turnip truck from Podunk City. He seemed so clueless that she almost wanted to rush right over and protect him from the hard, cruel world.

But she knew better than those swooning young things in the audience, clutching their autographed pictures as if they were sacred icons. This was all an act. A damn good one, she had to admit. But still an act. And it was time she came on-stage.

She slid up to the podium and put her arm around Neal's waist. He seemed to start slightly, then a faint flush crept over his skin as he turned toward her. For a moment, she thought she saw a shadow in his deep, dark eyes. She knew it was just part of his trap for unwary females, but it almost touched her anyway before she caught herself. She turned to the safety of the audience.

"I'm really looking forward to this tour, also," she said to the crowd below her. "But Mr. Becker was teasing you. Can you imagine me in a bus with this hunk for the next six weeks and no fireworks?"

The female members of the audience sighed and squealed, then were drowned out by the catcalls of the male half. It sounded as if most were offering to show her their own fireworks. She laughed and slipped in front of Neal, pulling his arms around her as the photographers in front of the stage scrambled for the right angle.

For a split second Neal seemed to fight her—just playing the shy boy, she knew. His arms were rigid as he held himself slightly away, but then he pretended something inside him started to melt. His arms relaxed and he let them hold her, really hold her.

And Lordy, did it ever feel good. His chest was hard and strong against her back, his hands possessive as they held her prisoner in his embrace. His breath teased the back of her neck, sending shivers down her spine. She felt so safe and secure, it was terrifying. This guy was good. Exactly as he was rumored to be!

She had her part to play, though, and snuggled deeper into his arms. Her heart fluttered slightly—in warning or antici-pation? She ignored it.

"Mmm," she said to the crowd, the purr in her voice loud enough for the mike to pick up. "This is the kind of animal I like."

Neal's arms tightened around her, but it was only because

he leaned closer to the mike. "I think I'm going to be in heaven by the end of these six weeks."

The words were what she'd expected, but the tone wasn't. A tremble was in his voice, a low, almost unnoticeable quiver that made him seem vulnerable. The man should give up veterinary medicine and stick to acting. He'd be winning Oscars right and left.

But she could act, too. She pulled away from him with a frown. "Six weeks? Honey, I don't need even six minutes to send you to heaven."

The crowd roared with laughter while Neal flushed. Those eyes seemed to flash a cascade of emotions in a split second. But then she caught a signal from one of the crew to wrap things up and slipped completely from his arms.

"Come on, darling," she said. "Time's a-wasting."

Waving to the audience, she led him off the stage to a mixture of catcalls and applause. At the bottom of the steps, where the press was waiting, she let go and was surrounded by reporters. For a moment, she missed the security of his solid presence, but that was crazy. She'd been standing in the sun too long if she was wanting to lean on a man.

"You're looking awfully perky this morning," Cooper said as she came up next to Colleen. A *Worldwide* photographer circled for the best shot.

"And why shouldn't I be?" Colleen turned to give the cameraman the angle he wanted. "It's a beautiful day."

"And was it a beautiful night?" Cooper asked with a glance toward Neal Sheridan.

Colleen laughed aloud. Cooper's uncertainty was a victory. "Gracious, Cooper, not yet," Colleen said. She felt a little wild in her certainty. Nothing would happen that she couldn't handle. "Love is like champagne. It only lasts for a little while. If you're too impatient for that first taste, it'll be flat by dessert."

Cooper watched her, then glanced in Neal's direction. "I guess I'll just have to keep a close eye on things, then, so I'll know when that bottle is opened."

A close eye? Some of the bubbles in Colleen's euphoria burst as she looked at the two luxury buses parked a short distance away. Her stomach tensed. "You're not going on the press bus, are you?" she asked Cooper. The woman's eyes narrowed, and Colleen raced on. "I mean, a reporter of your stature—"

Cooper barked out a laugh. "Honey, you're our bread and butter. Or should I say, champagne?" The smirk on her face was calculating. "Colleen Cassidy's adventures sell our newspaper better than three-headed aliens from outer space. You're where the story is, and that's exactly where I'm gonna be."

Damn. Colleen's stomach twisted some more. She tasted again the cup of coffee that had been her breakfast and felt like she was walking into a shoot-out with only a water pistol. But she gave Cooper the sweetest of smiles.

"I'll see what excitement I can stir up," Colleen said. "I sure don't want to let your readers down."

Nick watched the rows and rows of cornfields pass by. No matter what anybody said, they weren't getting any closer to the 4-H Rodeo and Roundup in Springfield, Illinois. They were caught in some gigantic loop that was sending them past these same fields over and over and over again.

He wasn't tired, that was certain, even though he hadn't been able to sleep more than an hour or so last night. He'd never felt so alive, so alert, so ready for anything.

Well, maybe not *anything*.

Colleen's voice floated from the back of the bus where she sat at a table with Ashley, her publicity manager. He felt again the warm softness of Colleen's body pressed against his. He remembered the sweetness of her lips and the fiery laughter in her voice. Long-buried emotions tugged at him. Long-suppressed desires churned through his blood.

Hell, why not anything? He'd heard what Colleen had said to that reporter, about love being like champagne. He had to start thinking like that himself. Quick little sips of love wouldn't hurt. Even whole bottles of it. It was only in wanting to own the vineyard that things went wrong. He was never going to want that again, but it didn't mean he had to avoid champagne altogether.

"So, how you doing, Doc?"

Nick turned from the bus window and to look at the man who'd dropped on the recliner beside him. It was Brad, their tour manager. A firecracker of a man with the energy of a seven-foot basketball player stuffed into his average-size frame.

"Great," Nick said. "Just trying to get a handle on all the excitement."

"Yeah, these bus rides can get to a guy."

Brad's voice said he thought Nick was being sarcastic, but he hadn't meant it that way at all. The tour was exciting. The attention. The acclaim. Colleen.

"Speaking of excitement." The tour manager settled himself in his seat. "I like the way you and Colleen play off each other. Don't get me wrong, sparks are flying. But you seem— I don't know—hesitant. You seem different than on your show."

Nick couldn't help frowning. Damn. He'd thought he'd been doing pretty good. He'd better get on the ball if he didn't want people to be suspicious.

"I know most of our stops are family affairs," Brad said. "But you don't need to tone down. You aren't too outrageous for our audience."

"Good to know," Nick said with a burst of bravado. He thought he'd been playing the part pretty well, but obviously not well enough. "I didn't want to offend anybody."

Brad laughed and slapped Nick on the knee. "No chance of that. Everybody loves the public Neal Sheridan." He winked as he rose from his seat. "I'll check with Colleen about your private ratings."

The tour manager returned to the seat across the aisle and buried his nose in some papers, leaving Nick to go back to staring at the passing landscape. Oh, boy, now what? Soft laughter floated from the back again, filling the bus like some exotic fragrance.

He'd better put on the big push to be Neal. He had two objectives for this trip—have himself a hell of a time, and not screw up his brother's reputation. Well, he was enjoying himself so far, but obviously he wasn't doing as well on his other objective. Time to rectify that.

He got to his feet, nodding to the two security guards in the row behind him. In the back of the bus was a full bathroom and a small bedroom, and in front of that was a small kitchenette area where Colleen and her publicity manager, Ashley, were seated at a table, sorting through photographs. Neither looked up at his approach. That might have stopped Nick, but not Neal. He sat in one of the empty captain's chairs. Ashley smiled at him. Colleen didn't even look up, her face shaded by the Chicago Cubs baseball cap she was wearing.

"New publicity photos?" he asked.

Ashley nodded. "The old ones were almost six months old." She pushed some his way. "We can't decide which ones to give away through her fan club and which ones to use with press releases."

"Nice," he said as he pulled them over one at a time. Though *nice* didn't come close to an adequate description of them. Colleen in leather. Colleen in lace. Colleen looking so hot and sexy that he was surprised the photos weren't smoking. He felt he was, just from looking at them.

Ashley got to her feet. "Want something to drink?" she asked. "We've got just about everything in the fridge here."

"Nothing for me," Colleen said, proving she could indeed talk.

"Any kind of soda would be great," Nick said, and looked at Colleen. "I hear we're saving the champagne for later."

She glanced up. God, she had the most expressive eyes. Purple velvet that went from wide and almost worried-looking to laughter and sensual in the flick of a moment.

She leaned back in her chair, pushing her cap up in the back so that the visor threw a shadow over her eyes. "So you're a champagne connoisseur, are you?'' she asked, her voice husky and low.

"But only the best vintage," he said, his eyes trying to find hers again. Was there a glimmer in the shadows? A hint of the fire within?

"That goes without saying." Her voice was a whisper, a promise.

A sudden pop near him said Ashley had brought his drink and had opened it. Murmuring his thanks, Nick picked it up, not letting go of his tenuous hold of Colleen, and took a sip. It was cream soda.

The bus, the countryside bathed in sunshine and summer, Colleen—everything fled, and all he heard was Donna. Her laughter and her soft apology when he'd picked up her can of soda by mistake. She loved the stuff. He hated it.

"Neal?"

She used to threaten to slip it into his cola cans or into his coffeemaker at work. She'd claim she had put it in the soup or the stew or any other meal he said he'd enjoyed. It had been a silly little game. A little joke. But then again, it had been everything. It had been one of the hundreds of little things that had made up the fabric of their relationship.

"Neal?"

He started at Colleen's voice and found her watching him, the baseball cap pushed from her face as she frowned.

"Is something wrong?" she asked, then glanced from the can in his hand to Ashley. "You gave him cream soda? I've never met a guy who liked the stuff."

He smiled and forced down a long drink of the soda. "Hey, no, it's fine. I said any kind, and that's what I meant."

Colleen looked ready to press the issue—something he definitely didn't want. He glanced down, and one of the photos caught his eye. One in which Colleen didn't seem to be posing at all. Her eyes seemed wistful as they looked into the camera, and her lips looked like they had never been kissed.

"My vote goes to this one," he said.

That did the trick. "Not that one," Colleen cried. "That one's awful."

"This looks like the real you," he said.

"The real me?" Colleen scooped the photos into a pile. "You've got to be kidding."

He stood, picking up the can of soda. "Pictures don't lie."

"They lie all the time," Colleen said, a touch of annoyance in her voice. "Our industry depends on it."

Nick shrugged, saluted both women with his soda can and made his way to the recliners in the front of the bus. He sank in his chair, putting the stupid can of soda in the drink holder next to him, then leaned back and closed his eyes.

Well, he had certainly blown that. Showed that he had better pay attention to what he was doing or the ghosts would sneak up even here. It was a stupid mistake on his part and one he could have easily avoided by being more alert.

And now he had even more ground to cover. Well, no problem. His role was simple. The Fourth of July was Neal's day, after all. Fireworks, fireworks and more fireworks.

Damn that Neal Sheridan, Colleen thought as the security guards were herding their group through the fairgrounds.

Why should she care if cream soda put him in a trance? She didn't. She'd only asked after him to be polite, not because she'd been concerned when that devastated look had come over his face.

But devious sneak that he was, he'd taken advantage of her courtesy and looked into her unprotected eyes. He had to have looked, since he said that one picture showed the real her.

Lisa said he wasn't to be trusted, but Colleen had had no idea just how low he'd go. She'd met cads before, but they all paled in comparison to Neal Sheridan. Pretending to be upset so he could get a look into her eyes!

"Can I take a picture of you two?" A young woman rushed past the security guards, her eyes glowing. "Please?"

The guards—a man and a woman—held her back, but Neal waved them away. "Sure," he said. "Go right ahead."

Colleen saw annoyance flash across Brad's face and knew he was thinking about their schedule. And from the groan of the photographers and video people trooping behind them, she knew they were dying in the heat. Neal, however, looked totally unaware of the commotion he was causing.

"Always glad of an excuse to hold on to a beautiful woman," Neal said. "Colleen, darling, come on over here."

The woman—who looked old enough to know better—giggled. Colleen was more inclined to throw up but knew she had to play her part even if Neal was a jerk. With a sigh, Colleen went over and let Neal's arms fold around her from behind.

She was wearing a knit halter top—one of her signature styles—but suddenly it felt too skimpy, as if she had nothing on at all. As if the fabric had melted away, leaving her bare skin to turn hot and steamy with his slightest touch. She leaned back, trying to escape those arms, but met the hard muscles of his chest. She was sizzling in front and behind.

"Don't you think you should take off your sunglasses?" he suggested, his breath tickling her ear.

Wouldn't he just love that? "No, I don't," she responded, ever so sweetly. She moved her head a few inches to stop the silliness in her stomach that his breath on her neck was causing. "You wouldn't want me blinded by your smile, now, would you?"

His arms tightened a touch as his lips brushed against her cheek. "Seems only fair, since your beauty is blinding me."

"Oh, this is so cool," the woman with the camera said, gushing.

Colleen smiled, though it was a strain. Her knees had the wobblies, and her heart had gone into overdrive. His musky scent seemed to drive coherent thought from her brain.

She closed her eyes and took a deep breath. This was not happening to her. Hundreds of leading men had held her—the industry's top studs, no less—and the only tingling she'd ever felt was her foot going to sleep. She was not going to succumb to some bounder's charms when she'd stayed safe this long. She opened her eyes, her smile bright.

The woman must have had a roll of six hundred shots, but finally she was done, and Colleen freed herself from Neal's embrace. Her skin still seemed on fire, and she rubbed it hard, as if stimulating the circulation would help.

"Gee, thanks," the woman said.

"No problem," Neal said. "If you want—"

Brad moved between them and the woman. "Dr. Sheridan and Ms. Cassidy would really like to chat with you," he said. "Just come to the rodeo pavilion at four. We'll be posing for pictures there and signing autographs at the same time."

Before the woman had a chance to answer, Brad was hurrying Colleen and Neal away. Colleen allowed her steps to lag slightly as she pretended to watch a horse-jumping event through the Fourth of July bunting adorning the grandstand. This was crazy. She was letting her agitation turn everything upside down. Neal was a crud. She had dealt with crud before. She could do it again.

Brad led them into an area of animal barns, then into one of the buildings. The heat plus the animal smells was not a good combination.

"This should go pretty fast," Brad said as he hurried them through the shadowy interior.

Colleen toyed with the idea of taking her sunglasses off, but a quick glance found Neal watching her, so she decided against it. She could see well enough.

She followed Brad down an aisle lined with cows in stalls. They looked different here—bigger, meaner—than they did when she was filming a scene for her show. Which was crazy. A cow was a cow. The difference had to be the smells. Everything was cleaned up when she was filming, and they arranged it so she only had to be around actual animals for a few minutes. Sometimes, not at all.

"All you two have to do is pose for a few pictures with a steer," Brad said. "Then with some sheep before we do the photo and autograph thing at the pavilion. After that, we'll eat at the barbecue. We can decide then if we want to stay to watch the fireworks.''

A man opened a metal gate and let them into a makeshift arena where a big black steer stood. A herd of TV cameramen and photographers followed in their wake.

The animal stood only about shoulder height, not so big after all. Colleen walked toward it. She could have sworn its eyes were not friendly. But that was what she thought about every animal they used in the show, and they were all gentle as could be. Besides, its handler—a teenage girl who looked like she was going to faint at the sight of Neal—had the animal on a leash.

''Nice animal you have there, miss,'' Neal said.

''Thanks,'' the girl said, her face going pale, then bright red. No doubt from the thrill of having the great Neal Sheridan talk to her. Colleen tried not to gag.

''Colleen, go stand next to Neal,'' Brad suggested. ''And take off the sunglasses.''

The steer bawled suddenly, and Colleen jumped, widening her berth around the animal. Which did she want to avoid more—the steer or Neal? She stepped in something squishy under the straw on the floor and winced, then backed off again as the animal tugged at its rope. The girl had to be stronger than she looked.

''Easy, Bum.'' The girl patted the steer's side as she crooned to it. ''Everything will be all right.''

Neal looked annoyed. ''This animal is getting spooked,'' he said to Brad. ''You need to get some of these people out of here.''

''It's just one shot,'' Colleen pointed out, and moved closer to the animal than to Neal. She slipped her sunglasses off, feeling naked and vulnerable without them. ''Let's get it over with.''

''We'll be quick,'' Brad promised.

The TV cameramen were turning on their spots, and the news photographers started snapping away, flashbulbs lighting up the place. She smiled at the cameras, then froze when Neal's hand was on her arm.

"Don't stand too close," he said. "These lights are—"

She jerked away from his touch with a shrill laugh. "I have been—" But in stepping away from him, her foot landed in another squishy something and she slipped. She waved her arm to restore her balance—and hit the steer.

The animal let out an enormous bellow as if it had been beaten. It bucked and jerked and pulled at the rope, then turned toward Colleen. She stared into its evil, angry eyes, unable to do more than gasp ineffectually as it lowered its head slightly.

"Look out," Neal shouted, and shoved her aside as the animal charged.

# Chapter Three

"**I**'m fine. Really I am," Nick said. His head ached, as well as other parts of him, but then this emergency-room gurney was none too comfortable.

The doctor grunted and continued shining the light into his eyes. "You were knocked out for a good five minutes, by all accounts."

"I was resting," Nick said. "I wasn't knocked out."

"I see."

The doctor put the light away and studied the X rays hung on a light box. Nick didn't bother to watch him, just stared at the ceiling. He'd taken worse bumps when he'd played football in high school.

"Doctor." A nurse pulled the curtains of the cubicle open. "There are some people who'd like to see the patient for a few minutes, if possible."

Colleen pushed past her without waiting for an answer. John and Ashley followed on her heels, but Nick barely noticed them. The tiny examining area was suddenly filled with Colleen—her beauty, her energy, her delicious soft scent. She was still wearing that skimpy halter top that had sent his blood racing when he'd held her for those pictures at the fairgrounds. It was starting to race again just at the thought.

"Are you really okay?" Colleen asked.

He forced his eyes to her face. It was the color of the sheet he was lying on. Her playful teasing attitude was gone.

"I'm fine." He sat up to prove the truth in his words, and to get a better angle to look in her face. The world wobbled, but he ignored it.

But Ashley came over and pushed him down as she turned to John. "We need to get some pictures of the two of them together. You know, Neal lying here and Colleen by his side."

Nick was still for a moment as the world slowed its spinning, annoyed that he did feel better lying down. "What in the world for?" he snapped.

"You're a hero," Ashley replied. "This is great PR. We couldn't ask for better." She disappeared through the curtain, the clicking of her heels on the tile fading as she hurried away.

Colleen moved to Nick's side. His eyes wanted to linger on the tanned expanse of bare arm near him. His fingers ached to touch that skin and feel its cool soothing. He forced his gaze to her face and knew a deep and desperate longing to feel the softness of her cheek, to bury his face in the fire of her hair.

His stomach was churning. He turned to John. "Come on." He had to get out of here. Get someplace where he could pull himself together. "I didn't do anything."

"You saved Colleen's life," John said.

"I saved her from getting a few bumps. That was all."

"You went down hard," Colleen said.

"So I'm not too light on my feet." Her voice sent shivers down his spine, but not the kind that came from being chilled. No, sirree, the temperature in here must be close to two hundred degrees. "You weren't supposed to notice."

"You were knocked out."

"Just a slight concussion," the doctor said. He made some

notes on Nick's chart and closed the metal folder with a snap. "But we'll keep a close eye on him tonight just to make sure."

"A close eye?" Nick repeated. He didn't need anybody keeping an eye on him, close or otherwise. He wanted to be alone. "I'm not staying here overnight."

Ashley was back with a photographer and a cameraman. "Colleen, hold Neal's hand and give him one of those 'my hero' looks." She put Nick's hand in Colleen's as the cameras started flashing.

Colleen looked at him, her violet eyes filled with shadows. "If you're hurt, maybe you need to stay."

Her hand in his was doing wild and wicked things to his heart, things that she oughtn't be doing to a wounded man. And it didn't help that from this angle, his gaze wasn't on her face.

"I'm not hurt," he insisted, and tried to sit up.

"So, how's the big hero?" A tall woman in her mid-thirties suddenly burst into the room.

Colleen's hold on his hand tightened, but then she let go to push him gently down. "He's doing fine, Cooper," she said over her shoulder. "But they want to keep him overnight for observation."

Colleen's touch sent waves of fire washing over him, drowning him in heat until he was sure he was going under for the last time. He gazed at her, wanting to look again in her eyes, but from where he lay, all he saw were her breasts. They were covered in some thin fabric, and he could almost see the texture of her skin, the roughness of her nipples.

He closed his eyes, his hand clenched with his sudden need for control. This was all Neal's fault. Somehow he'd really stepped into his brother's life. Neal might be a breasts man or a legs man, but Nick was a soul man. He'd always prided himself on seeing a woman's personality, on not being some hormone-driven magnet drawn to every beautiful woman around. Yet Colleen's nearness made every cell in his body ache.

"He's got to stay overnight?" Cooper asked. "Too bad. Some lady's going to be lonely."

Nick didn't like her sly, suggestive tone and he sure didn't know when she thought he could have set up an assignation, but he was too beat to care. He felt like he'd been tossed on the horns of a bull all afternoon and just wanted to go to his hotel room and sleep.

"I'm not staying here overnight," he growled. "I'm fine."

The doctor made a face. "Someone will need to check on you periodically. I'm not releasing you without that promise."

"Fine. Whatever." Nick sat up. Colleen took his arm as he swung his feet over the edge of the gurney. He willed her touch to have no effect on him. That was about as effective as trying to blow a tornado away.

"What somebody?" Cooper asked. "Why not Colleen?"

"What?" Colleen's hand tightened on his arm, almost cutting off the circulation, then she relaxed. "What a great idea, Cooper. I've always wanted to play a nurse."

She turned to Nick, her smile wide and bright as she slipped her arm through his and cuddled close. Her breasts brushed his arm, putting lower parts of his anatomy in charge of his thinking.

"I'll stay right by your side all night long," Colleen said, her voice all soft and cooing. "I'll make sure you don't suffer a nasty relapse or anything."

Nick groaned. And he had been counting on sleep?

"You sure you're okay? I've never done this before." Colleen turned off the light by the king-size bed, hoping it was a nurselike thing to do. Truth was, she didn't need to stare at his broad naked chest any longer. She knew he was wearing running shorts under the covers, but her mind was working overtime.

"I'm fine," Neal said.

His voice was tight, like he was anything but fine. Colleen debated questioning him further, then decided against it. It was bad enough that it was her stupidity in bumping the steer that had gotten him the concussion in the first place. She didn't need to keep pestering him, too.

She went into the bathroom and changed, putting on a T-shirt and shorts, and she took out her contacts. It didn't look like Neal had moved when she came out, so she curled up at the end of the sofa with her book and tried to read by the light coming from the bathroom. Investment banking was definitely more understandable with brighter lights. And in a room by herself.

"I should be taking the sofa," he said suddenly.

Colleen started and lost her place amid an explanation of amortization. "You're the one with the concussion," she said. "Besides, sofa beds are comfortable. It's no hardship."

"Then I should help you open it up," he said

Criminy, he was like an agent sniffing out a casting call. "I don't want it open yet," she said.

He quieted down after that, though Colleen really couldn't say he relaxed. She shouldn't have snapped at him. He'd only been trying to be nice. What if he was in real pain from the concussion? What if he went into a coma? She should never have let Cooper goad her into doing this. She wasn't qualified to take care of somebody injured, yet she'd let her stupid pride get in the way.

Colleen stared at the bed. Though the only light in the room came from the bathroom, she could see Neal lying on his back, still as the dead. His arm was over his eyes. She peered at him for a long moment. Long enough for some loud vacationers to go from one end of the corridor outside to the other. Neal didn't move.

Oh, Lordy, it was comaville, for sure.

She put her book down and tiptoed across the room. It was hard not to notice how big he was. Even in the dark, he looked tall and strong and—

*Cut it out,* she scolded herself. She was here to keep an eye on his health, not his body.

He didn't move when she stopped at the edge of the bed,

so she turned the light on. Still no reaction, so she gently raised his arm. His eyes were open, staring at her.

Could you have your eyes open in a coma? "Are you okay?" she asked.

All he did was stare into her eyes.

"Neal? You didn't go into a coma on me, did you?" She started to bend down to see if he was breathing when he sat straight up. She flew back a step.

He frowned. "What color eyes do you have?"

"Damn it, anyway," she cried as she sank onto the edge of the nightstand. She put her hand over her heart. "You gave me heart failure. I thought you went and died on me."

"Are your eyes really green?"

His words suddenly penetrated the rushing in her ears. "What are you talking about?"

"Your eyes. They were violet earlier."

He practically scared her to death over her eye color? "I wear contacts," she snapped. "I color coordinate my eyes with my outfits." And to keep nosy people from looking into her soul.

"Why are you ashamed of your natural eye color?"

Colleen got to her feet. This guy was unbelievable. She'd almost let herself forget that he wasn't to be trusted. "I'm not," she said, and turned the light out. Whoever heard of being ashamed of eye color? "They're just a plain ordinary color. Now if you're not dead, I'm going back to my book."

"Okay, sorry." The rustle of bed linen quickly followed.

"It's okay," she said and settled into the corner of the sofa.

"Thank you for staying here with me," he said. "You probably would have had more fun at the fireworks display."

She waited, holding her breath, for him to make some suggestive remark about fireworks. But none came. That in itself had to be proof he wasn't feeling very good.

"You're welcome," she finally said and went back to her book.

She read one whole chapter, and not having understood any word that had more than three letters, read it over again. She still didn't get it, but this time she suspected it was due to the man across the room, not the subject matter. She looked at him.

At times, he seemed the exact opposite of what she thought he would be. He seemed genuinely nice, not always on the make or looking to puff himself up at someone else's expense or so ego-driven that he never noticed anyone else. He seemed concerned about other people's feelings. In fact, he'd called his father when they'd gotten to the hotel room a few hours ago, worried that with all the news cameras around, his family would find out about his concussion and be worried. Yet Lisa had said he wasn't to be trusted. Was this all pretense?

Colleen gave up her book and trying to figure Neal out. She took a long, leisurely bath, then gave herself a facial and did her nails, stopping every little while to check on Neal.

He seemed quiet each time she looked. Was he sleeping or just pretending? His breathing was even, as if he was asleep. Not that she was any expert on guys sleeping.

When it got close to the time to wake him, she reviewed the printed paper the hospital had given her. It was brief and to the point. Wake every two hours. Check reflexes and pupil response. Pupil response? How was she supposed to do that? With a flashlight. A little diagram showed her.

Rats. Why hadn't she looked at this earlier? This nursing gig was harder than she'd thought. She checked her watch again. Ashley, Brad and John would still be at the fairgrounds' fireworks display, so they couldn't get her a flashlight. She picked up the phone and dialed the hotel's front desk.

"A flashlight?" the man said once Colleen had explained what she needed. "Why? Don't the lights work?"

"The lights work fine," Colleen snapped. "That's what the doctor told me to use."

"The doctor? What are you going to do with it?"

"Would you just get the flashlight, please?" she said coolly. "And deliver it to Dr. Sheridan's room immediately."

After hanging up, Colleen crept over to look at Neal. His breathing still seemed regular, which meant he could be in a coma but probably wasn't dead. She hurried to the door and stepped into the hall.

Within a few minutes the elevator door opened and a tall, lanky man in blue coveralls stepped out. "Here's your flashlight, Miss Cassidy," he said, and held out a huge, black, heavy-looking thing. "Seven batteries. Extra-large bulb."

Colleen took it in her hands. It wasn't a flashlight—it was a spotlight. It was something you'd use to search for airplanes in the night sky. "This is awfully big," she said.

The man appeared not to have heard her. "What you gonna do with it?" he asked, his voice eager. "Some Hollywood kinda thing?"

Colleen looked at him. What would it be like to be just a regular person, asked regular questions? "Yeah," she said, knowing it was useless to protest. "Thanks."

She slipped into the room, closing and locking the door behind her, then hurried to Neal's side. He looked the same as when she'd left him. Eyes closed, breathing slowly and deeply.

Her hand went out to touch his shoulder, but somehow it wouldn't. She couldn't. He looked so solid, so safe and so dangerous. She felt she'd be threatened just by letting her fingers rest on his bare shoulder. As if somehow all her defenses would be weakened and she'd be vulnerable to his charms. Crazy, but the way she felt.

"Neal," she said.

All he did was groan. Her heart skipped several hundred beats. Did people in comas make sounds?

"Neal." She spoke louder and poked him with the flashlight. Just a little. "Neal, wake up."

"Huh? What?"

Neal's face was in the shadows, but he spoke, so his eyes must be open. She turned on the flashlight, shining the beam directly in his face.

"Hey." He brought one arm across his eyes as he turned away. "Turn that damn thing off."

"Neal, stop that." She pushed his arm away and tried to pry an eyelid open. "I have to see your eyes."

"Ow!" He rolled away from her. "What the hell are you poking your fingers in my eye for?"

"I've got to see if you're in a coma."

"No, but I *am* blind now." He sounded irritated. The distance he'd sped from her across the bed agreed.

She sighed, letting her arms drop. She was doing it all wrong. She knew she would. She was good at pretending stuff, not being real. And she'd never been good at caring for things—any things. Suddenly her hand began to shake and tears welled in her eyes.

"I don't have any idea how to be a nurse," she told him, her voice shaky. "I never even played one in a movie. I don't like touching icky stuff like eyes and guts, even when it's pretending. You should have stayed in the hospital. You're probably going to go into a coma and die, and it'll all be my fault."

She wasn't crying, because she never cried. And she wasn't feeling silly or embarrassed or scared, because she had nothing to be embarrassed about. No, she was just tired and nervous and probably allergic to people in danger of comas.

"I'm not going to go into a coma and die," Neal said softly.

And somehow—in spite of his being blind and possibly suffering from a coma—he was getting out of bed. He turned on the light on the nightstand and slowly took her in his arms. She didn't fight it at all. It felt so good, so right.

This was the last place she ought to be, she knew, but she stayed anyway, continuing not to cry and not to feel stupid and embarrassed and scared. His bare chest was just right for laying her head against, the mat of brown hair soft against the hard muscles. His arms were solid and strong, perfect to keep her from toppling over.

She felt his lips brush her hair—felt the tremor all the way down to her toes—and let the sweetness ease her worries. The way he held her made her feel cherished, like she was delicate and fragile. Nobody had ever made her feel like that.

His arms tightened on her, or maybe she snuggled closer into his embrace. Either way, when his lips touched her forehead ever so gently, it seemed only normal to lift her face to his. To meet his lips with her own and let the sweetness surround her.

Except that it didn't stay all sweet and soft and gentle. As his mouth touched hers, she felt like she'd been hit by lightning. Something happened to make every inch of her feel alive. Alive and craving his touch. Her knees felt wobbly, her arms weak. This was just like it happened in her movies, except that was make-believe and this wasn't. This was some sort of magic and—

What the hell was she doing?

She jerked away from him. "Hey, now—"

There was a muted thud, and a look of pain crossed Neal's face. "Damn!"

She looked down just as another—softer—thud announced the flashlight had bounced from his foot to the floor.

"Oh, no." How could she have dropped that thing? "I'm so sorry," she cried and grabbed it as if that would stop Neal's pain.

But he just fell back on the bed with a groan, his eyes closed. Her heart really did stop. She was sure of it. Damn. Could a foot injury bring on a coma? It was all her fault for being such a ninny in his arms.

No, it was his fault for taking advantage of her in a weak moment. She should let him lay there in his coma.

But even as she had the thought, she was scrambling onto the bed, kneeling at his side and shaking him roughly. "Wake up, damn you," she snapped. "You can't be in a coma. I won't let you."

His eyes flew open and he shoved her hands aside as he sat up. "Did you take lessons in nursing or is your technique a natural one?"

She sat on her heels. "I told you I wasn't a good nurse."

"But I didn't know you meant lethal."

She stared at him glaring at her. Her stomach was flapping

like a loose sail in the wind, her hands were wet with sweat, and her heart rate had gone from zero to eighty million beats per second. Finally, she got slowly from the bed and put the flashlight on the nightstand.

"You know, we're going to have to do this again in another two hours," she said.

"God, no," he cried. His voice echoed with horror.

She turned to face him. He looked as horrified as he'd sounded. "I mean, just waking you up."

"Not poking me in the eye and dropping the flashlight on my foot?" He still sounded aghast, but there was something in his eyes. Just the hint of laughter. The barest suspicion of it.

Which was more than enough for her, thank you. "We can skip those, just like we can skip you being he-man," she said, and turned off the nightstand light with a satisfying click.

"Fine by me." Now his voice sounded like he was laughing.

She stomped to the sofa through the darkness and threw one of the seat cushions onto the floor, then the other one. She'd lay down for a while instead of trying to read. She could wake herself every couple of hours, no problem.

Six more hours, that's all she had left with this guy. No, what was she thinking of? It was six more weeks! How was she going to last? He was awful. Lisa was right. No decency, no integrity.

But his arms sure had felt wonderful around her.

"Want some help?" Neal called through the darkness.

Colleen jumped. Surely he couldn't read minds, too? "No, thank you," she said, making her voice smooth and pleasant. "You just rest. Two hours will be up again all too soon."

"And I sure need the rest to survive your exam."

Colleen said nothing as she threw down the back cushions and reached to find the strap to pull the mattress out. Nothing. She used both hands, feeling along the length of the sofa. There was no strap. There wasn't even an opening where the mattress would—

Damn. This wasn't a sofa bed. She had assumed the sofa would be convertible into a bed, but she hadn't actually looked. She frowned through the darkness. And the stupid thing wasn't even long enough to stretch out on. She turned, not able to see the wide expanse of bed next to Neal, but knowing it was there.

"Having trouble?" His voice sounded concerned. No, it sounded inviting. It sounded trustworthy and safe and too damn sexy.

She threw herself onto the cushionless sofa, probably bruising one of her better features on the rock-hard surface. "No, not at all," she said lightly. "I can't go to bed yet. I need to meditate."

"You meditate?" he asked.

"Whenever I can find a quiet moment," she said, hoping he'd take the hint.

And the first things she'd meditate on were all the reasons she shouldn't sneak into bed with Neal once he was asleep.

Nick wasn't sure how he did it, but he didn't move for almost four straight hours. Not once Colleen, wrapped in a light blanket, crept onto the bed next to him and stretched out.

At first, he thought he was dreaming. Beautiful women never crawled into his bed in Three Oaks. But then he knew he wasn't. If this was a dream he would have given himself more light. Then he'd be able to watch her as she slept rather than just sense her presense and have to be content with the scent of her nearness and the soft rush of her breath in the air.

By the fifth hour, the only part of his aching body that wasn't throbbing was his eyes—and that was because the darkness in the room was so complete. He'd thought that Neal's life would bring him a little excitement and the chance to sleep through the night. Well, there was no way getting concussed and then nursed back to health by Colleen could be called a *little* excitement, and spending the night in the same bed with her certainly wasn't a prescription for sleep.

Colleen stirred and rolled on her side. If he lay just right, he could see the gentle curve of her hip in a faint glow from the window. He let his gaze slide along her silhouette until his body burned from wanting her. What was he doing?

Somehow he got off the bed and into the bathroom. He gulped down equal amounts of air and cold water, really needing a cold shower but afraid that would wake her for sure. And that was the last thing he wanted.

He barely knew Colleen. He didn't know her real eye color. Or what her middle name was. They'd never argued over what to watch on TV or shared a meal of leftovers. How could he be lying in bed, watching her sleep? How could his body be responding as if they shared a lifetime of memories? Those things might not matter to Neal, but Nick believed that he and his brother were light-years apart in some ways.

He willed himself to relax. When that didn't work, he did some push-ups on the bathroom floor. Then some deep knee bends and sit-ups. If tonight was typical of Neal's love life, then Nick was going to be in great shape by the end of the tour.

Nick stopped in mid sit-up. What was that Neal had said in Portage? Love was nothing but a pet food.

He was wrong, of course, but so were all those slogans. Or maybe just misinterpreted. Love is all you need—if you were into pain and loneliness. There's nothing like love—for bringing misery. Nick wasn't looking for that. Never again. So maybe he needed to adopt Neal's definition of love. Or maybe it was all of Hollywood's.

Nick took a deep breath, got another cold drink of water and walked slowly into the room. Colleen's even breathing said she was still asleep, but just hearing her soft breaths was enough to send his blood surging. Nick slipped into bed, settling himself so that he lay facing her.

What would Neal do in this situation? He would wait, Nick decided. Colleen joining him in bed was a clear sign, but she was tired—they both were tired. He'd wait until morning, though the pain was agonizing.

Dawn came slowly after excruciating hours of Nick's feeling burned by Colleen's every breath. But finally the room turned a pale pink, then gold as the sun crept over the horizon. Nick felt his breath start to quicken, and the fiery knot in his belly grew tighter. She'd wake up soon and then smile at him and invite him to—

He was drenched in sudden sweat and rolled on his back with a strangled sigh. He wasn't into quickie affairs, no matter what his body was shrieking right now. He closed his eyes. But neither did he want this monk's life he'd been leading. So where did that leave him? Either he jumped off this cliff and accepted the gift Neal's life was offering him, or—

"Neal?"

His hands clenched and he took a deep breath, trying to become Neal inside and out. Trying to erase a thousand million memories from his subconscious. Then he rolled over to face Colleen, hoping his eyes didn't betray the panic of a man in free fall.

"Well, hello there, sleepyhead," he said softly. "Or should I say Sleeping Beauty?"

But she was already sitting up. "What time is it? I was supposed to check you every two hours."

"Hey, I'm fine," he said and slid a little closer. He touched her hand gently. Just the barest caress was enough to set his skin afire. "More than fine, actually."

She pulled her hand away to lay it on his forehead. "You're hot," she said. "And sweating like a pig. You must be coming down with something, and it's all my fault."

This didn't sound like any lover's talk he'd ever heard, but he would forge on. "I'm fine," he assured her and reached for her hand. "Let's just relax a little—"

But she was out of bed and out of his reach, switching on a light. She dug amid the sofa pillows, then pulled a piece of paper from under one. "A fever, a fever," she muttered. "It's not even on here! What kind of help is this?"

Nick fell back against the pillows with a sigh. He'd fought with a demon for hours, only to find out he'd been shadow-boxing.

"I'm fine," he told her. "I don't have a fever." He felt like an idiot, but that wasn't fatal, last he'd heard.

"Maybe it's part of the coma," she said.

"I'm not in a coma," he said. She obviously wasn't listening to him, so he gave up his soft, seductive tones. "I poked myself in the eye every two hours just to make sure."

"You don't have to be so hostile," she snapped.

No, he didn't, but damn it, he was in agony. Agony that she was sure to see if she came close to the bed. He carefully rolled over so that he was facing the other way. "I'm going to go shower." He was up and into the bathroom before she could respond.

The cold shower did the trick for his body, but not for his soul. He felt drained and weary. He'd been ready to shake off the shackles of the past. So what had gone wrong? He'd thought his words were pretty good. It must have been the delivery. Somehow his uncertainty must have showed. Well, he'd just have to do better next time.

When he left the bathroom, Colleen was ready to slip in, and he had another half hour to himself. What was Neal's technique? Humor. Compliments. An undercurrent of desire. And all delivered with confidence. Sounded easy. Sounded impossible.

He'd never done well on tests if he studied too much. This was the same thing—he was trying too hard. He went over and turned the morning news on, forcing himself to watch until Colleen came out of the bathroom. He glanced at her. She looked cool and wonderful, like a clear creek rushing over mossy stones, but he kept his reaction in check.

"Hazel," was all he said. "Very nice."

She picked up a pair of sunglasses and put them on. "Shut up." But she was smiling.

"That's pretty tough talk from someone so fragile-looking."

"Fragile-looking," she repeated with a laugh. "Maybe you're the one that needs glasses."

"Maybe you've played a part so long you've forgotten who you are."

Her lips tightened as the words left his mouth, and he silently cursed himself. He'd been doing great until that last remark. Where had it come from? Nick's cobwebby archives, not Neal's snappy repertoire, that was for sure.

"Are you ready to go?" she asked.

"Sure." He went ahead of her to open the door.

And stopped in shock. The hallway was packed with reporters. As soon as the door opened, they all started to clap and whistle. What in the world was going on? Nick stood there dumbfounded, but Colleen threw her arm through his and pulled him forward into the crowd. A burning heat shot through his loins at her nearness.

"So, Dr. Sheridan, what kind of a night did you have?"

He could barely think with her body pressed against him. He knew what kind of a night he'd wished he'd had. "It was—"

"Lovely." Colleen squeezed his arm. "Just lovely."

"Someone's pretty chipper this early," Cooper said.

Chipper? Only if that meant he looked like the wood chips that were spit out by the machine that ground up tree trunks. "Actually, Colleen—"

"Uh-uh," Colleen said, and stepped on Nick's foot. "Remember, a gentleman never tells."

Even with only ten minutes of sleep the night before, Nick was beginning to catch on. It was just more make-believe.

He smiled at her. "I guess I'm not supposed to say you hogged all the covers, then."

Colleen made a face. "Definitely not," she said, and everyone laughed.

"What did you need an industrial flashlight for?" a reporter shouted.

Colleen cuddled closer, so close that her every heartbeat echoed in his ears. Her every breath stole air from his lungs.

"I don't want to give away all my secrets," she said, her voice low and sultry.

"Come on, Colleen." The reporter was persistent. "Not all of us are Neal Sheridans. We can use all the help we can get."

Nick fought to keep hold of his sanity and still play the game. "Give it up," he said lightly. "You guys will never be me. Some guys are just born talented." And some were born looking like those who were.

The crowd laughed and let them through to the elevator. Nick knew he'd done great. He'd fooled them all. So why did he feel like hell?

## Chapter Four

"Oh, like, this is so totally—you know—like, just totally," the girl said.

"I couldn't have put it better myself," Colleen said with a smile as she autographed the poster and handed it to the girl.

"But just what was it you would have said?" Neal asked under his breath.

He'd leaned closer, setting off all sorts of alarms in Colleen's anti-hunk radar, but she turned to give him a bright smile. The very fact that her alarms were working today—as opposed to yesterday—made her feel strong. She was in control.

"You really need to listen better, darling," she said, and gave him a playful pat on his cheek.

They were still in Springfield—it was one of the two-day stops—at the grand opening of a new pet-supply superstore, sitting in air-conditioned splendor as they autographed Love Pet Foods posters. It was their second stop of the day—after a blessing of the animals at a local park and a lunch on the run. The nervous jitters Colleen had started the morning with were gone. Yesterday had been a fluke, she'd convinced herself. She'd worried so over Neal's reputation that she'd made all her worries come true.

"You guys make the greatest couple." The next person in line was a middle-aged woman with a camera. "I knew that article in *Worldwide* was a joke."

Neal had slipped his arm around Colleen's shoulders—setting off those alarms again—but seemed to pause. "What article?"

Colleen laughed and leaned forward to sign the poster—and coincidentally, move out of his embrace. "Maybe the question should be, which article? I think I'm *Worldwide*'s favorite topic."

The woman took a picture of the two of them, a copy of each poster and moved on to let a teenage boy step up to the table. He appeared to be trying to speak. His mouth kept opening and closing. No sound came out, but his face got redder and redder.

"I have the same reaction when I look at her," Neal said. His voice was surprisingly gentle, drawing Colleen's gaze against her better judgment. But Neal was facing the boy. "What's your name?" he asked.

"Bob," the boy managed to say, then his face went deadly pale.

Colleen turned to the boy, disturbed by something in Neal's voice and not wanting to dwell on it. "Don't pass out on me, Bob," she teased.

"She doesn't understand," Neal told him. "Men just don't have enough air to breathe around her, do they, Bob?"

Colleen wanted to tell him to stop being ridiculous, but something made her keep her mouth shut and sign the poster for Bob. The last thing she wanted was to get caught up in a discussion of anything with Neal. Yesterday was done. Over with. Lessons learned, the rest forgotten.

"There you go, Bob." She pushed the poster over to the boy.

He grabbed it as if she might change her mind. "I know everything about you," he blurted.

"Everything?"

"I know your first role was in *Deadly Gulch* when you were seven," he continued in a rush. "You were an orphan and Jessie Hayes raised you. You've been in thirty-four movies, seven TV shows and sixty-four commercials. You and Steele Blazes had a thing going a few years back but you dumped him for Mitch Tyler and then dumped him for Sinclair Davidson." He paused to take a quick breath. "You've lived all your life in Los Angeles, but your family can trace its roots back to Irish royalty."

"My," Colleen said, her voice faltering. He couldn't know everything, but he sure knew a lot. She didn't feel quite so in control anymore and was relieved when the boy hurried away.

"Steele Blazes?" Neal said. "You know, I've always wondered if that was the name his mother gave him."

Colleen fought back a laugh. It was almost as if he'd sensed her uneasiness and wanted to put her at ease. Not that she needed his help. And not that she was going to acknowledge it. She smiled at the two young girls who were next in line and signed another poster. She'd always taken care of herself and always would. No need for anyone's help.

"Now hold on to those," Neal said to the girls as they collected his poster.

*Hold on.*

Neal's voice broke into her thoughts, and Colleen remembered suddenly when he'd held her last night. When his arms had slipped around her so naturally, so comfortably, and her heart had been convinced that she'd found a haven.

Lordy, where had that come from? Colleen shook herself back to life and signed another poster as Brad came up behind their table.

"Another fifteen minutes," he said quietly.

Colleen nodded and signed her name again, handing off the poster with a quick smile.

But Neal turned to face Brad. "Fifteen minutes?" he repeated. "We need another couple of hours to take care of everyone."

*Take care of.*

Colleen found herself lost in Neal's voice again. He'd tried to take care of her yesterday when he'd warned her about the steer. He'd taken care of her when she'd fallen asleep last night, and when she'd totally botched her nursing assignment. He'd even taken care of her with the reporters, going along with her suggestive remarks.

"Love leads and we follow," Neal said, his arm brushing hers as he passed out another poster.

His touch awoke a strange wonder in her, his words a definite panic. "What did you say?" she cried. Love had nothing to do with any of this.

He gave her an odd look as he handed a poster to an elderly lady. "I just meant that whatever Love says we have to do, we do."

Colleen closed her eyes for a brief escape. "Oh. Love Pet Foods." Her mind had really gone out to lunch for a moment. She felt like a complete idiot.

"What else?" He frowned, his eyes shadowed as she felt him turn inside himself. "Oh, love, as in true love? Well, I guess that fits, too."

"I wouldn't know about that."

Neal's reaction wasn't what she expected. She thought he'd laugh at her or tease her. Not close himself away so visibly. Could he have lost someone he loved? But this was Neal Sheridan—king of the three-week romance! She busily scrawled her name across the bottom of a poster and handed it to a teenage girl.

"You've never been in love?" he asked once he'd handed out a poster also. His voice held surprise and something that sounded close to pity.

Pity? With a sudden jolt, Colleen was back in the driver's seat. It was just another of Dr. Studly Sheridan's tricks. "Poor little woman, never been in love? I have—" pause for dramatic sigh. "Let me show you what you're missing." *Fat chance, fella. Find some other woman to trick. Colleen Cassidy is too smart.*

Colleen didn't bother to answer Neal, but smiled at a young mother with her two kids. "Hope you didn't have to wait too long."

Colleen spent the rest of the time talking to the people in line and ignoring Neal. She barely noticed when his arm brushed hers or when he shifted in his chair and his knee touched hers. That shiver was due to the air-conditioning, not to Dr. Charming.

Her good feelings lasted through the rainy ride to the hotel and changing—in her own room this time—for the Humane Society dinner and the reception afterward. If anything, she grew stronger with each passing moment. More and more in control. So much in control that she wasn't afraid to walk into the banquet room with Neal.

"You have much family in Los Angeles?" he asked.

His words caught her by surprise. "Actually, the only family I know of are my Irish ancestors," she said.

"Oh." He gave her a look that increased her uneasiness. "Must make for lonely Christmas dinners."

It was an invitation to confide that she'd been offered dozens of times before. True, he did it better—the urge to tell him the whole Irish royalty bit was a fake, just like her name, was stronger than it normally was, but the habit of silence was stronger still.

She had no family. Her mother had died years ago, and Aunt Jess, who had been family by virtue of her love, was gone, too. And if Colleen's father or his family were still alive in Iowa, they were no part of her. She would turn her back on them, the way her father had turned his back on her mother all those years ago, when she'd been pregnant and alone.

Luckily, Colleen and Neal had reached the head table, and the moment passed. It was time for her to be on stage where she belonged, where her persona was created by her, not by the random whims of fate. So she provided sparkling dinner conversation, and Sassy Mirabel gave a short and snappy after-dinner speech while Colleen Cassidy did her best to shock—but not offend—the donors at the reception afterward. Jennifer Anne Tutweiler, daughter of the rejected and abandoned Jane Tutweiler of Los Angeles, California, wasn't heard from, but then she hadn't existed for years. Not even in Colleen's mind.

So why was that little girl with her dreams of a big family bumping around in Colleen's thoughts?

Because Neal Sheridan—damn him anyway—had woken her up. Luckily, Colleen knew that the longer she played her roles, the quicker Jennifer Anne would disappear again.

So Colleen made sure she was the belle of the ball. She was witty and concerned and outrageous. She teased Neal until he was speechless, posed for pictures with everyone and their uncle, and even donated her scarf for a raffle the society was holding next month. By the time Brad made their excuses and herded them out the door, she was exhausted. At their hotel, she let the others walk inside ahead of her, but Brad waited in the slight drizzle.

"You two did great today," he said, nodding to the doorman as they went into the lobby. "Super chemistry."

"Thanks." All she wanted was to get to her room and unwind.

A sprinkling of the tour media was in the hotel lounge area just off the lobby, having drinks and relaxing. And waiting for the hint of a story. Cooper was there, sitting with two other women while her eyes followed Colleen and Neal like a hungry lion.

"Neal says his head doesn't hurt anymore," Brad said.

"That's good." Didn't that woman ever sleep?

"I'm not sure if it is or not."

Colleen saw Cooper getting to her feet but forced her mind to Brad. "What do you mean you're not sure? Would you rather he had a concussion?"

"You have to admit it made for damn good PR," Brad said. "The way you took care of him, staying in his room, curing him. It was great."

"I didn't cure him," Colleen said sharply. "If you must know, I fell asleep."

"So how's the big strong doctor?" Cooper called, her piercing voice drawing everyone's attention. Even the silk plant in the corner listened up. "You going to need nursing again tonight?" She paused long enough to turn her gaze to Colleen. "Or is your nurse playing another game?"

Colleen could feel the woman's threat in the air, the unspoken accusation, but Neal just laughed.

"I'm fine," he assured everyone. "Colleen did a wonderful job. She deserves a night off."

Cooper snickered, and Colleen could see the next *Worldwide* story—a confirmation of the last one.

"A night off?" Colleen sashayed over and wrapped an arm around Neal's waist. "Honey, if you're too pooped, just say so, but this gal would have to be dead before she needs a night off."

Everyone roared, cameras clicked, and the moment passed. But all Colleen felt was a cloud of gloom gathering in the distance.

Chemistry. The only thing she could remember about high school chemistry was the tendency for stuff to blow up in her face.

Handling the tour was no problem, Nick told himself as he stood under the shower. Handling his reaction to Colleen was much more of a challenge.

She was so damned gorgeous. One look at her, one whiff of that faint flowery scent she wore, and he wanted to possess her. He wanted to bury himself in her soft moistness. He wanted to know every inch of that perfect body. And he wanted to bash in anyone's face who dared look at her.

This wasn't him! He'd never reacted to a woman this way before. But then Colleen didn't seem that interested in being possessed by him or having him bash in anyone's face for her. So maybe it didn't matter.

It was this crazy world of make-believe. Nothing had been

right or real or sensible since he'd met John last Friday night in Chicago. And Nick had made things even worse this morning when those reporters had been outside his door. Vultures waiting for roadkill.

He should have told them the truth about last night. Letting them think he and Colleen had made love might have made him look like the great lover, but it only complicated the situation.

Nick turned off the water, got out of the shower and dried, then dressed in shorts and a light shirt. He needed some time to get his head together. He needed to regain some control of this farce. Maybe a walk would do him some good. Or if it was raining harder, he'd see if the gym downstairs was open.

He was putting on some shoes when he heard a light knock at his door and went to open it.

"Hello, sweetheart," Colleen said.

Nick barely noticed the flashbulbs flickering in the hallway. With the TV spotlights shining in his face, he was lucky he could see anything. Although he didn't need to see Colleen to sense her presense.

"How are you, baby?" Colleen put an arm around his neck and pulled him down so she could lock her lips to his.

His blood pressure soared. His temperature skyrocketed. His sanity just plain fried. He knew nothing but the soft sweetness of Colleen's body pressed against his. Of her womanly scent that smashed his willpower into tiny pieces to be blown away by the hunger pounding through his blood.

The earth was trembling beneath his feet. The stars were exploding around them. Colleen's arms were moving him from the raging fire of his—

She shut his door and slipped out of the clinch like a vampire who'd tasted holy water. When had they come inside the room?

Colleen was obviously not suffering from the same dementia. She walked to the windows, dropping an enormous purse on the bed as she passed.

"You shouldn't leave these open." She drew the drapes closed.

"Okay," he said slowly. "Consider them closed."

Colleen's only response was to fall back on the bed. She kicked off her high-heeled sandals, put her right arm across her face and lay still.

Looking at her beautiful body stretched out before him, Nick felt the hunger again consume him. All he wanted to do was…was something he didn't want to admit. His second choice would be lying by her side and pulling her into his arms.

But he wasn't going to do either. Control was his goal here—of the situation and himself. He lost control whenever he got too close to Colleen, so he would stay away from her. He could ask her from this side of the room if she wanted to go for a walk with him.

But then a small movement caught his eye. As Colleen lay stretched across the bed, her left hand tugged slightly at the hoop earring in her ear. It was a small tugging, one she probably wasn't even aware of, but it made her look vulnerable. And awoke all sorts of memories.

Donna used to play with her rings when she was nervous. She denied doing it, but it never failed—when she got tense, the rings got played with. He remembered that last year, when they'd been trying to have a baby, how she'd finger her rings more and more as her period approached.

The usual pain flooded in in the wake of the memories, then receded, leaving the familiar ache behind. He was used to it now—eat, sleep, remember, hurt. It was the pattern of his life.

But rather than feel the expected weariness, he felt a surge of anger. This was supposed to be his escape. These six weeks, he was supposed to be free. He wanted to feel excitement and curiosity, the thrill of being respected and looked up to. He wanted to feel the rush of desire when he was near Colleen— she was one of the sexiest women he'd ever seen, for heaven's sake. Desiring her only proved that he was alive.

But something had changed. Now he looked at Colleen and

all he saw was vulnerability. She had built a damn near impenetrable wall around herself, but all he could feel was her raw pain.

Damn it, this wasn't what he wanted. He didn't want to know why she acted so tough or what had hurt her so deeply. He wanted to make wild passionate love to her. He wanted to laugh and tease and spend long steamy nights in her arms, with satisfying their physical needs the only thing they cared about. He didn't want to know anybody's secrets anymore.

"Look, I was just going for a walk," he said. "You're welcome to come with me if you want."

Colleen took her arm from her face and sat up, leaning on her elbows. The move accentuated the rise of her breasts, a curve that didn't need any help.

"You're kidding, right?" she asked.

He forced his eyes to her face. "About what? I thought some time alone would feel good."

She fell back on the bed. "Maybe it's different for you, but the only place I can get time alone is in my room."

"Oh." That was dumb. He should have thought of that. "I guess I wasn't thinking straight."

She turned on her side to watch him. Her every move was a mixture of sensual explosion and innocence, but she seemed totally unaware of it. "You know, you sure aren't what I expected."

"You aren't, either," he said, but before he could go on, the phone rang. It was Brad.

"Hey, some of us are going down to the lounge for a drink. Want to join us?"

He ought to. He ought to get away from Colleen while he was in this weird mood and stay away until he stopped thinking he could see into everyone's soul. But he couldn't leave. "I don't think so," he said. "My head's aching a bit."

"You want me to get anybody to look at it?" Brad sounded concerned, and Nick felt a twinge of guilt.

"No." He looked at Colleen. "I'm okay. My favorite nurse is here."

Nick watched her, trying to see if his words brought any reaction. None that he could see from Colleen, but plenty from Brad.

"That's great," he exclaimed. "Hey, man. That's super."

Why? What was so great about it? But Nick didn't ask. "See you tomorrow morning," he said, and hung up.

A bitter taste lingered in his mouth. The sponsor must want him and Colleen to appear attracted to each other. Love leads and they follow. He had been righter than he'd realized earlier.

"Does it really hurt?" Colleen asked. "Your head, I mean."

"Just a little." He sat on the edge of the bed. Far enough away so he couldn't see her face. So he couldn't decide he could feel her pain. Time to shift gears. "All right. If we can't go for a walk, how about a little wickedness?"

She sat up. Her eyes had narrowed. "You know, if your head—"

"I was thinking double chocolate fudge," he said, not letting her finish. Her voice had changed. She'd sounded cynical and weary, and he didn't want the load that would bring him. "With nuts, whipped cream and two cherries."

"Ice cream?" She sounded more than surprised. Stunned, even. "That's your wickedness?"

"Are you game?" he asked.

She sat up, the laughter on her face changing her from a distant, untouchable goddess to the girl next door. There was a light in her smile and a gleam in her eye. One thing hadn't changed, though—she was still so damn gorgeous that he could scarcely breathe.

She picked up her big purse as she got to her feet. "You call room service. I'm going to change into something more comfortable." With a bounce to her step, she hurried into the bathroom.

In "Animal Life" when she changed into something more comfortable, it was sexy, revealing, something lacy and low-cut. Something definitely not more comfortable for the men around. Just the thought of it made Nick sweat, even though he doubted that that was what she was changing into.

He called room service and ordered two hot fudge sundaes, promising to pay double for fast service. Two autographed pictures—"To Tammy with love"—were preferred.

Soon after he hung up, a soft sense of tension filled the room, announcing Colleen was back. Nick turned. Like yesterday, she had on shorts and an oversize T-shirt. Her feet were bare. And, just like yesterday, she looked so beautiful that he found it hard to breathe.

"No wickedness yet?" she asked.

"Really good wickedness takes time," he said.

"I see." She sat on the end of the bed, curling her feet under her. She grinned at him, an invitation to heaven, it seemed. "And are you an expert on wickedness?"

Right at the moment, he wasn't feeling an expert on anything except gasping for breath. But then the sundaes arrived, leaving him to wonder why he had wanted them in such an all-fired hurry. The waiter set up the table in the corner with a cloth and silverware, then served the two sundaes while Nick pulled some photos from the pack John had given him.

"What are you doing?" Colleen asked, and peered over his shoulder. "Who's Tammy?"

"The ice-cream lady," he said, and finished signing the photos. "I offered her my firstborn, but she only wanted pictures."

Colleen laughed, and the sound was like raindrops falling on the forest floor. It seemed to wake something deep inside him. Which was crazy, since everything deep inside him had been woken up by Colleen the first moment they met. Nick gave the photos to the waiter, then joined Colleen at their little table.

"This was a great idea," she said. "Nothing is better than a hot fudge sundae."

"Uh, right," Nick muttered and dug into his ice cream. There were a lot of things better than a hot fudge sundae, but it wasn't a discussion he wanted to get into. He chose to go a safer route. "You have any pets when you were growing up?"

She shook her head. "Just Tommy the imaginary dog."

"An imaginary dog? Guess you didn't have to take him out too much at night."

She shrugged, seeming intent on savoring a huge spoonful of chocolate off the top of the sundae. It clung to her lip, and she slowly licked it off, sending Nick's blood pressure into the stratosphere. So much for safety.

"What about you?" she asked. "I bet you had a zillion pets."

"At least." Wait a minute, he was Neal. Nick was the one who'd had cats and dogs and hamsters and parakeets and even some frogs. "Uh, yeah. I had a cat."

She gave him a funny look. "A cat is a zillion pets?"

"Sure." He struggled for a moment. "It had fleas. And worms. Believe me, zillions."

She laughed and patted his hand before going back to her ice cream. Why had she done that? How could he get her to do it again?

"Where did you grow up?" Nick asked. "No, wait. In Los Angeles."

Colleen nodded. "How about you?"

"I grew up in—" he took a deep breath "—on the east coast. Washington, D.C."

"Oh, yeah?" She sounded surprised. "I would have guessed the country. You seem so comfortable around the bigger animals."

"I didn't think we were around too many bigger animals," he said. "Just old Bum yesterday, and if I remember correctly, I didn't fare too well with him."

"That was my fault." Her voice was serious, regretful.

"No, it wasn't."

"And I never thanked you for rescuing me," she said. "I was acting really stupidly and would have been hurt if it hadn't been for you."

But he only heard the word *rescue*. That was it. That's

where he'd been going wrong. Nick was the rescuer. Neal was the lover. Not that he wasn't glad he'd been able to take care of Colleen yesterday, but if he had been doing a better job of being Neal, maybe she wouldn't have needed rescuing. He had to force himself to think like Neal, act like Neal, be Neal.

"It was no big deal," he assured her with a smile. "Though I can think of various forms your gratitude could take."

She gave him a brief look before going back to her ice cream. "When you were a kid, did your mom fall all over you every time you batted those big brown eyes at her?"

"What?" That certainly stopped him short. "What does my mother have to do with anything?"

"I figured that you got your way with some woman way back when and that's why you think it'll work now."

"I'm not trying to get my way with anybody," he said. His voice sounded a little huffy, and he forced himself to relax. "And my mom was a sweet, gentle lady. I never tried to pull anything on her."

"Sure," Colleen said. "You were the perfect kid."

"As a matter of fact, I was," he said. "I won awards for my perfection. They still talk about me in hushed tones."

She grinned at him. "Like how perfectly you use industrial flashlights?"

They laughed together, and it was sweet. The constraints were down for a moment, and they were just two people getting to know each other. Nobody was hurting and nobody was vulnerable. They could talk about all sorts of things and not veer onto dangerous ground.

"Actually, my parents divorced when I was six," Nick said. "It was hard on us all."

She reached over and covered his hand with hers. "Did your mom have it rough?" she asked.

The touch of her hand drove all coherency from his mind. "I guess. I never really knew—" Neal, Neal, he had to be Neal "—my father."

"Who does?"

The laughter was gone from the room, like birds before a

thunderstorm, leaving only a weary sadness in Colleen's eyes. There was a wealth of questions in the air, but he wouldn't ask them. She'd shut some door in herself, shut it and locked it tight. Even if he had the key, he wouldn't use it. He was out of the caring business.

"I'm ready to hit the sack," she said, standing. "I thought last night's way worked pretty good. Share the bed but have our own blankets."

"Yeah." Nick stood up also. Last night had been agony, but he would die before he admitted it. "Sounds like a good plan."

## Chapter Five

It was raining. Pouring, if the noise of the water hitting the window was any indication. Colleen closed her eyes and snuggled deeper under the covers. Closer to Neal's solid warmth—

Her eyes flew open. No other muscles were allowed to move. It was morning. Dim light filtered through and around the drapes, letting her see her purse on the chair, the table where they'd had their sundaes last night and way too much of her side of the bed. Sometime during the night she had crept across the bed and right up against Neal!

She eased herself away from him, slowly crossed those miles of bed, then stood up. He hadn't moved. He must be asleep. Oh, please let him be asleep! She made a quick dash into the bathroom to freshen up enough for the dash to her room. That was the only reason for her heart to be pounding—just all the dashing around she had to do.

There were no photographers outside Neal's door, or hers, either; she rushed inside and locked her door. She wasn't responsible for what she did in her sleep, was she? Of course not, but she'd have to make sure that everyone understood that. She didn't want anyone thinking she had the hots for a certain doctor. Especially the certain doctor. Ashley came by as Colleen was drying her hair.

"I think we need to go real sexy today," the other woman said as she looked through Colleen's clothes. She pulled out a pale yellow halter-top sundress. "Maybe this one for the day." Then she took out a black evening dress. "And this one for tonight."

Colleen turned to look at her choices. They were nice dresses, ones she liked. Ones she felt good in. What would Neal think of them?

"Think Neal would like them?" Ashley asked, echoing Colleen's thoughts.

"Who cares?" Colleen snapped, both to herself and to Ashley. "I need to please my public, not him."

"It looks to me like they're one and the same," Ashley said and went digging through the shoe bag. "Or maybe you haven't seen that smitten look on his face when he watches you."

"Don't be silly." Colleen tossed her hair dryer into a case and started to put on her makeup. "This is all make-believe, remember? Great PR. An act of love."

"Yeah, but we both know that you have your limits where love is concerned."

Colleen froze, her mascara brush poised above her right eye. Ashley couldn't know. It was impossible. Colleen forced her hand to move and dabbed mascara onto the eyelash. "What's that supposed to mean?" she asked.

Ashley stopped putting aside the change of clothes for inside the bus. "Nothing," she said. "Just that I know you wouldn't throw yourself at Neal because the sponsor wanted you to."

"Oh, that love," Colleen muttered, and concentrated on finishing her makeup. What was the matter with her lately?

Ashley broke into laughter. "What other love do you have limits on?" she asked.

Colleen grinned—with relief and for effect. "You got me there." She tossed her makeup into the bag and slipped on the dress Ashley had left on the bed. Once she was dressed, she got her purse and her trusty pair of sunglasses.

"You won't need those today," Ashley said. "It's raining."

"I always need them," Colleen said. "What's the first stop today? The vet school?"

"The University of Illinois at Urbana Champaign is this evening. We're at Decatur for lunch, then a children's pet fair."

"Sounds like fun."

And it might have been if it hadn't been pouring rain when they pulled into town. And if it hadn't come after several hours in the bus watching Neal out of the corner of her eye. And if that hadn't come after spending the night in his arms.

Not in his arms! She corrected her wayward thoughts, but once the idea had been planted, it wanted to dance and grow and tease. What would it be like to lay in his arms all night? He seemed so gentle and caring, so very—

Untrustworthy. It was all part of his game. Why couldn't she remember that?

"Did I tell you how beautiful you look this morning?" Neal whispered as they went to the front of the bus.

She felt her cheeks flush—a totally stupid reaction from Sassy Mirabel. Sassy or Lucinda or Tanya had better start taking over. She gave him the flirtiest of smiles. "It's the closest thing I have to a nurse's uniform," she said. "Does it make you feel better?"

He looked flustered, then recovered. "Actually, it makes me feel shaky. Like I need complete bed rest for days, weeks even." His eyes grew darker. "With very specialized nursing."

She laughed and patted his cheek. "Poor baby. Too bad I'm booked for the next six weeks." She could handle him like this—all brash and cocky. That was what she was used to.

She stopped at the door of the bus and watched as first the security guards got out, then Ashley and Brad went to greet the crowd gathered at the door. The bus had pulled up as close to the door as it could, which still left about fifty feet of rain to race through. Teenagers from the school were waiting with large umbrellas, but that wouldn't—

"You can't go out in those shoes," Neal said. His voice had lost its playful tone and sounded a bit officious to her. "Your feet will be soaked before you go two feet. And with those sunglasses on, you probably can't even see where the puddles are."

She looked at the river of water racing along the route they'd have to take, then at Neal the Untrustworthy, and then pushed her sunglasses a fraction of an inch higher on her nose. "Well, I guess I'll just have to put up with wet feet."

He sighed and moved past her to the door. He stepped into the rain, then turned and scooped her up in his arms. As a teenager scurried along at their side with a huge umbrella, Neal carried her to the doorway.

Colleen was aware of reporters and cameramen hurrying along, too, and the laughter of approval from the crowd at the door, but mostly she was aware of Neal's arms around her and how good they felt. She'd been carried before, rescued often in the course of her movies and TV shows, but this was nothing like those times. This felt real. This felt safe. This felt like she was wrapped in the arms of a man who cherished her.

What a crock! She had to have turned her hair dryer up too high. This was all for show, she knew, and judging by the amount of film being used to capture it for the newspapers and fan magazines, it was a damn good one. And to make it even better, she slipped her arm around his neck and laid her head against his shoulder. Just for the split second or so that was left before they got to the doorway.

Neal put her down amid another flurry of snaphots. She smiled at the cameras and at him. Her heart was racing and her cheeks felt like they were on fire—due to the rain and the surprise of Neal's action and the crowd's pleasure, but she'd better be careful. Someone might think she was taking this seriously.

"You know, you really should take better care of yourself," Neal said. His voice was scolding, as if he was annoyed with her, but he leaned forward to wipe a raindrop off her cheek. More cameras clicked around them.

Criminy, she didn't need him to decide she was falling for him, but she didn't need him to play daddy, either. "Why should I when I have you around?" she asked, with a super-sweet smile.

His eyes—dark and disapproving—glared at her. She wasn't sure what he was angry about, but she knew with blinding clarity that she couldn't afford to let him win. She lifted her chin, and after a moment, it was over. So fast that she wondered if it had occurred at all. The crowd surrounded them, pulling them inside the building.

"You sure looked happy back there," Cooper said.

Colleen turned. The woman had slipped up unnoticed. Scary. Colleen was usually more aware of things like that. Her safety depended on it.

"And why wouldn't I be?" Colleen asked. "I didn't have to walk through all those puddles."

"Is that all?" Cooper pushed, her eyes searching and sus-picious. "You looked like a young girl who'd found her Prince Charming. You know, sort of innocent and virginal."

Colleen laughed loud and long. "You're delusional, Coo-per. The bus fumes have gotten to you." She hurried to catch up to the others.

"Hey, there, whatcha doing?" John sank into the chair next to Nick and looked at the papers in Nick's lap. "Going over your speech, eh?"

"Yeah." Actually, he'd been staring out the bus window, watching the rain race down the panes of glass and vowing that Colleen was not going to turn him inside out all the time.

He glanced at the speech he was supposed to give at the University of Illinois veterinary school this evening before he presented them with a check from Love Pet Foods. When he'd seen this stop on the schedule, he'd thought it would be a highlight of the trip. Now he couldn't keep his mind on it. He couldn't keep his mind on anything but the way Colleen felt in his arms—and then it certainly wasn't his mind doing the reacting.

"Something the matter with the speech?" John asked.

Nick forced his attention to Neal's manager. "It's fine. Brad's even got stuff in here about the great research they're doing on blood parasites. It's perfect." Nick paused, not knowing what else to say. "I guess I'm just excited about seeing their facility."

"Oh." John gave him a strange look. "Well, anyway, I just wanted to say you're doing a great job."

Doing what? Being a babbling idiot for Colleen to run ragged? But Nick didn't ask. There were some things, he'd learned, that he didn't want to know. "Thanks."

"Keep this up, and contract negotiations will be a breeze."

Nick stared at the man, feeling even more weight descend on his shoulders. Neal was up for a new contract and let Nick step in for him anyway?

"Brad's not involved in the new contract, but he has major input." John gave him a surreptitious thumbs-up sign. "Way to go." He returned to his regular seat and his papers.

Nick leaned back with a weary sigh. Now he had another burden to add to the load—to not lose Neal's job for him. That meant keeping Brad happy, which meant pretending that he and Colleen had a thing going, which meant playing along with her flirting even though he'd vowed yesterday that he was going to be in control.

Which meant he probably wouldn't get one decent night's sleep this whole trip. Well, sleep was vastly overrated, anyway.

Putting the speech aside, he ran his hand over his jaw. He needed to shave before they got to the vet school dinner. He rose to his feet, promising himself he was going to do things his way. Brad might be running the show, but Nick wasn't some puppet to dance when Love wanted. He had his own agenda, and right now, it was seeing the labs at the University of Illinois and talking with some of the researchers there.

He moved toward the back of the bus, then stopped short. Ashley was at the kitchenette table going over some papers, but Colleen wasn't in sight, and the bathroom door was shut. She was probably redoing her makeup for the next stop. No big deal, he'd just wait until she was done.

He sat across from Ashley. "You ever make a decision on those publicity photos?" he asked.

She nodded. "The leather one."

Nick leaned back. "I didn't think she'd pick that one I liked."

Ashley put her pen down. "She's very savvy about what her public likes, and I've learned to trust her. She's never wrong."

"Never?" Nick thought about the way she danced with the reporters. Colleen always led. She gave them what they wanted, or maybe it was what she wanted them to want.

"Trevor Madison is a great agent, but Colleen's been in charge of her career, not him," Ashley said. "I met her almost ten years ago, and even in her early twenties, she knew exactly where she was going. I think she was born with a career plan in one hand and a bank book in the other."

He tried to be impressed with Colleen's determination, to see how strong and capable she was. But he found himself instead wondering what had made her so self-reliant at such an early age. Who had failed her when she was young? All the things he didn't want to wonder about.

"Well, I guess I'll go back and read my speech again before I shave," he said, getting to his feet. "I'm looking forward to this evening."

"Wait a minute," Ashley said before he'd taken a step away from the table. She pulled a large envelope from her pile of papers and dumped out the publicity photos he'd seen the other day. "Here. You can have this, if you want."

She handed him the photo of Colleen he'd admired. The

one that wasn't posed, that seemed to show all the inner secrets of her soul. He stared at it a long moment, half wanting to give it back. To claim that he hadn't liked it much, after all. But the other half of him—the Nick half—wanted to take that lost, frightened lady into his arms and tell her that everything was going to be all right. And where was Neal's half—the one that would admire her beauty and see only how to make her laugh and smile? And wasn't that too many halves?

Damn, what had happened to the control? "Thanks" was all he said, then hurried to his seat. He stuck the photo into the papers Brad had given him, hoping out of sight, out of mind.

And it almost did. He and Brad got to talking about other ways Love could support pet programs, then he talked contract with John—just in general terms. He managed to shave and shower before they got to Urbana and felt fresh and ready for anything by the time they got to the banquet hall.

He and Colleen were seated at the head table, but apart this time, and though he felt a slight ache in his heart that his eyes couldn't feast on her beauty, he was glad. It gave him a chance to talk shop with the head doctors. He felt so confident—so Neal—that he even promised to do a segment of Neal's show next season on tick-borne diseases and their prevalence among greyhound racetrack rescues.

But then he went up to make his speech and present the check. It started great. He could feel his energy build and his enthusiasm grow. "And with these small advances come greater challenges and higher stakes. The work done here at the University of Illinois is a good example of how—"

He turned to the next page of the speech and found Colleen's picture. "—of how...of how—"

There was something in the way the light hit her face. Something in the angle he was seeing it from. Something that broke through the stupid barricades he'd been trying to put up against the fear in her eyes. Something so lost and needful and yearning that it wanted to break his heart.

"—of how working on small problems can lead to big solutions," he finally managed to say. Somehow he finished the speech and presented the check. No one seemed to notice his stuttering, but he felt shaken to the very core. How could he be Neal if Nick kept butting in?

"Great job, doc," Brad said afterward. "We just need a few shots of you and Colleen and the good doctors, then we can head back."

"I'm going to stay awhile," Nick said. "Dr. Derwent here has offered to show me around. I'll catch a ride to the hotel later."

Colleen joined them as Nick was speaking. "Just don't go saving any more ladies from rampaging steers," she said, tucking her arm into his. "One bump on the noggin per trip is enough."

The others laughed as she cuddled up to him, and he tried to. But it just wouldn't come. Her touch sent his blood pressure soaring, as always, and her scent drove his senses wild, but he could hear a tremor in her voice that said she was all alone.

He put his arm around her as they posed for the pictures, smiled for the camera and said all the right things, but his heart was heavy. No matter how he tried, he couldn't stop being himself, couldn't stop seeing beyond the smile and hearing behind the words. Everyone was using her for their own purposes—Love, Brad, the press. And he was no better. To maintain Neal's reputation, he was using her, too.

Once the photos were over and the others were dispersing, Brad slipped up behind Nick. "Don't be too late," he said softly. "The press'll be waiting, you know. And we don't want them thinking you're cheating on our Colleen."

Nick nodded as he watched Brad slip off to other chores, but suddenly he'd had it. There was only one way to free himself of Colleen's spell, and that was to shut his guilty conscience up. And the ever-present press was the way to do that.

Colleen stretched out on her bed in her comfy old T-shirt and shorts, settling back for a good hour or so of reading her investment banking book. It was heaven to be able to have all the lights on. Now maybe she'd make sense of what she was reading.

She read a paragraph—a hard paragraph—and then read it again before staring across the room with a frown. She should have gone on that tour with Neal. Maybe she would have learned something for her show. "Animal Life" was doing great—high in the ratings and nominated for a few People's Choice Awards—but it never hurt to try to improve. Next chance she had to learn more about real vet work, she would.

She went back to her book and reread that same paragraph, stopping when some people went down the hall. They hadn't made much noise, but it had been hard to concentrate nonetheless. It was quiet in her room, too quiet. The slightest noise was an interruption. At least when Neal had been around, her aggravation with him kept it from being so deadly quiet.

Of course, there were better ways to keep the little noises from distracting her. She didn't need someone around. Putting her book down, she went over to flick on the television. "Worldwide's Wide World" came on, the tabloid newspaper's television counterpart. Definitely not her favorite bedtime watching. She was about to change the channel when her face came on the screen. It was some footage shot at the fair in Springfield.

"On tour in the Midwest with Sassy Mirabel and Dr. Neal Sheridan," the voice-over was saying. "Now we've all heard that saying—where there's smoke, there's fire. Well, let me tell you, there's been plenty of smoke on this tour so far, but is it a fire or is it a smoke screen?"

Colleen took her hand off the channel selector. What were they talking about?

"Just minutes ago, we talked with Dr. Neal Sheridan about his torrid relationship with Colleen Cassidy."

The scene shifted to the hotel lobby downstairs. Neal was wearing the tux he'd worn earlier, and probably sending female hearts all across America aflutter. A clock in the background showed ten-thirty—an hour ago—so they must have caught him when he returned from his tour.

"I think we need to set a few things straight here," Neal was saying.

Her stomach twisted into a knot. She didn't like the sound of that.

"You all seem to be under the impression that Colleen and I had some exciting times the last few nights," Neal continued. "Well, nothing could be farther from the truth."

The knot tightened. What the hell was he doing?

"Are you saying that you didn't spend the last two nights together?" Though the camera was on Neal, Colleen knew that was Cooper's voice. Colleen's hands clenched as if they could somehow hold back Neal's words.

"We did share a room the last two nights," he agreed. "But that was all we shared."

Colleen sank onto the foot of the bed, complete disbelief washing over her. He couldn't do this to her! He was going to ruin her!

"I had a concussion and needed someone to check on me periodically. Colleen volunteered. That's all there was to it."

Colleen's eyes blurred for a moment, then anger kicked in. That scumbag! He was probably mad because she hadn't leaped into bed with him when he'd flirted. Well, she'd worked too hard to get where she was today. She wasn't going to let some jerk destroy it all.

He was still talking. "Colleen Cassidy is a gentle, compassionate lady. End of story."

End of story? Ha! That's what he thought. Neal was spouting more nonsense, but Colleen didn't wait to hear the rest of it. She tore out of her room, raced down the back stairs to the second floor and pounded on Neal's door. He opened it long minutes later, looking groggy and half-asleep.

"We need to talk," she said and pushed past him into the dark room. She didn't care that besides being half-asleep he was also half-naked. He could be all naked, and she still wouldn't care. Her treacherous cheeks burned, and she spun to face him as he flicked on the entryway light and shut the door.

"What did—"

"Damn you, Neal Sheridan," she snapped. "You ever step on my lines again and I swear, I'll kill you dead."

"What?" He looked confused. Well, actually, he looked exhausted, but that wasn't her fault.

"What do you mean, what? You know what you did."

He frowned, crossing his arms over his chest and leaning against the wall. "Humor me," he growled. "Pretend I had a concussion and my brains were scrambled."

She wanted to hit him. She wanted to throw something large and heavy at him. She wanted to tell him to put a shirt on, and some big thick baggy pants, too. Those little running shorts he had on were not conducive to an adult conversation. Of course, there were other things adults might do....

She moved away, went into the room and sat on the edge of the rumpled bed. "You're not going with the program." She carefully looked at a spot on the wall just past him.

"I'm not what?"

He was purposefully being dense. He was trying to get her all riled up, but she wasn't going to play his little game. "We both have big reps," she said calmly. "And you're wrecking them."

"I'm destroying our reputations?"

"Don't act dumb," she snapped, then took a deep breath. She had to stay calm. "You and I have images as easygoing folks. Fun people."

"And I've changed that?"

"Changed?" She snorted. "No, you haven't changed it. You've totally screwed it up."

"All I did was tell the truth," he said.

"The truth!" she cried. The hell with calm—this guy didn't deserve calm. "What in the world would you do that for?"

"Why wouldn't I?" He looked so outraged, so morally wounded that she couldn't stand it.

"Oh, get off your high horse," she cried. She picked up a

nearby shape in the darkness—a shoe—and threw it at him. Damn. He caught it.

"I think you owe me an explanation."

"I don't owe you anything." She dove for another shape.

But he had read her mind and went for it at the same time. She was off balance. He was too fast, and suddenly they were tangled up together. His arms were around her, his broad bare chest pressed against her. She tumbled backward onto the bed with him on top of her.

And then he was kissing her. Oh, Lordy, was he kissing her. He was kissing her like she had never been kissed before, never even dreamed of being kissed before. He was rough and strong and insistent. His lips demanded every breath she'd ever taken, every secret she'd ever whispered. His mouth swore that the song from her lips would be his.

She told herself to push him off, but instead she wrapped her arms around him. Sliding over his bare skin as he crushed her beneath him. His mouth devoured her, moving so relentlessly against hers until she lost all power to think. She gave herself up to the hungers that raged through her, to the exploding desires that flooded her to the very core.

She was caught up in a flood, awash in the rising power of his passion and without the strength to resist. Without the slightest desire to resist. His hands awoke all sorts of sleeping dreams, releasing them to be washed along in the current of his desire. Racing along to some dark whirlpool.

He moved away suddenly, as if just awakening, and she sat up, shaking as if she'd barely weathered a storm. It took a moment to catch her breath and then another moment before she thought there was a chance she could speak.

"I'm sorry about that," he said stiffly from somewhere in the shadows. "That isn't what you came here for."

What did she come here for? Some things were a blur. "Don't go all sensitive on me," she snapped, trying hard to pull herself together. Sassy Mirabel did not go to pieces over a kiss. "All I want is for you to be yourself."

He laughed, obviously finding something humorous in the idea. "And what is that?"

"Like every other guy in the world—callow and shallow and addicted to large public displays of affection?" That summed up about every guy she'd ever met—and some she hadn't. She got to her feet. Slightly unsteady, but able to walk. "I'll see you tomorrow."

"Sure you don't want to stay?" His voice was cynical, as if he was trying to hurt someone, but she had the strange idea it wasn't her. "What'll we tell the reporters?"

She went to the door. "That we fought."

"I'm not sure I can keep lying."

"Who said it's a lie?" She hurried out before her heart could tell her she was a fool.

The continuing rumble of thunder told Nick to quit faking it and just get up. He was never getting any sleep. He should just accept the fact and get on with his life.

He slowly got out of bed, not needing a light to see that the other side of his bed was empty. Hell, the room smelled empty. Just as empty as his house in Three Oaks. He walked to the window and opened the drapes wide. If somebody wanted to take a picture of him, let them.

It was still raining, spilling out of a sky so overcast it was almost black. People in Three Oaks always said Neal brought rain when he visited. Maybe Nick was doing such a good job of being Neal, he had the gods of rain fooled. Yeah, right. He dropped the curtains and stepped away from the window.

What had gone wrong last night? He sighed. The better question might be, what hadn't?

He had wanted to stop feeling that she needed him to rescue her from some dark, mysterious something. It had seemed simple. Until they'd kissed. Until she'd told him she wanted callow and shallow.

Hell, why was he fighting it? If callow and shallow was what she wanted, then that's what she would get. And it would fit in with his plans, too. A little fun and protect Neal's reputation, those were his goals. What would safeguard Neal's reputation better than some callow and shallow flirting with the young women on the media bus?

Colleen was already at breakfast, surrounded by reporters, when he got to the coffee shop. Some of them glanced up when Nick entered the restaurant, looking as if they were going to move to make room for him, but Colleen ignored his presence. She saw him—he knew she had—but then she deliberately turned away.

Proof that he definitely didn't want to get involved with her. When they'd spent the night in the same bed, she was all chummy in public. When they'd kissed and slept in separate rooms, she treated him like Genghis Khan. There had to be simpler ways to have fun.

He glimpsed a tall blond reporter at a table by herself. Mickie, Nicky, Kelly... What was her name? He knew she was with an independent news service but she wasn't wearing her name tag.

"Hi," he murmured, slipping into the seat next to her. "If you put your name tag on right now, I'll make sure you don't get arrested."

"It's Sally Anders," she said, smiling.

"I knew that. I was just trying to protect you. You may not know it, but Illinois is quite tough on media personnel walking around without their name tags."

Sally laughed. "What's really going on with you and Colleen?"

Her question caught him off guard. "With me and Colleen? Nothing."

"Right," Sally said. "You guys make like Romeo and Juliet for three days and now nothing?"

Damn. If there wasn't a story to report, the reporters would make one up. "Last I heard, we were both single and unattached," he said, getting to his feet. "Free to get involved or not get involved, as we see fit."

"Why'd you make that statement to the press last night?" Sally asked. "You two have a fight?"

"Later," Nick said with a wink, and headed toward the entrance, his appetite gone. Great. A lot of good talking to the press did last night. They believed what they wanted to anyway.

"Hey, Neal, come tell us what's really going on," a reporter called.

Nick stopped. It was someone at Colleen's table. And even from this distance he could see Colleen was upset. Her smile was wide and bright, but by his reading, a hair too wide and too bright.

"Come on, Colleen," another reporter said. "Something has to be wrong. Last night Neal claims you two aren't an item, and this morning you aren't talking to him."

Damn. For once she wasn't wearing those stupid sunglasses, and he could see she was glaring at him. Her eyes were spitting out the warning not to come near, that she could handle it. Like she had so far? With a weary sigh, he walked to the table.

"Who says we aren't talking?" he said. "With all you guys around, it's hard to get a word in edgewise."

"So give us the scoop. Are you two an item or not?"

"Colleen and I are as close as we've ever been." That was depressingly true. But as the media crowd stared, he took Colleen's arm and helped her to her feet. "Absolutely nothing has changed in that regard." He bent and kissed her on the lips— giving him a jolt but apparently not doing a thing for her. "Has it, sweetheart?"

Nick hadn't expected any undying gratitude, but a smile and a pleasant word would have been nice. He got neither.

Colleen turned to the reporters and gave them both. "See, I told you guys," she said with a laugh. "Not everything is a story."

The reporters couldn't feel it, but Nick sure could. Wrapped around all her sunshine was a tall, cold, barbed-wire fence meant to keep him out. That was fine, though. Just the way he wanted it.

He kept smiling, saying hello to the people in the lobby,

signing a few autographs and all the while leading her to the bus. Once onboard, they separated, taking their usual seats without a word.

Colleen was exhausting. She had more moods than all of Three Oaks put together. If he was lucky, she'd stay mad at him for the next six weeks. He closed his eyes and sighed when the rest of the crew got on and the bus pulled out of the parking lot.

The ride took a couple of hours but once there, Danville turned out to be a busy stop. First they toured a major hog farm, then they had lunch with the county veterinarians' association. After lunch they spoke to a 4-H session at the local high school. And at every stop it was the same thing.

"You two speaking yet?"

"Come on, what really happened?"

"What's the matter, Colleen? Doesn't Neal like to party?"

"What happened, Doc? Why aren't you giving Colleen the usual three weeks?"

He wanted to tell the reporters to bug off. To find some real news to cover. But he played along, denying anything was wrong. Colleen did the same thing, but he couldn't help notice that her tension grew as the day wore on. It was little things— playing with her earring, an air of distractedness, a laugh that rang slightly false.

Why was she letting the pressure get to her? She was the professional here. She should be used to it. Obviously, something was wrong, and it wouldn't be long before the reporters sniffed out that fact. Then they really would give her no peace until they found out what it was—or made something up.

He fretted, glancing around the bus as it sped to the last town of the day and the motel where they'd spend the night. Was he the only one aware of her tension? John was dozing across the aisle, Ashley and Brad were going over some papers in the seats in front of him, and the two security professionals were playing cards at the kitchenette table. No one acted like anything was wrong. He looked at Colleen.

She was staring out her window at the miles and miles of

cornfields. It was probably just the way the evening sun was coming through the window, but the longer the shadows grew, the more fragile she seemed. Like a dogwood tree breathtaking with blossoms that would be stripped bare by the next strong wind.

He sighed. Like it or not, he was going to have to fix it with the media. And the next town would be the perfect setting.

# Chapter Six

Clutching the key Brad had given her, Colleen stepped down from the bus and ran through the evening drizzle to her room. She'd been dozing on the bus, not even sure where they were, and woke up in time to hear Brad apologize for getting them rooms in this strip motel. The place looked clean but far from luxurious, with all the rooms opening out onto the parking lot. She was too tired to care, though. This had been a hell of a day.

"Going to be alone again tonight?"

Damn. Another half second and she would have been safely in her room. Colleen turned with a smile. "Hi, Cooper."

"It doesn't get any better as you get older," the woman said. "The loneliness, I mean."

"Who's lonely?" Colleen asked brightly. "I need a little breather, that's all. A little time to myself is heaven after being on show all day."

"Sure. Why not?" Cooper said. "But remember, when you're believing that nonsense, you're in trouble."

Laughter raced across the parking lot, causing both women to turn. The media gang seemed to be heading for a country and western bar across the street, Neal along with them.

Nerves ate a sudden hole in Colleen's stomach. It was going to be awfully hard to maintain her pose if the great Dr. Studly preferred drinking with the reporters to private snuggling with her. Of course, part of the problem could be that she wasn't actually offering him any snuggling.

"Guess I might as well join that sorry bunch," Cooper said. "Only thing worse than drinking your beer to country music is drinking your beer alone."

Colleen didn't know what to say. She'd caught a fleeting glimpse of a vulnerable Cooper and it was like seeing a party hat on a barracuda—disconcerting, to say the least. "Have fun," she said. "Hope the food's decent."

"Honey, you set your expectations too high and you get nosebleeds when you hit reality." After that bit of wisdom, Cooper turned to the drizzle.

Colleen hurried inside her room, shutting the door with a weary sigh. Cooper was wrong. There were worse things than being alone—and one was having your happiness depend on another.

Aunt Jess had told her women were born to be lonely, and the sooner you got used to it, the better off you'd be. If Colleen's mother had listened to that wisdom, maybe she wouldn't have run off with every guy who winked at her. But if her first love— Colleen's bastard of a father—hadn't turned his back on her, maybe she wouldn't have needed love so desperately.

That was a trap she was never getting caught in, Colleen thought as she moved away from the door. Trouble is, in trying to avoid that snare, she'd gotten herself into another mess. How was she going to get her party-girl reputation back?

Colleen took a shower, then changed into shorts and a T-shirt. She supposed she could join the others at that bar, work at having some wild fun, but it was so hard to know who to trust. Hollywood was easier. You weren't living with two dozen people for six weeks. There she could start a few rumors and step aside. Here, the rumors weren't enough. Everybody wanted a body count, and pictures.

Colleen picked up the phone and ordered a pizza from a joint advertised on the cover of the phone book. Neal was probably hoping to hook up with the blond reporter he'd talked to this morning and wouldn't want her around, anyway.

She had just settled down with her book when there was a knock at the door, and she tensed. Who was it? A fan? Some nutcase from the bar? Damn Brad and this open-air motel. Where were the security people, anyway? She slipped into a pair of sneakers and tiptoed to the door.

"Colleen, it's Neal. Open up."

She looked through the security peephole, then opened the door.

"What do you want?" she asked. It came out softer than she intended when she saw he had a single red rose in his hand. What was going on?

"I've come to beg your forgiveness," he said.

"My forgiveness?" She stepped out of the doorway into the fading light of evening and realized that he wasn't alone. Half the media crowd must be here, too. "For what?"

"I've been an ass." He handed her the rose. "It's a poor second to your beauty, but then everything would be."

She took the flower from him—how could she not when his eyes pleaded so?—though she had no idea what this was all about. The media crowd either knew what was going on or didn't care about specifics when a good photo opportunity came their way. The cameras were all clicking, and the spots from a video camera threatened to blind her.

"You didn't have to do this," she said.

"I had to do whatever it took to get back in your good graces." He reached out a hand. "May I have this dance?"

"Dance?"

Even as she asked, Neal turned and waved. And music filled the parking lot, coming from a big pickup truck parked close.

"This is crazy," she said as he led her toward the parking lot. But her heart was racing, and she felt like laughing.

"Ah, but it will stop all the questions," he said under his breath and folded her into his arms.

"That's why you're doing this?" She felt a quick flicker of disappointment, but forced it back. Or maybe the gentle drizzle washed it away as he swept her along with the music. It didn't matter why he was doing this.

"You said a public display of affection, didn't you?" he whispered.

His breath was soft on her neck, a teasing tickle that sent fingers of delight down her spine. She felt echoes of the hunger that had shaken her last night when he'd kissed her. A little voice tried to warn her to be careful, but she refused to listen. What was there to fear out here in the rain, in a motel parking lot, with a dozen reporters and camera people watching their every move? Taking pictures of their every move?

It suddenly did matter why he was doing this. He was doing this because she'd asked him. He was doing it because he was willing to play the silly games Love Pet Foods demanded of them. This was a performance he'd staged for her sake. For their sakes. For Love's sake. She started suddenly as the words of the song seemed to ring out over the parking lot.

"And love is the answer..."

She smiled at Neal. "You pick this song on purpose?"

He stopped to listen to the words, then laughed. "You think love is the answer?"

His quiet laughter did something strange to her stomach, seemed to tie it in a knot. She was glad the reporters were far enough away that they couldn't hear her words. And that the growing darkness kept her eyes hidden from even the most telescopic camera lens.

"It depends on the question," she said. "Yes, if they're asking who's my sponsor."

He looked at her, his eyes taking on a sad look. "You've never been in love?"

It was a strange question coming from the king of the three-week romance, but then she understood. Dancing here in his arms in a rainy parking lot, she got a sudden peek into his soul. That was what drew women to him—he fell in love. It didn't last, but for that three-week period, he made you feel you were everything to him.

It was empowering, this sudden understanding. She had nothing to fear from him. He could look into her eyes all he pleased, but the love—if there was any—would all be on one side. She would stay safe. The knowledge made her feel free, made her feel giddy and silly.

"Just don't fall in love with me," she told him softly. "I don't break hearts on purpose."

"Love is just a dog food, eh?"

She pulled back slightly to stare into his eyes. There was such a wealth of sorrow there that her heart wanted to break. Surely it wasn't from all his three-week romances. "Yeah, it is just a dog food," she said slowly. "Only a crazy romantic would think otherwise."

He just smiled—a slow, sad smile.

And she couldn't take anymore. "Speaking of crazy," she said with a burst of briskness. "If we get any wetter, we'll catch cold."

"We can't. They don't let things like that happen here."

She frowned at him. "Here?" Then looked around her at the motel parking lot.

The sun had set, and the evening shadows were swallowing everything. Down the street, she could see the neon signs of the restaurants and motels flashing against the coming night. The Eiffel Tower Inn. Louvre Paints and Wallpaper. The House of Crepes.

A fear crept into her stomach, slowly reaching out with icy cold fingers to chill every inch of her. She stepped back from his arms. "Where are we?"

"Paris," Neal said. "Paris, Illinois."

His voice was bewildered, as it should be. They'd all been given schedules, and Brad had talked about the various stops all day. She hadn't listened. How could she have been so stupid?

"Paris! I can't be dancing in the streets of Paris!"

"Actually, this is a parking lot."

But he was looking at her like she'd gone nuts. And maybe she had. It was just a silly coincidence. No reason to panic.

"You're right," she said, and tried to laugh. "And it was a great idea. The media sure ate it up."

She could feel their eyes—and cameras—on her. And on her they would stay for the next five weeks. She looked at the rose that Neal had given her and then at the truck, still blaring music from its sound system. He knew how to play the game, all right. The question was, could she trust him? Did she have a choice?

"Think we've put on enough of a show?" she asked him. "I'd really like to talk something over with you."

"We could have talked later," Colleen called from the bathroom. "You could have gone over to that bar, if you had wanted."

"Why would I want to do that?" Nick asked.

He glanced around her room, looking for something safe to stare at. Not the double beds or her clothes draped over a chair. Not the jewelry dumped onto the nightstand. He finally picked up the TV station card that was standing on the television set.

He and Colleen had put on their show for the media, and it had worked out great. Neal couldn't have done it better. Things would settle down now, and he'd be free to relax. As long as he stayed out of Colleen's room, that is.

She came out with two towels, handing him one. "Maybe you ought to go to your room and change," she said. "You look soaked."

"I'm fine," he assured her, needing to see this thing through.

He dried off his arms and face, then dried them again rather than watch Colleen towel dry her hair. He didn't want to be part of that intimate an action. He took his towel into the bathroom, hung it on the rack carefully, then came into the bedroom.

"Actually, this is probably for the best," he said. "It would look odd if we had this grand reunion scene and then I left to go out with the guys. Or went to my room by myself."

She smiled, but it never would have won an Oscar. "Yeah, I guess you're right."

A blind man would have seen that something was wrong, but he was not going to ask. Just as he was not going to ask her why she'd gotten so flustered outside, either. He was finally getting his role down pat.

"So what now?" he asked. "You want to go get something to eat?"

There was a knock at the door and she brightened slightly. "That must be the pizza I ordered. Eating here okay with you?"

He felt the walls of the room close around him, saw the beds looming large and no dinette table available, but held himself in check. "Sure. Sounds great."

So they sat on one of the beds, sharing pizza and diet cola. It was altogether too cozy for Nick's taste, but Colleen seemed to relax. And whatever had been troubling her seemed gone. Without his help, he noted, which ought to convince his rescuing reflexes to stop trying to take over.

Of course, there were other reflexes that were leading the revolt just now. Mainly because Colleen didn't look anything like the drop-dead-gorgeous woman on the Love posters. But with no makeup, her hair hanging in damp ringlets around her face and no sultry look in her eyes, she was ten thousand times more beautiful. And more dangerous to him.

He took another slice of pizza. "What did you want to talk about?"

She was picking up a piece for herself and acted like she hadn't heard him. "You know, this is just like a slumber party."

"I never had too many of those." He kept his eyes on the pizza, as if counting the mushroom slices.

"I did one in *Two Bits, Four Bits*," she said.

He glanced at her. "In a movie? Didn't you ever have a real one? I thought all girls did."

"Only ones with normal childhoods." She ate her pizza, then wiped her hands before looking at him. "You know, I've been thinking…" She took a deep breath and tried to smile. "Love really is trying to throw us together. And that horde of reporters isn't helping any."

"Helping?" Nick grimaced. "Aiding and abetting is more like it."

She grinned "We can't exactly skip out on the tour."

"Or do it incognito."

"So how do we handle it?" she asked.

Her grin was intoxicating, her laughter addictive. The first thing he had to do was get off this bed.

"You done eating?" he asked.

When she nodded, he picked up the box and the napkins and tossed them onto the dresser before pulling up an easy chair. He sat down, putting his feet on the end of the bed. Still too near her for his peace of mind, but his brain was able to function somewhat.

"I'm glad you brought this up," he said slowly. "Love and the media sure seem to have a plan for us. I think we need to come up with one of our own."

She leaned against the headboard, a shadow falling across her face. "It's not that I object to having some fun," she said, her voice careful. "It's just that I don't want it orchestrated by someone else."

"No arranged marriages," he said.

She nodded. "Right. We can pretend all we like, so long as we both know it's just pretend."

Nick looked at her. Either he had totally misread Neal's life or he had misplayed the role since he'd gotten to Chicago. The latter was totally possible, Nick had to admit to himself. He had been out of the dating game for years—assuming he had ever been in it—and could easily have put his foot in his mouth numerous times and driven Colleen away.

Yet given what he'd seen of the press and their ability to fabricate a story out of nothing, maybe the stories about Neal's love life had all been a lie. Or greatly exaggerated. Hell, all that stuff about Colleen's life could be pretense, too. Maybe she wasn't the wild party girl. Maybe it had all been set up for publicity reasons. From what he'd learned of her in the past week, it suddenly seemed not just possible, but likely. So she wasn't rejecting him, she was just putting their relationship on its correct ground.

"Okay," he said briskly, glad to finally understand. "So we play it cool. Put on some public displays and maybe spend some evenings together like this one, but maintain our independence."

She sat forward, and light fell across her face. She was smiling. "No more tantrums like this morning, is what you're saying?"

"Well, I'm not sure I would call it a tantrum."

"Only because you're too nice."

Nice wasn't what he was feeling. A little embarrassed, perhaps, that it took him so long to catch on. And a bit regretful, too, that his attraction to Colleen would stay his secret.

"So we pose however they want for the pictures," he said briskly. "But we know it's all a game."

"Just like playing a part on TV."

"Exactly." He got to his feet. "Think I can safely go back to my own room now?"

"Hey, we're independent, remember?" She got off the bed and walked with him to the door. "And maybe we're really quick, too. We ran in here after we danced and made mad passionate love while we ate pizza, and now we're ready to be independent again."

He stopped, his hand on the doorknob. Something in him couldn't let those words go unchallenged, though he knew he should leave. "I don't make mad passionate love fast," he said. "Certainly not while I'm eating pizza. And I would not hurry out an hour later. I think you've had the wrong kind of lovers in the past."

She turned red. "Sounds like it."

"And love is not just a pet food," he told her, his voice sounding bitter with its certainty. "It's a living, breathing monster that consumes you until you can't think straight. Anyone with half a brain should run from it as fast as they can."

Before she could respond, he bent down and brushed her lips with his. A thrill of desire raced through him, tempting him to pull her into his arms, but he fought it. Even if he didn't know the rules, he had his own warning ringing in his ears. Love was something to run from, to avoid, to fear. It didn't matter how his body reacted to her nearness, she was a trap waiting to spring on him.

He reminded himself as he walked down the wet sidewalk to his room. The parking lot was deserted—no media people hanging about to capture yet another picture of them—and he felt totally alone. But it was a good feeling. He felt free.

His wandering took him past the motel lobby, and he ducked inside. After buying a newspaper, he stopped to look through a rack of postcards.

"We got stamps if you want to send some postcards," the man at the registration desk offered. "And we can put it with our mail to go out tomorrow morning."

Why not? Neal deserved to know how great things were going. Nick pulled a Sights to See in Gay Paree postcard that showed smiling cows and pigs and ears of corn and wrote his own name and address on it. *Am getting quite an education in Love.*

"So how are the lovebirds?" Cooper asked late the next morning.

Colleen smiled at her. "Just fine," she said. "Couldn't be better."

"Then why is he over there and you're over here?"

"Because we are two separate people with two separate lives."

Cooper didn't look pleased with the answer, and Colleen felt nerves dancing in her stomach. It had sounded so good last night, but would it work? It must have—at least this time—for Cooper moved toward the media bus, and Colleen climbed on her own.

Colleen sank into her seat with a weary sigh. Neal was still on the sidewalk, talking to three women wearing Charleston Animal Rescue sweatshirts. He looked so caring, so trustworthy, but it had to be an act. Nobody was that nice, that decent. Except for Lisa's Mr. Perfect, of course, but Colleen was willing to bet her last People's Choice Award that even he had feet of clay.

Neal's statement nagged at her—that she'd had the wrong lovers in the past. He must be on to her, though there was no way he could know there had been no lovers in her past. She was going to have to watch him carefully. Sooner or later, he'd show his true colors.

"Everybody here?" Brad called, then looked out the bus window and caught sight of Neal. "Damn. We've only got an hour to get to Toledo."

Brad hurried off the bus to get Neal. Colleen watched as Brad was forced to almost drag Neal away.

Whatever Neal was talking about was something he sure seemed to believe in. Colleen bit her lip, suddenly torn. Someone that passionate couldn't hide his motives, and Neal was certainly passionate. He had causes he was devoted to, and exposing her as a fake wouldn't be one of them. It just didn't fit. She was comparing him to Steele and Mitch and Sinclair, and maybe he was nothing like them. It was possible.

She smiled at Neal when he finally got onboard, then settled in with her book. She had the urge to go sit with him but talked herself out of it. The bus was private time, not show time. There wasn't anybody around to impress. She forced herself to try to read her book until they got to the pet parade in Toledo.

"You must be an expert in investing by now," Neal said as they walked up to the stage set up in the park.

"Not quite," she said, her suspicions sprouting again. Did

he know that she was worried about the day her star would fade? How would he use that against her?

She was getting paranoid, reading the worst into every innocent thing he said. Her worries faded as they posed for picture after picture. It was the gentle touch of his arms as they encircled her, though the way her heart raced was far from gentle. Maybe this was part of his plan. Maybe he was trying to make a list of her weaknesses. Maybe she'd seen one too many cornfields and had become delusional.

By the time the day ended, in Effingham with a humane society fund-raiser, Colleen no longer knew what to think about Neal. She was going to have to work harder at finding his Achilles' heel. So she gushed and posed and snuggled and played the game to the hilt. And was exhausted when she went to sign autographs at the end of the evening. Neal was an expert at the game. He never once let his guard down. Never once showed his real self.

"It's so exciting to meet you," a woman gushed to Colleen.

"We always watch your show," another added.

"You and Dr. Neal make such a wonderful couple."

Colleen smiled and signed the Love posters brought in for her. It was good to know someone was fooled by their performances.

"You need to get him to be on your show with you," one of the women said.

"Yeah, dump Jeffrey. He's a jerk."

Colleen stared at them. All last year, they'd gotten hundreds of letters wanting Jeff elevated from bit player to costar. "I thought everyone liked Jeff."

"That was before we saw you with Dr. Neal."

"Before we knew you were falling in love with him."

A new panic sprouted in Colleen's stomach. "I'm not falling in love with Neal."

The women shook their heads.

"We saw 'Worldwide's Wide World' last night and saw you two dancing in Paris," one said.

"And heard how you won't dance in Paris until you're in love."

Colleen tried not to groan as her stomach churned. Damn that Cooper. "That's not exactly what I said."

"We think it's so wonderful."

Colleen didn't say anything more, knowing it was a lost cause. She hoped Neal wasn't hearing about her love, too. She'd just been showing off when she'd made that stupid statement to Cooper, using examples from old movies to prove a point, but she should have known that Cooper would remember every word she said.

What bad luck to end up in Paris last night! If it had been in Effingham, Cooper wouldn't have been able to make a big deal of it.

But by the time Colleen and Neal were walking through the hotel lobby that night, she was able to laugh over the incident with him. Oh, not her silly statement and Cooper's fixation on it, but that he was being voted in as her hero.

"Jeff can keep the job," Neal said dryly. "I don't think I'm up to it."

She didn't know what that meant, but it definitely rankled. "You wouldn't want to be my costar?" she asked.

"Not in a million years." He pushed the button for the elevator. "I know my limitations."

So much for his mighty charm. He must save it for women he figured he could bed, and he'd eliminated her. "I'll have you know everywhere I go, men are offering to trade places with Jeff."

"They must be stronger than me."

"Strong? They don't have to be strong." The elevator doors opened and she stepped inside.

He leaned in and pushed the button for the third floor, holding the door open with one hand. His eyes were dark with something she couldn't read. "Oh, believe me, working with you every day, pretending to care about you, they need to be very strong."

His voice touched something deep inside her. His eyes suddenly were alive with a million shades of caring. She didn't know what to say. Didn't know if she even could speak. But she was saved the necessity because he stepped back and the elevator doors closed.

Damn him. Once he was gone, a full load of anger washed over her. She was never going to know what was going on in his head.

Thursday was a repeat of Wednesday. A pet fair in Salem, then on to a pet store grand opening in Mount Vernon and then a dinner at Southern Illinois University in Carbondale. Smile, smile, smile. Pose, pose, pose.

Cooper seemed to be everywhere, too, her eyes always narrowed in suspicion as she watched Colleen with Neal. Colleen knew what the woman was looking for—a crack in Colleen's armor. Colleen had to pretend Neal wasn't driving her crazy.

And Neal was even more devious than she expected. Colleen could think of no other reason for his sudden solicitousness.

"I'm going to be a little late," he told her after dinner. "Nelson has a problem he wants me to look at."

Colleen looked up to see a heavyset man across the table wave at her. "What kind of problem?" she asked.

"A mare," Neal replied. "With an inflammation in her ankle."

"A horse?" That was stupid. Everybody in the world knew a mare was a horse. But it was all Neal's fault. If she didn't have to keep such a close eye on him, she might be able to think before she spoke.

Then Colleen turned slightly and saw Cooper off toward the side of the banquet hall, watching. Between the reporter's persistence and Neal's deviousness, Colleen couldn't rest. She turned to Neal.

"Of course, you have to go," she told him, clutching his arm as she had clutched Linc Burton's in *Night of No Hope* when she'd been urging him to save the orphans from the flood. "I just hope you can help the poor thing."

He looked a little startled at the passion in her voice. "It really isn't anything that serious."

She threw her arms around him and held him close for a long moment. Her knees got wobbly and her stomach tied itself up in knots. Either she was really into her little performance or her traitorous body was enjoying itself a little too much. She pulled back from Neal.

"Let me know how she is. I won't sleep for worrying."

He gave her an odd look before leaving with Nelson. When Colleen turned Cooper's way, the woman was gone. Colleen smiled and made her way over to Ashley and John. Maybe Cooper was finally getting the idea that there was no story.

But if there was no story, why couldn't Colleen sleep? Her room was right next door to Neal's, and she found herself lying in bed, listening to the silence. Eleven o'clock. Midnight. One o'clock. How long did it take to check a swollen ankle? He probably was out drinking. Or in the arms of some all too willing farm girl. He'd come back reeking of beer and perfume.

Not that she cared, but he'd better be discreet. All she needed was for Cooper to get one whiff of Neal fooling around and—

Colleen heard a noise in the room next door and hurried to the connecting door. She knocked, and the noise stopped. Probably trying to pretend he wasn't there. She hadn't been born yesterday. She knocked again.

"Neal," she whispered. "It's me. Open up."

He opened the door, and all her righteous indignation fled. His white dress shirt was streaked with blood!

"What happened?" she cried, and pushed past him into the room. "You were mugged! Damn these small towns, they pretend they're so safe. You should have taken one of the security people with you."

Neal laughed and took off his shirt. For someone who was mugged, his skin was remarkably bruise-free. Remarkably muscular, too.

"I wasn't mugged," he said, dragging her thoughts from

his muscled chest. "When I was checking out the mare, a cow began to calve. It was a breech and kind of tricky for a time, but we got the calf out, and she's just fine."

He was so pleased, riding so high you'd think he got nominated for an Oscar or that his show got picked up for syndication.

"I see," she said, though she didn't. What she did see was that he was so much more than an actor. He was real. She was all pretense. Everything about her was pretense. She felt like such a fraud.

"It was so great," he said. "No matter how many times I help with a birthing I still feel that wonder."

"I wish I could have seen it, too."

He laughed. "That's what you always—"

Suddenly his face went bleak, and he got his cream soda look. She knew he wasn't looking at her, but at something—someone—in the past. But the devastation on his face scared her.

"Neal?"

He came out of it quickly enough, though his eyes no longer held that joyful fire. "You weren't really waiting up for me, were you?" he asked, sounding more weary than anything else. "I thought you were just saying that for show."

"Of course I was," she assured him. "Gracious, I've been asleep for hours." She yawned as provocatively as Sassy Mirabel could. "And I think I'm going to get back to bed."

Sleep didn't come too fast, but that didn't stop Colleen from dreaming. He hadn't been out cheating on her, he'd been out saving a calf's life. Maybe he really was different from the other guys she had known.

And what had made him so sad all of a sudden? She'd never seen a person's eyes hold so much misery. She had wanted to take him in her arms and hold him until the pain went away. The idea was scary. She wasn't a comforter; she didn't do well with other people's emotions. She turned over and pounded her pillow into submission.

What she really needed was a breather in a real town. A big town. A town that had buildings taller than the cornstalks.

Somehow she made it through the next day. Pickneyville. Murphysboro. Illinois's miniature version of Nashville. Or was it Pickneyboro and Murphysville? All she knew was that sometime well past eleven that night, they pulled in front of their hotel in downtown St. Louis. Two days in civilization. She would regain all the sense she'd lost out in the wilds of Illinois.

While Brad checked them all in, she and Neal followed a bellhop to their rooms. Hers was first, and she tipped the man well enough to get a hearty thanks, then he took Neal off in the opposite direction.

"See you in the morning," she called after Neal, then closed the door, relieved to finally be amid civilization. She'd be herself again in no time.

She unpacked a few things, hung up her clothes for tomorrow, then collapsed on the bed. This had been the craziest week. She was glad it was over and could only hope that the next week would pass fast and smoothly.

Her thoughts were interrupted by a knock at the door, and she got to her feet and hurried over. Maybe Neal wanted to do something tonight. A great idea, actually. They could go to a nightclub, maybe, or some trendy jazz bar. She'd regain her strength faster in familiar surroundings. She pulled open the door.

"Hey, doll," Steele Blazes said with a grin. "What's happening?"

## Chapter Seven

Nick stared at the late night talk show host babbling on about something. The audience was roaring with laughter, but Nick didn't get it. Maybe it was the emptiness of the room. It didn't feel right to fill it with his own laughter.

He turned the TV off and walked to the window. The Mississippi River was off to one side, and the Gateway Arch was all aglow in the darkness. It was a night for romance. A night to walk along the river and listen to the song of the stars. So why was he in here?

Once he'd understood the rules of the game, he thought he had played by them pretty well. And he could continue to play by them even if the field changed a little. He and Colleen could go out and have a good time and nothing would change. He wouldn't forget that it was all pretense. That is, if she felt willing to take a chance.

He stepped into the hall and strode to Colleen's room. He took a deep breath, then knocked gently. There was no answer, so he knocked again, a little harder. But still no answer.

He knew Colleen was a sound sleeper but this was ridiculous. Either she was wearing earplugs or she wasn't in her room. Maybe she had gone out already.

Nick frowned and turned away. There was no reason, of course, she should have sought him out to share her evening on the town. They were merely tour partners, not even friends. But still it irked him that his first thought had been of her, while hers obviously hadn't been of him.

He went to the first floor, not about to go to his room in defeat, and took a quick look around the lobby. Colleen didn't seem to be around, but neither was much of anybody from the tour. He looked in the main dining room, the all-night coffee shop and the lounge. Nobody looked familiar. Maybe he should just go upstairs.

"Dr. Sheridan? Neal?"

Nick turned. It was one of the reporters. "Hello, Ms. Cooper."

"Just Cooper is fine," she said. "Now why are you wandering around the lobby at this hour of the night?"

She was tall and blond and very attractive. A little tired around the eyes, maybe, but weren't they all after a week of the tour? Maybe he need look no farther for companionship.

"Just trying to unwind a little after all those hours on the bus," he said. "How about you?"

"Same here," she said with a smile. "Do you mind if I join you?"

Even though he'd already had the thought, he had a moment's hesitation. But why not? He'd done fine all week convincing everyone he was Neal. Nothing was going to happen in the next hour to screw everything up.

"I know it's old-fashioned of me," she said, misreading his hesitation. "But I don't feel comfortable eating alone. Especially in a strange town at this time of the night."

That decided it. A gentleman didn't let a woman go out alone this time of the night. They didn't do things that way in Three Oaks.

"I'd be honored." He offered her his arm and headed toward the coffee shop. "I just want something light. Would the coffee shop be—"

"I know a better place," she interrupted. "It's not far from here."

Nick stopped. He thought she had just said St. Louis was new to her.

"Some friends told me about it," she quickly added.

"Isn't this a little late to be walking around?"

"We'll take a cab."

They walked through the lobby toward the main entrance. Nick couldn't help but glance in the coffee shop as they passed, almost wishing Colleen would see him and know someone valued his company, but there was still no sign of her. Which was just as well. He was acting like a junior high kid and not being fair to Cooper. He was escorting her, after all, and she deserved his attention.

They went outside and over to the first cab in front of the hotel. He opened the back door for her. A man was already in it.

"You remember Jud Baldwin, don't you?" Cooper said as she got in. "He works with me."

Nick felt a tickle of worry flit along the back of his neck. If she knew Jud was going along, why did she need Nick as an escort? He paused, unable to rid himself of his uneasiness.

"Neal?" She looked out the taxi door at him, a question in her voice and in her eyes.

Damn. He had to stop looking for problems everywhere. He was forgetting he was Neal Sheridan. Women might not flock to Nick Sheridan's side, but they did to Neal's. Okay, Colleen didn't, but she was a star in her own right, so that didn't count. He climbed into the cab.

Cooper gave the driver an address, and they pulled away from the hotel, heading west.

"How are things going with you and Colleen?" Cooper asked after a moment.

"Fine."

"Just fine?"

ANDREA EDWARDS                                        115

The tone of her voice bothered him, but he knew not to show it. "What's wrong with fine?" he asked with a smile. "Where I come from fine is good."

"And where is that?"

He'd learned a lot in the past week about handling questions. "Oh, come now, Cooper," he said. "You probably know more about me than I do. You have the whole world in your files."

Cooper threw her head back and laughed.

Nick swallowed a sigh of relief and turned his attention to the dark streets. The neighborhood was rapidly turning shabby, but his hope that they were just passing through on their way to something better died when the cabbie pulled to a stop.

"You want I should wait?" the man asked.

"Yes," Cooper replied. "Please do."

They were in front of a place called Big Charlie's. A blue neon winking fish hung above the door. Beneath it hung a smaller, red neon sign, flashing just one word—Girls. This was not exactly what he had expected.

"What did your friends say about the food here?" Nick asked Cooper.

She smiled and winked. "They said it was a fun place. Chock-full of surprises."

"Go ahead. Order anything you want," Steele said, flashing his smarmy little grin. "I'm buying."

Colleen almost laughed out loud. Steele Blazes was a hustler, skulking on the fringe and living off the energy of others. His offer to buy must mean that hell had frozen over. But if she laughed, Steele would start whining and pouting and then it would be even longer before Colleen got out of this dump.

"I'll have a soda, please," she told the waitress. "In a bottle, and I'll open it myself."

"Ya want some ice and a glass, honey?"

"No, thank you. Just the bottle will be fine."

Once the waitress was gone, Colleen looked at Steele, but he was staring at a scantily clad woman dancing on a small tabletop stage. Steele was around six feet—tall but not as tall as Neal—with dark brown hair. He was around Neal's age but looked older. Maybe it was due to Steele's profession, but no, Neal was in the public eye, too. The difference was that Neal hadn't let it touch his soul. Of course, it was possible that Steele never had a soul. The waitress brought their drinks, then hurried away without asking if there was anything else they wanted.

"Nice place you brought us to," Colleen said, looking around at the bar's dark, dingy interior.

"I wanted something private. Someplace where people didn't really know us and we could have a heart-to-heart."

This didn't feel good. She and Steele didn't need a heart-to-heart. They had worked together in a couple of third-rate sci-fi flicks some years back and had had the same agent for a while, but Trevor had dropped him when Steele had shown more interest in alcohol than in his craft. Unfortunately, before that had happened, Colleen had agreed to one of the stupidest things imaginable. Now it appeared it was coming back to haunt her.

"What do you want, Steele?"

"Aren't you gonna drink any of your soda?" he asked, looking at her unopened bottle.

"Look, you said you wanted to talk. So talk or I walk."

Steele made a face as he glanced at the dancer gyrating on the platform above them. "You're still an uptight chick, aren't you? You should learn to relax before you have a heart attack or something."

Colleen looked at her watch. "You have fifteen seconds."

"Okay, okay." Grinning broadly, he held up his hands in mock surrender. "Whatever you say, boss lady." He leaned forward and began talking in a low voice. "As you know, I got this great part."

She didn't know but said nothing.

"I play Sonny McBride on the 'The Wicked and the Wild.' It's a new character. My first episode is in September. Right after Labor Day."

"I'm happy for you, Steele," Colleen said. "But you could have left a message with my service. You didn't need to follow me to St. Louis to personally deliver that information."

"Like I said, the only reason I came out here is so we could talk. You know, like private."

Why? Steele had never been shy about asking for money over the phone.

"This is a great part." He took another sip of his drink. "I play a cop with a shady past who's romancing the governor's daughter."

"That's great, Steele." She had no interest in getting a blow by blow of his part and stood up. "Now I really have to—"

He put his hand on her arm. "I need a good dose of PR, Colleen. I'm only in five episodes right now, but I know I can make it permanent. All I need is to get noticed. You know, get a few letters. A few lines in the right columns. An article in *Worldwide News*. Now that would really help." He paused to drain his glass. "Like it did for you."

Her stomach fell with a thud as Colleen sank down into her seat. Back when she'd been working those bit parts and auditioning every day, Trevor had decided she needed some good PR. Something exciting. Something that would put her in the public eye. That something had been Steele.

"I'm sorry," Colleen said. "There's nothing I can—"

"Aw, come on, Colleen." If anything, his whine had gotten worse over the years. "All we have to do is play the passion thing. Just like we did before."

Colleen shook her head. "I'm through with those games."

"Colleen, you gotta. This is a good part. If I get it going, I'll have something I can ride for a couple of years. Maybe more. And then other stuff'll come. Just like it did for you."

She slowly stood up. "I can't."

His face suddenly turned hard. And mean. "You know, there are people who are wondering about you."

She froze, her stomach twisting in sudden fear. "What people?" she asked.

He shrugged. "People. Important people. Ones who were

willing to pay nicely for a few little tidbits and would pay big
bucks if I offered them the truth.''

The scumbag. He was the one who had sold stuff to *Worldwide News*. It had to have been him. He must have told them
there had been no romance, that they'd never kissed or held
hands except in public. The headlines last week had claimed
she was frigid and couldn't find love unless she paid for it.
Next week's would be that she was a silly virgin who was
more suited to play Mother Teresa than Sassy Mirabel.

The whole carefully constructed life she'd built for herself
would be destroyed. She'd be lucky to get a job doing voice-
overs for used car lot ads.

''This time we do it right,'' Steele was saying. ''You know,
the sex thing. And I'll make sure that no one thinks you're a
freak.''

''You bastard,'' she hissed.

Her hand flew through the air, and she slapped him. She
had expected the stinging in her hand and the look of shock
on Steele's face, but she hadn't expected the world to explode
in a blur of blinding light. For a moment, Colleen feared that
she'd caused Steele's head to explode. But only for a moment.

''Aw, aren't they the cutest lovebirds you've ever seen?''

It was Cooper's voice she heard, but it was Neal's face she
saw. Staring at her with dark, unreadable emotion as the flashbulbs and TV spots lit up the dingy bar.

She turned to Steele. ''You two-bit scum. You set me up.''

''Not me,'' he protested. ''I'd never do that.''

She picked up the soda bottle from the table. If they wanted
pictures, she would give them pictures. Pictures that would
put her on the front page of every newspaper in the world.
Pictures that would kill her TV show and any chance to make
it in her lifetime. But she didn't care. She was not going to
be manipulated by every piece of male scum that crawled upon
this earth.

Colleen swung the soda bottle, determined to bash in
Steele's head. Wanting to make him pay for tricking her into
trusting him, even for a minute. But even as she swung the

bottle, she was encircled by arms like steel cables, lifted bodily off the floor and carried out the door.

What the hell? She was so shocked she didn't start kicking and screaming until the warm night air hit her face. They were outside.

"Damn you," she screamed. "Put me down."

Neal did, but she landed almost facedown in the back seat of a waiting cab. He pushed her over enough so he could climb in, too.

"Get moving," she heard him growl. "Now."

"Uh, sorry, buddy," the cabdriver said. "The other lady told me to wait for—"

"I'm not asking, I'm telling," Neal snapped. "Get this cab out of here or I'll do it myself."

Within a split second, tires squealed and they pulled away from the curb. Colleen heard angry voices and sat up in time to see Cooper and a crowd of people pouring out the door of Big Charlie's.

Colleen fell back against the seat, her heart still pounding and fury still racing through her blood. She needed to yell and scream at somebody, but there was only Neal. Which was fine. This was all his fault, anyway. She never would have trusted Steele if Neal hadn't weakened her instincts by pretending to be so noble.

"What the hell were you doing there, anyway?" she cried. "Why were you following me?"

Neal barely looked at her. "I wasn't."

Colleen snorted. "Right, you were at that dump visiting an old college friend."

"And you were visiting your sick mother."

Her temper was cooling. She still wanted to strike out, but the force was no longer with her. She slumped in the seat.

Damn that Neal Sheridan. She hated the way he always rushed in like some kind of stupid TV hero. He was probably the one who had set her up and was offering *Worldwide* some exclusive story about her.

But even as she thought it, she knew it wasn't true. He

wasn't just acting noble—he was noble. He was everything he seemed to be. No pretense, just solid, true hero material. Lisa had said he wasn't to be trusted, but she wrong. She didn't know what real scumbag men were like. Just as she didn't know what a fake Colleen really was.

"All I wanted was a little snack before I went to bed," Neal said, turning to look at her. "I went to your room but you weren't there."

"How was I supposed to know you wanted to go out?"

"You could have asked. Unless you had another type of company in mind."

"I didn't look for Steele. He just showed up." And she'd had to go out with him. She'd had to find out what the hell Steele Blazes—and that was the stupidest name—was up to.

But there was no explaining it all to Neal. To tell him the truth would only be to tell him what a fake she was. What a fraud. And once he knew that, he'd look at her with the same disgust that had been in his eyes when he'd looked at Steele. It shouldn't matter how he looked at her, but it did.

The cab pulled up in front of the hotel, and while Neal was paying the driver, Colleen scrambled out the other side. "I'm going to bed," she called over her shoulder at him and hurried inside.

Nick walked through the lobby. He was heading toward the elevators, but truthfully, his room was the last place he wanted to be.

What a jerk he had been to believe her that night in Paris. But then, she hadn't said that her reputation was based on pretense. No, he had jumped to that conclusion all by himself. Why else wouldn't she want to spend time with him? It couldn't be that she didn't want to waste her time on the great and charming bumbling idiot from Three Oaks. Or that she had other men—any man?—whose company she preferred to his. Ones with fancier hair and slicker manners and more moronic names.

Laughter drew his eyes toward the dimly lit hotel lounge.

There were just a few people in it—a group of young guys near the door, some couples and several lone drinkers. It was dark and private. Why not?

He chose a table in the far back and sat in the chair that was partially hidden by some sculpture. Not that it would keep him hidden if someone was determined to find him, but it might protect him from chance encounters. He ordered a beer and sat back farther in the shadows to drink it.

"Mind if I join you?" a woman asked.

He froze. Hadn't this just happened a few minutes back?

"Look," the woman said. "I just want to enjoy a drink and relax a little in peace, but it seems that a woman alone in a bar at night can't do that."

He sighed and wanted to tell her that that line had just been tried, too. He'd fallen for it once, but even a hick from Three Oaks knew better than to fall for it again. But still, that group of guys near the door had loud mouths and bad manners....

"Sure, sit down," he said and took a long drink of his beer. But he'd be in charge right from the start. "What paper do you work for?"

"Paper? I'm an accountant. I'm here for the CPA convention."

He took a better look at her. Late thirties probably, conservative suit. And she didn't look the least bit familiar. She still could be a reporter, though.

"You here for the convention, too?" she asked.

Did she really think he was that dumb? Not that recent events had proven otherwise. "No, I'm here with Love Pet Foods," he said, and waited for her exclamation of recognition.

"Oh, yeah?" She made a face. "Hope you don't mind me being honest, but I'm not a fan of Love."

Neither was he, lately, not in any form. But "Oh?" was all he said.

"Their regular dry cat food is too rich for my Punch, and the light stuff makes my Judi constipated. I just use a grocery store brand."

"Not a generic brand, I hope."

She looked embarrassed even in the dim light. "Well, the way they go through it…"

"But those generic brands are all filler," he said, and leaned forward. "There's hardly any nutrition in them."

"Well, it can't be good for Punch to be overweight, either."

"I bet you free feed. Put down a measured amount and pick it up after a half hour."

"They'll kill me."

He laughed, thinking of his own cat. "Pansy wanted to when I first started that, but she got used to it."

"You've got a cat, too?"

He stopped, his beer halfway to his mouth. What was he doing? Neal didn't have a cat. "Well, actually it's my brother's cat," he said.

She smiled at him and reached over to take his hand. "You don't have to pretend. I think a guy with cats is cool."

He wasn't sure what the proper response to that was, but he was sure he had finally slipped into Neal's life. The life of fun and games and no need for pretense. This was what he had been looking for. This was the life of no cares and no commitments that he'd been needing.

A burst of laughter came from the group near the door, and the woman frowned toward them before smiling at Nick. "Why don't we go on up to my room?" she said. "We can exchange cat stories and have our own little party."

He sat back in his chair and looked at her. He needed to say something cool and suave and witty. He needed to charm her with a bit of worldly wisdom. He needed to shake some sense into her.

"How do you know I'm not some kind of nut?" he asked. "Or that I'm not carrying some disease?"

She looked startled.

"What would happen to Punch and Judi if something happened to you?" he asked. "They're totally dependent on you, you know."

She pulled back, definitely no longer in the mood for a

private party with him. "I just thought you seemed like a nice guy," she snapped and grabbed her purse. "Obviously I was wrong."

Nick sighed and held up his hand in supplication. "Wait. I'm sorry." He took a deep breath. "No, actually I'm not. You should be careful, but I didn't mean to lecture. Or to throw your invitation back in your face like that."

He reached for her hand, which lay like a lump of ice in his. "I think spending time with you here was delightful, but I'm afraid I am some kind of a nut, and it's time I went back to my room. Alone."

Her hand softened in his. "Are you sure I can't change your mind?" When he said nothing, she got to her feet. "Well, it's been interesting."

He watched as she left the lounge, knowing that he was probably an even worse nutcase than he suspected. A lovely lady wanted to give him herself, and all he could think about was Colleen. And how she might like the Steele Blazes of the world, but he wouldn't become one just to get even with her.

He would keep his distance from now on, though.

"He's really a nice guy," Ashley said to Colleen. "You could see him playing a small town vet. Where he knows everybody in town. Takes care of their animals and forgets to bill people."

They were at a county park west of St. Louis. She and Neal were scheduled to pose for poster photos, and animals and handlers were all over the place. Temporary pens and cages had been set up in just about every bit of shade that there was—puppies, kittens, ponies, ferrets, what have you. And a pack of kids. Of course, wherever Neal was, there were kids.

Colleen made a face as a makeup artist powdered her nose. Why did everything Neal did have to remind her he was a nice guy, and she was nothing but a fake? And remind her she had acted like a jerk last night.

"He's just a good actor," Colleen said. Maybe if she said it enough, she would start to believe it. She looked at the smock covering her and flicked a tiny bug off one of the better parts of her anatomy.

"Aw, come on, Colleen. He doesn't have to spend all that time with the kids. He could do a few smiles for the cameras and then scram."

The mention of cameras caused Colleen to cringe. As yet, no one had said word one about last night's incident except for Steele. He'd called around nine o'clock this morning— very early for him—but she'd hung up and hadn't answered the phone since. She'd been handed a stack of telephone messages when she'd left the hotel, but she'd thrown them all out. Who would be calling her but Steele?

"Okay, people." Brad came over to the shelter where the dressing rooms had been set up. "We want to start shooting ASAP. Go to the potty if you have to and get over to the set." He turned to Colleen. "We'll be doing doubles with you and Neal first. Then we'll do singles."

Suddenly Brad frowned and looked at Neal, still talking with the kids. "You know, it would be nice if you two stayed together. That way I wouldn't have to repeat myself."

"Just trying to make sure you earn that big salary," Colleen said, but from the odd look Brad gave her before he hurried off in Neal's direction, she knew she hadn't quite pulled it off.

Damn that Neal. She'd owed people apologies before but it had never discombobulated her so. She felt like she'd taken a swipe at an altar boy. The makeup artist brushed Colleen's cheeks lightly, then slipped the smock off so Colleen could stand up.

"You okay?" Ashley asked. "You seem tense today."

Colleen forced a bright smile and waved at the wide expanse of nature around her. "It's all this clean air," she said as they started to walk toward the set. "Can't breathe air I can't see."

That one fell short, too, and the look Ashley gave her was more pitying than anything else.

"You and Neal fight?" Ashley asked.

Colleen was tired of having her life on public display. She

needed an act that would get them all to lay off her. She tried for the brave but weak look of Lola when she was dying of scarlet fever. "If you must know, I had too much to drink last night and I have a monumental hangover."

Ashley didn't seem to know her role called for sympathy. "Was that before you attacked Steele or after Neal carried you out of the bar?"

Colleen dropped her act. "You know?"

Ashley laughed. "Honey, everybody knows. Even if I hadn't seen the *Worldwide* headline of 'The Fight for Colleen's Hand—Who Will She Wed?' Brad talked of nothing but at our meeting this morning. He said he couldn't ask for better publicity than that shot of Neal carrying you out of the bar."

"'Who Will She Wed?'" Colleen repeated as she sank onto the edge of a picnic table that had been set up for the photos. "What kind of nonsense is that? I'm not marrying anybody."

"Who cares?" Ashley said with a shrug. "The press is eating it up. You want some lemonade?"

Colleen shook her head. "Not unless it comes laced with arsenic."

Laughing, Ashley left, leaving Colleen to watch Neal as he approached, surrounded by kids. She took a deep breath and slowly let it out. She owed him an apology. Not a major, groveling-on-the-ground one, but just enough of one to get them back on solid footing. Maybe if they could pretend that last night never happened, the rest of the world would, too.

Neal seemed to be really enjoying himself, but he probably got a decent night's sleep last night. No worries that his career was in danger. But then he probably hadn't ever done anything he regretted. He probably had never been haunted by his past. He stopped in front of her.

"Can we talk?" she said.

One of the photographer's aides hurried up and handed Colleen a squirming puppy, then gave an older dog on a leash to Neal.

His eyes had never left hers, though they weren't even as

warm as the North Pole. "I understand we have the freedom of speech in this country," he said. "Guaranteed in the constitution."

Great, she thought. He was in a foul mood. Just her luck. She shifted the puppy in her arms. "I'm sorry," Colleen said stiffly. "I'm just not accustomed to being hauled around like a sack of dog food."

"Colleen, you sit there on the end of the table, will you?" the photographer called. "And Neal, you stand behind her."

"You would have preferred a visit to the police station, facing an assault charge?" Neal asked once they'd gotten into place. His breath danced along the back of her neck as he spoke.

"Steele wouldn't have done that," Colleen said, and bit off the defensive anger that was trying to rise. She took a deep breath, gritted her teeth and forced her voice to be pleasant. "I said I was sorry."

"Yes, you did." His voice held no forgiveness. "And so graciously, too."

"Smile, folks."

Colleen smiled at the camera. She hoped her smile reflected the joy of the puppy and not the anger radiating from the man behind her. This sharp-edged Neal was new to her. She wasn't sure how to react. Luckily, the photographer was only taking an instant shot to check their positions.

"After I checked your room, I took the elevator to the lobby," Neal said, as the others gathered around the developing print. "And ran into Cooper. She told me she was hungry and knew a place not far from the hotel. She had a cab waiting outside. There was a photographer in the taxi, but I didn't think anything of it at the time."

She knew he'd been an innocent victim of Cooper's maneuvering. It couldn't have been anything else. He didn't have an ounce of guile in him. Though she didn't know how he could be so naive as to believe that cockamamie story. She wouldn't have fallen for it past the third grade. Sometimes Neal seemed like a babe in these television woods.

"I suppose I should have questioned things." Neal shrugged. "But I didn't, and before I knew it, things went to hell."

"That's putting it mildly," Colleen said.

"Great shot, people," the photographer called. "Let's do it for real."

So he danced around them, taking dozens of shots as aides rushed in to distract the dogs and fix Colleen's hair and brush a bug off Neal's shirt. Colleen smiled and cooed and played with the puppy and melted for the camera as she was paid to do, but her heart was heavy. She didn't like having Neal mad at her, but damn it, she'd apologized. What else did he want from her?

Finally, it was time to set up a new pose. Neal got to lay on the grass with a basket of kittens in front of him while Colleen sat behind him with three spaniels. This was a better pose, an easier one. She didn't have to look at him, or feel his nearness right behind her.

"Great, people. Just great." The photographer took his sample shot.

"I gave you my version of what happened," Neal said over his shoulder, his voice sharp. "Some people call that sharing."

Colleen looked at him, crossing her arms suddenly and clutching them to her chest. An almost irresistible urge to run away danced in the shadows of her mind with an equally irresistible urge to confide in him. Which would never do!

Taking a deep breath, Colleen straightened her shoulders. "Look, I'm sorry you got caught up in all this," she said. "It won't happen again."

She'd said her piece, apologized like she should have, and it was over. Last night's episode, she meant, since there wasn't anything else to be over.

"Smile, people. Big, big smile, now."

They were on the road again, and just as well, Nick thought. St. Louis had been educational, if nothing else.

He could feel the bus turn onto the interstate and pick up

speed, rushing toward Steelville. They were supposed to have gotten yesterday off, but the rains had come sooner than expected on Saturday so they hadn't gotten all the pictures shot. Then, on Sunday, the sun had kept going in and out of the clouds, making it bright one minute and dark the next. The photographers had been dissatisfied, and everyone else was in such a bad mood that no one had eaten together yesterday evening.

At least, he and Colleen hadn't. He'd spent last night watching a Cubs baseball game in his room. He didn't know what Colleen had done. Maybe she'd been out with Steele again. Not that he cared one way or another. No matter what that *Worldwide* headline said; he and Steele were not competing for Colleen's hand.

"Hey, Neal." Brad sat in the seat next to him. "The drivers wanted me to express their appreciation for your being on time this morning."

Nick probably should have laughed, but his heart wasn't in it. "Thanks." He closed his eyes and pretended he was trying to doze.

Brad didn't say anything, but Nick knew he was still there. Finally the tour manager cleared his throat. "I don't want to interfere in personal stuff."

Nick opened his eyes and looked at him. Brad's words said he didn't want to, but his tone of voice said he would.

"But I don't want you guys to kill a good thing."

Nick chose not to respond. It seemed safer that way.

"This *Worlwide* series about you and Steele as rivals is great. We need to play it up, but that's hard to do when you two aren't talking."

They exchanged stares for a long moment.

"You know what I mean?"

"Yeah." Agreeing seemed easier than arguing.

Brad got up and went to where Colleen was sitting. No doubt, he was going to give his go-team message to her, as well. Nick leaned back again, but turned his head to stare out the window as they went around a wide curve.

- ◆ **Exciting Silhouette romance novels — FREE!**
- ◆ **Plus an exciting mystery gift — FREE!**

# YES!

I have scratched off the silver card. Please send me all the free books and gift for which I qualify. I understand that I am under no obligation to purchase any books, as explained on the back and on the opposite page.

With a coin, scratch off the silver card and check below to see what we have for you.

## SILHOUETTE'S

# LUCKY HEARTS

### GAME

**DETACH AND MAIL CARD TODAY!**

NAME

PLEASE PRINT CLEARLY

ADDRESS                                                     APT.

CITY                          PROV.                  POSTAL CODE

**Twenty-one gets you 2 free books, and a free mystery gift!**

**Twenty gets you 2 free books!**

**Nineteen gets you 1 free book!**

**Try Again!**

# The Silhouette Reader Service™ — Here's how it works:

Accepting free books places you under no obligation to buy anything. You may keep the books and gift and return the shipping statement marked "cancel." If you do not cancel, about a month later we'll send you 6 additional novels and bill you just $3.96 each plus 25¢ delivery per book and GST.* That's the complete price — and compared to cover prices of $4.75 each — quite a bargain! You may cancel at any time, but if you choose to continue, every month we'll send you 6 more books, which you may either purchase at the discount price... or return to us and cancel your subscription.

* Terms and prices subject to change without notice.
Canadian residents will be charged applicable provincial taxes and GST.

If offer card is missing, write to: Silhouette Reader Service, P.O. Box 609, Fort Erie, Ontario L2A 5X3

0195619199-L2A5X3-BR01

SILHOUETTE READER SERVICE
PO BOX 609
FORT ERIE ONT
L2A 9Z9

Canada Post Corporation/ Société canadienne des postes

**Postage paid**
If mailed in Canada

**Port payé**
si posté au Canada

**Business Reply**

**Réponse d'affaires**

0195619199       01

MAIL▶POSTE

That was all he needed, Colleen being nice to him because the sponsor said to. Ranked right up there with—

He frowned. It was probably his imagination, but he could have sworn that little blue car back there had been around when they'd left St. Louis. Was it following them?

## *Chapter Eight*

They'd had a luncheon meeting in Steelville, another pet parade in Potosi and dinner with an association of pet and feed store people in Farmington. Now it was almost midnight, and they were all bedded down in a motel in Fredericktown, where not a creature was stirring. Not even a reporter. Colleen was finding that although Missouri wasn't as flat as Illinois, the roads were just as long.

Groaning, she kicked off her shoes and collapsed in a chair by the window. The drapes had already been drawn, so she didn't have to worry about how she looked. Besides, she didn't have any lights on, so it was doubtful a lurking photographer could get any kind of picture. Not that she really gave a damn. She was beat.

And it wasn't just the tour. Sure, multiple cities in one day was a definite grind, but she and Neal had the routine so under control that they could have done it in their sleep. What was really wearing on her was Neal and his mopey attitude. Although she had to admit that hers wasn't any better.

They were handling the public appearances just fine. Holding hands, smiling at each other, flirting. As if *Worldwide's* continuing series about her trying to choose between Steele and Neal was true. Brad had told them a number of times today that they were doing good. But there used to be something behind that public face. Not anymore. They didn't say one word to each other when they were on the bus. Of course, Brad could care less about that. He worried about how they came across when the cameras were rolling.

Colleen closed her eyes and shook her head. What a business. All illusion, built on a solid foundation of sand. Lies, fabrications and good old-fashioned BS. But it had always been that way, so why should she be bothered now?

She was about to throw herself out of the chair when there was a light tap at the door, bringing her up and across the room in a flash. Neal had seemed especially cool at dinner, but he had to warm up some time. She was ready to let bygones be bygones. No reason he couldn't do the same. A little voice reminded her to check the security peephole, but she already had the door open.

"Hi, doll," Steele said.

The bastard. She was so mad she was almost ready to burst into tears. The two-bit lowlife.

He'd been following her all day, his little blue rental car a fixture in their rear window. And when they'd rolled into town, he'd become part of the crowd that had greeted them. He couldn't join them at the luncheon or dinner, but he had been part of the people lining up to see the pet parade along Main Street. Now here he was, almost eleven o'clock at night and still harassing her.

"Get away from me," she snapped. "Or I'll have you arrested for stalking."

"What stalking?" he said. "I ain't threatening you. I'm just an old friend wanting to have a chat."

"Steele, I don't want anything to do with—"

"Come on, Colleen." His whine was so grating that she

was about to scream. "I just need a little help. I've already done the same for you."

She wished they'd never played that mad, passionate romance thing, but there was no way to undo the past. But that didn't mean he owned her for the rest of her life.

"Hit the road, Steele. There's nothing I can do."

"Like hell you can't."

"All right," she said tiredly. "Maybe I can, but I don't want to and I won't."

Steele stood at the door staring at her, the anger obvious in his face, but that was too bad. She couldn't and wouldn't play his sweetheart for the newspapers. There had to be some other way he could get his publicity.

"Talk to Trevor. He should be able to help you."

"He ain't returning any of my calls."

Trevor had been the one who'd come up with the idea. He might not think he owed Steele, but he sure owed her some peace of mind.

"Let me talk to him," Colleen said. "I'll see what I can do."

"No 'see' to it, doll. Just get it done."

Steele was doing his tough-guy imitation, and Colleen didn't know whether to laugh or cry. It was pathetic, but he was probably seeing his soap opera part as his last chance to catch on. And desperate people were dangerous people.

"I said I'll try, but you'll have to give me a couple of days."

"I've already given you a show of your own."

That was nonsense. Yeah, their little passion gig had gotten her some notoriety, but she'd also paid her dues, in full with interest.

"Two days," she said. "You know how hard Trevor is to get hold of."

"Two days, doll."

He backed away and pointed a finger at her, thumb up like a gun. Another minute and she would have torn what hair he had left out by its roots. She slammed the door shut and collapsed onto the bed.

After a fitful night, she thought of calling Trevor. But it was six o'clock in Missouri, which would make it four in L.A., and one never called Trevor before eleven in the morning. She'd have to figure out some way of calling him later.

And she tried. Not in Ironton, where the main event was a visit to a large commercial kennel. She thought she'd have time to slip away because the plans called for Neal and the owner to do the talking, demonstrating advanced dog training techniques to a bunch of high school kids. But the kids all wanted her autograph, so she couldn't get near a phone.

Lesterville was a horse show where the plans were for her to stand around for a while, but Brad had found out that she could ride a horse. Before she knew it, she was involved in showing proper riding technique to the attendees.

"I didn't know you could ride," Neal said as they ate hamburgers and fries at the fair's concession booths.

*There's a lot you don't know about me,* she wanted to say, but she smiled and continued eating.

"I thought you said you grew up in L.A.," he said. "Where did you learn to ride? Summer camp?"

She was about to tell him Lisa's father had taught her but was suddenly afraid of the questions that might start. "I was in some westerns," she told him. That was the easier answer and the quicker. Maybe she could find a phone around here—

"Let's go, people." Brad marched in on them. "Back to the buses. We're running late."

Colleen considered insisting on getting her phone call in. After all, even those arrested for a crime had the right to a telephone call, but she knew that Brad would have told her to use the cellular on the bus. And that wouldn't do anything for the privacy she needed.

Bixby was a cutest pet contest. Between judging and signing autographs, she had no time at all.

"Cover for me, would you, please?" she asked Neal when

they rolled into a shopping center in Salem, Missouri. He gave her a questioning look but didn't say anything as she dashed off.

Colleen found a pay phone in a drugstore, out of sight of the pet store where Neal was signing autographs. She called her agent's office and left the number of that night's motel, saying she had to talk to Trevor. She was at the pet store before anybody missed her.

They had a nice dinner in Rolla with some University of Missouri biology professors who were doing animal nutrition studies for their sponsor. It was a small, quiet dinner, and she thought Neal was starting to warm up to her again, but when they got to the motel, they went their separate ways. Just as well. She needed to talk to Trevor in private.

But when the call came through, it jarred her out of a deep sleep. "Yeah," she croaked into the receiver.

"You called me, babe."

She blinked rapidly, trying to make out the time while her brain searched her memory to identify the voice. It was 2:37 a.m. "Trevor?"

"You left word for me to call," he replied.

Groaning, Colleen sat up in bed. "I meant at a decent hour."

"Better be careful, sweetheart," he said, snickering. "You're picking up some bad farmer habits."

Yeah, like trying to get a good night's sleep. "I got problems, Trevor. Steele is threatening to expose me."

"You mean that little thingy you and he did for *Worldwide* a couple of years ago?" Trevor snorted. "He's a nobody that's got nothing. That's old news, and nobody cares."

"Then why is Cooper following me?"

"She wants to see how the natives live in Flyover Country."

"She also has pictures of me slapping Steele," Colleen said.

"Yeah, I've been following her 'Who Will She Wed?' stories. Great publicity."

"It's insane," Colleen said. "I'm not marrying anybody.

And I'm much more worried about Steele telling everyone that our big romance was a phony.''

"Life's a phony, kid. Forget him. Or if he bothers you too much, have your boyfriend punch him out."

She knew he was talking about Neal, but given the way he felt about her, Colleen knew he wouldn't do anything for her. Certainly not something like getting in a fight with Steele. No matter what Cooper kept writing about them all.

"That would make for great PR," she snapped.

"You know what they say, sweetheart. The only bad PR is no PR."

The dial tone told her the conversation was over, as if she needed any hint. Colleen hung up and turned on the light. Now what was she going to do? Steele was going to get more desperate and more obnoxious. She'd always been proud that she could take care of herself, but she couldn't help thinking that, at a time like this, it would be nice to have a boyfriend. The kind that would punch out the lowlifes of the world for her.

Nick did a good job of holding on to his anger, using it like a shield to keep Colleen from drawing any closer to him. The fact that she was barely speaking to him made it even easier. That would be the last time he tried to help her out of a jam. From now on, he was Mr. Noninvolvement.

And it didn't matter that Colleen looked tense and weary, more so each day. Or that Steele was in the audience every place they went, lurking as if looking for ways to slip close to Colleen. She told Nick to stay out of it, and he would. He'd learned his lesson.

His resolve slipped a little in Lesterville, when he kissed her for the cameras. She fit in his arms so perfectly, and the way she clung to him just a moment longer than necessary suggested to his silly heart that she secretly wanted his help. Which was the stupidest thing he'd come up with in years. She was an actress, for goodness sake. It was her job to convince people of the unbelievable. All she'd probably been doing was giving Cooper more fodder for her *Worldwide News* stories. Or else she was just trying to make Steele jealous.

He'd thought she must have succeeded when she slipped off from that pet shop in Salem—to meet with Steele, he was sure. But a moment later he'd spotted Steele lurking around the parakeet cages, quite obviously unhappy.

Nick watched him, growing more and more irritated. Damn it, if Colleen loved him so much, why didn't that jerk do something about it? So what if Love wanted their two spokespersons to be playing it up for the camera? A real man wouldn't let that stand in his way. Nick certainly wouldn't let anything get in his way. But it was none of his business—he'd been told that and didn't need another telling.

But still, when Colleen came back to the pet shop a few minutes later, she seemed so tense, his conscience nagged at him. If he saw someone driving toward a cliff, wasn't he duty bound to warn them? Surely he could give her some advice without getting involved. He waited until they were on the bus, then walked to where she was sitting and dropped into the empty seat next to her.

"You look tired," he said, and waited for a response that never came. Okay, he would try a different tactic. "Is something the matter?"

"Considering it's ninety-five degrees out, we've been in two parades today already and we still have two more events to look great in, I'm perfectly fine," she snapped, turning to look out the window.

Looking for Steele's car, no doubt. Nick took a deep breath. The guy looked like a jerk, acted like a fool and had about as much backbone as an earthworm, but if he was what Colleen wanted...

"Look, if you want some time with your boyfriend, why don't you just tell Brad?" Neal said. "Or tell Steele to meet you for our break in Bramson—"

She turned to face him. "My boyfriend?" she asked. "What are you talking about?"

Her confusion was a bit much. "I'm not stupid. I've seen Steele at every stop so far. Neither of you look happy—"

"And so you decided we were suffering from sexual frustration? Thank you for your diagnosis, Dr. Freud."

Her anger stung. He would like to point out that if she chose a *man* instead of that jerk, maybe she wouldn't be having these problems, but he forced the words to stay unspoken. "I was only thinking of you," he said instead.

"Well, you don't have to. It's not in your contract." She settled in her seat again.

He should just go to his own seat and forget Colleen and her troubles. She didn't want his help, and he did have some pride. But he leaned his head back and closed his eyes.

Could it be he had too much pride? And that maybe that pride was getting in the way? Colleen and Steele used to be a pair, even that kid in the pet show grand opening had known that—so they used to be in love. She snuck out with Steele in St. Louis, but when Nick found them, she was on the verge of hitting him with a bottle—now that wasn't love in Three Oaks, but Nick had thought it might be in Hollywood. Steele was moving from town to town with them but unable to get close to Colleen—hell, in Three Oaks a sixteen-year-old boy had a hundred moves to get him by a vigilant mother. With Colleen's cooperation, Steele ought—

"Steele's not your boyfriend, is he?" he asked her suddenly. It was all clear now.

She turned long enough to glare at him. "Look, this really isn't any of your business."

How could he have been so stupid as to have believed what was in the newspaper? He knew the part about him was all lies. Why hadn't he ever considered that the rest might be, too. Hollywood or Three Oaks, love was love. "He's not." Nick frowned, a sudden anger churning in his stomach. "So that means he's following you. Is he harassing you? Threatening you?"

Colleen sat up. Her eyes looked startled, worried. "It's a

personal matter," she said, her voice unsteady. "And none of your business or anyone else's."

He stared at her for a long moment. He tried to will her to talk to him. Tried to think of the words that would make her trust him. Tried to break down that stubborn wall of independence she'd surrounded herself with. But she wouldn't give in.

Though his heart ached for her, he let her go this time. With a curt nod, he returned to his seat. She hurried to the bathroom to clean up for the next stop. By the time she came out, they were passing a sign that welcomed them to Jefferson City.

At least she'd be relatively safe from Steele here. Dinner and their appearance on a local news show were private, so Steele couldn't try anything. And maybe over the course of the evening, he could convince her to confide in him.

"You know, if I knew what was going on, I might be able to help," he told her in a quiet moment during dinner.

"I think dinner's going on," she said sweetly. "And thank you, but I can cut my chicken myself."

Her smile was enough to drive a civilized man back to his barbaric nature. He felt like picking her up and carrying her out of there. He was probably the one person on this whole tour she could trust with her life, and she was acting—

He sighed and went back to his meal. How was she supposed to know he was the one she could trust when she was surrounded by those she couldn't? He'd have to take care of her without her knowing it.

And it wasn't that hard. A few words with the hotel manager, a few with the security guards. He thought of talking to Brad but decided against it. Brad saw everything in terms of PR, not safety and privacy.

The next morning, Nick called Colleen about ten minutes before they were all to meet for breakfast. And felt his stomach eat a hole in itself. The phone rang and rang and rang. He was too late. Steele had been there and—

The receiver was picked up, but no one spoke. Damn. It

was all he could do to stay in his room instead of rushing to hers. "Colleen?"

"Neal?"

"Yeah." His heart started beating again, and he slumped on to the bed in relief. "Yeah, you know, tall guy who's been riding around on a bus with you for the past three lifetimes."

"I know who you are," she snapped.

Did she, now? But even her anger was welcome after his fears. "Our breakfast plans have been changed. I'll be by to pick you up."

Nick called one of the security guards and met him outside Colleen's room before knocking on her door. She opened it cautiously, giving the guard a curious glance.

"You ready to go?" Nick asked.

She nodded and closed the door behind her.

For a long moment, Nick said nothing. He stood in front of her, looking into her eyes. The worry was still there, no stronger but no weaker. He guessed that was a good thing and took her arm.

"You look rested," he said. "Sleep well?"

"Fine, thank you." She let him lead her toward the elevator as the security guard went ahead to press the call button.

"No interruptions?"

"No." Her feet slowed, her look suspicious. "Did you..."

"Yes?" He smiled at her, an answer ready for anything she might accuse him of.

But she shook her head and got into the elevator. "I was just trying to remember how many days until our break in Bramson," she said.

"An eternity," he said, and pressed the button for the lobby. "Have you been there before?"

She shook her head.

"Country music Las Vegas."

"You don't sound thrilled," she said.

"Hey, I'm thrilled about going any place where we can eat something other than chicken for a change."

"We have had more than our share of it over the last ten days, haven't we?"

"In more ways than one," he muttered as the elevator doors opened.

He was afraid she would ask him just what he meant by that, but the first thing he saw was Steele glowering at them from across the lobby. She must have seen him, too, because she suddenly clutched his arm.

"Something wrong?" he asked.

She loosened her hold and laughed. "You have to learn not to question a lady's entrance, sweetie. Bad form, you know."

But Nick's gaze had gone from the smirk on Steele's face to the worry deep in Colleen's eyes. Steele didn't think Colleen had anybody, that was clear from his attitude. But gut-wrenchingly worse was Colleen's belief she didn't have anybody, either.

Well, he might not be able to convince Colleen she could lean on him, but he sure as hell could show Steele she wasn't alone. He could pretend just as well as either of them.

Without another thought, he pulled Colleen into arms and took her lips with his. He kissed her like she was everything in the world to him, like the sun rose and set in her smile and the stars only came out to sing of her beauty.

The fiery rush of desire that swept over him was part of his act, proof of how well he was pretending. Just as the tightening of her arms around him meant nothing but that she was playing along. Yeah, his heart was pounding and his knees were feeling wobbly, but that was what happened in a kiss. A good kiss, that is. When the fire in his loins demanded he pull her closer, he broke away.

"What was that for?" she gasped.

"Didn't you see the cameras?" His voice was no steadier than hers, but he pretended not to notice as he glanced around them. Luckily there were a few people with cameras nearby. Steele was no longer in sight—a fact that pleased Nick no end.

"No, I must have missed them."

"Can't afford to do that in our business," he said. "You have to be alert, you know."

"I'll try to pay better attention from now on," she said.

His heart was still racing when they got on the bus later, and that fire came alive again whenever he glanced Colleen's way. Maybe it ought to scare him, make him fear he'd broken his resolve, but she looked so much better that it was worth a little discomfort on his part.

He sat with her on the bus. Maybe she needed him to be there. Lending his support wasn't really getting involved.

"We're on a very continental segment of our journey today," he told her. "Our first stop is Versailles, then Warsaw, and we finish in Lebanon."

"I wonder if they eat chicken," she said.

"Nothing else. But they call it by very fancy names."

She laughed as if she couldn't help it, and he took it as a good sign. A sign that maybe he could go a step further.

"You know, when I was a kid, there was this dog that was the meanest thing I'd ever seen. He was always out waiting for me when I did my paper route after school, and I used to go out of my way to avoid riding my bike past that farm. Finally one day, I decided that I had to stop letting him rule my life and I stood up to him. When he came charging at me, I stood my ground and told him to go home. And he did. It was scary, but in the end, I won."

She stared at him for a long, silent moment. Probably thinking of how it applied to her and Steele.

"I thought you grew up in Washington, D.C.," she said slowly. "How'd you get a farm on your paper route?"

Colleen found that the next few days zipped by. Steele was still hanging around, though he hadn't approached her. Neal or one of the security guards was always around. Not that their protective net was necessary—she had decided it was time to stop running away. She would deal with Steele. Just as Neal had dealt with the mean dog in that silly story he'd made up.

Farms in Washington, D.C. She smiled as she thought of it. The man was such a lousy liar.

Sunday afternoon, they made just one stop—in Gainesville, home of a talking dog—then they would head to Bramson, where they'd relax until going back on the road Tuesday morning. Colleen could hardly wait. She and Steele would sit down and have this whole thing out. She was going to have to risk him telling about their romance because she wasn't going to play games with him again.

"That dog couldn't talk any more than my goldfish can," Ashley said, collapsing on the picnic bench next to Colleen. "But this ice cream alone would have been worth the trip here."

Colleen nodded. It was unlike Brad, but he'd been so pleased with the footage of Colleen and Neal with the talking dog that he'd suggested they stop at this little picnic area on the outskirts of Gainesville. There wasn't much there—a little ice cream shop, souvenir store and a gas station all sharing the parking lot next to the picnic benches—but Colleen would have been content to spend the next day and a half there, sitting on a bench and soaking up the sun.

"Maybe Brad has a secret weakness for fudge chocolate chip," Colleen suggested.

"Hmm, we need to remember and exploit." Ashley got up as she finished her cone, tossed her napkin into the trash can then walked toward the bus.

Colleen knew she should be getting to the bus herself, but she was too comfortable to move. Neal had drawn his usual contingent of kids and was trying to show them how to teach somebody's dog to sit. It looked like he'd be a while. Maybe she'd—

Cooper sat next to her. "I have a message from a friend."

Colleen frowned. It sounded like something out of a bad spy movie.

"He needs to talk to you," Cooper said, tipping her head toward the far north edge of the parking lot.

Grimacing, Colleen slowly turned her head. Steele was

parked behind the ice cream parlor. Well, she'd planned on talking to him in Bramson, but now was okay, too. No sense in waiting.

Slowly pushing herself up, she walked toward the back of the building. The security lady looked at her, but settled down when Colleen mouthed, "Bathroom."

"Well?" Steele snapped as she drew near him.

She could have said something snappy like, "Well, what?" But that would be too childish. "I'm sorry, Steele. I tried to get Trevor to lend you a hand, but it was no go."

"Damn." He slapped the top of his car and turned away for a moment, glaring at the green-covered hills almost as if he hoped to silence the birds' singing with his hard look.

"That's not acceptable," he said, turning to her.

"Steele," she said wearily. "There's nothing—"

"Not so fast, doll." A vein throbbed in his temple. "I could bring your whole sand castle crashing down, you know. All I have to do is tell the world that a nun knows more about loving and making a man happy than you do."

She knew he could, but she'd also come to realize she couldn't pay the price he was asking for his silence. "Do what you want, I can't stop you."

"Lucky for you, I got me another plan." He opened the car door. "Get in. I want to tell you all about it."

Colleen hesitated.

"Damn it, Colleen," he whined. "You owe me. Can't you at least listen to my plan?"

She glanced toward the buses. People were still standing around. She had time.

"Don't worry," he said. "I can always give you a ride to Bramson."

She sighed. She didn't want to go with him, but she did owe him something. He hadn't been responsible for her success, but he had helped.

"I don't want this to take too long," she said, getting into his car.

"You got it, doll."

Steele pulled onto a narrow dirt lane that wound around the back of the gas station before taking them to the county road. He took a right at an even narrower blacktop, following the twisting road through a wooded area. An occasional pasture with horses and cattle was the only thing that broke the solid mass of woods on either side of them.

"I thought you were going to tell me your plan." She was getting a little concerned as they climbed higher into the hills. The sun had disappeared behind the clouds, and it looked like rain again.

"I will," he said. "I'm just looking for a spot to pull off."

Finally, Steele pulled to the side of the road in a narrow area at the edge of a curve. He got out of the car, came around to her side and led her out of the car to a log by the side of the road. The shoulder was loose gravel, and she had to step carefully in her high-heeled sandals. A moderately steep hill, covered with bushes, fell to a stream below.

"What's your plan, Steele?" She stared down the hill. "Sell your exposé of our phony relationship to Cooper and *World-wide News?*"

"I got something even better," he said.

"I hope it doesn't involve me," she said.

"Involve you? Doll, you're the star."

"Not anymore," she said with a weary shake of her head. "I'm sorry I couldn't help you, Steele. Take me to the buses and let's each of us go their own way."

"Can't do that."

"I beg your pardon?"

Colleen could feel a chill creeping up her spine. Steele was a blowhard, afraid to stand up to anybody or for anything, but something in his eyes made her uneasy.

"You see, my plan is—" he paused with a fine sense of drama that even the most mediocre actor had "—to rescue Sassy Mirabel."

"What?" She stared at him, dumbfounded.

"And rescuing her is gonna buy me space on every front

page in this U.S. of A. Not to mention a million minutes of airtime.''

''You've lost it.'' Colleen turned away. ''I don't need rescuing.''

''But you will, doll. You will.''

The crunch of gravel told her he was coming toward her, but he was upon her before she'd completely turned. Close enough to give her a shove and send her slipping and sliding and tumbling down the incline.

Damn him! Colleen tried to grab at the bushes, but her feet in those stupid sandals slipped in the soft surface, giving way each time she almost gained her footing. She fell onto her butt, then was on her side as she slid into bushes and twigs and rocks and grass, not stopping until she was at the bottom of the incline, just a few feet from the stream.

''Don't worry, darlin','' Steele called down to her. ''We'll be back before dark.''

''You bastard.''

But her shout was lost in the noise of the engine and the tires on the gravel shoulder. Then there was silence. Dead silence.

''That scumbag,'' she muttered as she got to her feet. ''No wonder I hate men.''

The heel had broken off one of her sandals, but it hardly mattered, since they were the worst thing for climbing up a slope. Her hands were skinned, two nails were broken, and her legs were a mess of dirt and scratches. And what skin wasn't torn was now being chewed on by bugs. She'd probably hurt like hell if she wasn't mad enough to strangle somebody.

''I'll ruin him,'' she vowed as she started up the slope, climbing gingerly since her sandals were in her hands. ''I don't care—ouch—what stories he tells about me. I damn will make him pay—ouch—for this. Triple ouch!''

She moved her foot next to a branch before putting more weight on it. The damn bushes were full of these little invisible thorns that tore at her skin, and every blade of grass she brushed against was home to a million hungry insects. She trudged upward.

"He won't get—scat—away with this." She smacked a bug, leaving a bloody streak on her arm but a cry of victory in her heart. "Nobody—go eat somebody your own size—uses me like this."

She finally made it to the top, though she felt like she'd carried half the hill up with her—and half the hill's insect inhabitants. She swatted them away as she limped to a log near the edge. With a weary sigh, she lowered herself.

"Damn."

She looked around. Not a soul in sight. No sound of approaching cars. Nothing. She'd walk to civilization if she had shoes, but it looked like all she could do was wait. And hope that those dark clouds overhead would be content to wait, also.

Damn. Maybe she'd just kill the first man that came along.

"What do you mean Colleen's not here?" Nick snapped. "You were supposed to be keeping an eye on her."

The two security guards wore a mixture of defensiveness and embarrassment on their faces, but Brad pushed them aside and pulled Nick to the front of the bus with Ashley following along. "Chill out, Neal," he said. "It's not like she's missing. She just went on to Bramson with a friend."

"And did you ask if this friend was the one that's been following her the last week?"

Brad looked a touch uneasy. "I didn't actually talk to her myself," he admitted. "Cooper just told me—"

"Cooper!" Nick exploded. "She's the one that set us up in St. Louis, and you believed her?"

"Cooper likes a good story," Ashley assured him. "But she's not going to get involved in something dumb."

Nick gave them both a look. It was all he could do to keep from throttling someone. But then movement outside the bus caught his eye. Cooper and her favorite photographer were heading toward the gas station.

Without a word to Brad, Nick hurried off the bus. He felt the others following him, but he didn't care. He hurried after the reporter. He would get some answers from Cooper whether she liked it or not. But before he had a chance, a blue car limped into the gas station on a flat tire. Steele's car. Nick's breath caught for a moment, but Steele was the only one in it. Damn.

Steele was out of the car and in the middle of a laughing conversation with Cooper by the time Nick reached them. He didn't bother with the niceties.

"Where's Colleen?" Nick demanded.

Steele smirked at him. "Well, well. If it ain't the big whip vet."

"Just answer my question." Nick knew Cooper had stepped back, not to give them privacy but to give her photographer more room. He didn't care.

"Don't see where it's any of your business," Steele said, sneering like the villain in a cheap gangster flick. "Colleen and me, we're old friends from L.A. and old friends like to get together." He turned and waved over the gas station attendant.

"Maybe I didn't make myself clear," Nick said, anger keeping his voice quiet. "I was not giving you an option." He put his hand on Steele's arm. "Now tell me where she is."

"Quit bugging me, man." Steele tried pushing Nick's hand off, but it wasn't going anywhere. Ignoring it, he looked at the attendant. "I need this tire fixed fast."

Nick flung the actor against the side of the car. "You aren't paying attention. No one is going anywhere until I go get Colleen."

He had gotten Steele's attention, at least. The man's eyes were wide, and his face had paled. "Are you crazy?" he asked.

"Just a little," Nick replied. "And the longer I wait, the worse my condition gets."

"Well, I ain't scared of you," Steele said.

He shrugged off Nick's hand, then, after a quick glance at the cameraman, he lunged forward, shoving Nick back a few steps.

Nick had had it. Fear was eating a hole in his stomach, and this guy was jerking him around. He pulled back his right arm and let Steele have a sharp blow to the jaw. Quick. Hard. And neat.

Steele went down like a pin-pricked balloon, sagging onto the pavement and rubbing his chin. "Hey," he whined.

Nick stood over him, fists clenched. The cameraman was going crazy, taking shot after shot, but Nick didn't care. "Where is she?"

Steele told him then. Complex directions about country roads and hills and curves were interspersed between bursts of whining and complaining. Nick turned to the gas station attendant.

"How soon can you get this tire fixed?"

"Depends on how long you want it to take," he said with a grin and tossed Nick a set of keys. "You take the pickup over there and I'll work on this one until you tell me it can get done."

The pickup was probably about ten years old, its exterior a mixture of dark green paint and rust blotches. "Does it run?"

"Like a dream, and you can use it for as long as you want."

Nick grinned at the man, then stopped. Everyone was off both buses, watching. Cameras all in use, as well as cell phones. A stop-the-presses alert? He'd certainly given them enough news to fill up several editions of their various papers and TV shows.

"I need your cell phone," he called to Ashley. "And a number to reach you all here when I find her."

In a matter of minutes, he was speeding down a narrow country road in a pickup that roared like a demon from hell. Like it or not, this time Colleen was going to tell him what was going on.

# Chapter Nine

Nick rounded a curve and there Colleen was, sitting on a log and holding a rock about as big as a grapefruit. She looked irritated, but fine. Emotion filled his throat and his vision blurred as he pulled the truck off the road and brought it to a stop. He cleared his throat a few times, then got out.

She stood up, barefoot and with scratches all down her legs and arms. Anger churned in him—he'd let Steele off too easily—but he tried not to let it show. Neal never lost his cool, no matter what the situation.

"I don't think the bus stops here," he said. "But if you want, I can give you a lift."

She threw the grapefruit-size rock at him. "Damn you," she cried as the rock fell short. "I really hate you."

Nick ignored her verbal welcome as he watched the rock roll away. "It's a good thing you throw like a girl. That thing could have done me serious harm."

"Just when I get things under control, you have to come barging into my life."

Her eyes—brown today—were flashing like the heat lightning dancing over the hills to the west. Her fists were clenched so tight, the knuckles were white. She was as nervous as a colt on the Fourth of July.

A few raindrops began to fall, and he knew he had to end this stalemate. "Maybe we ought to start all over from the beginning here," he said softly.

"Okay," she said. She sighed wearily, her smile sweet and gentle.

As her fists softened into hands, Nick felt his nerves unwind. All he had to do was be cool and everything would be fine. In a tense situation, his instincts were at least as good as Neal's. Maybe better.

"I don't how far back to the beginning you want to go, but could you hand me that rock, please?" Colleen pointed to the missile she had thrown at him. "I'm embarrassed by my poor showing and I'd like to show you I can do better."

So much for starting over. The rain was a full-fledged drizzle by now. He went to the passenger door and pulled it open. "Get in the truck," he snapped.

"Who died and made you boss?" she snapped back.

This time he'd really had enough. He was rescuing her. Why was she arguing? He strode across the gravel shoulder and swept her into his arms.

"Put me down," she screamed, fists pounding on his shoulders. "Damn you, Neal Sheridan. Put me down."

"I'll be glad to."

She stopped beating him and waited.

"I can put you down in the truck—" he paused "—or I can put you down in that gully."

Her eyes had a sheen, and he thought there was a slight quiver to her lips. He didn't like being a bully, but things had to be resolved. She'd been playing games about Steele all week, and it was time they ended.

"Your choice," he said.

Colleen folded her arms across her chest, and he stood there. The seconds stretched out into eternity, long enough for his arms to get tired. Long enough for their clothes to start getting damp from the rain.

"Well, where do you think I want to be put?" she said. "I've rolled down that hill once today, and it wasn't a bit of fun."

Nick set her in the truck, where she folded up like an old rag doll. He closed the door, then got in on the driver's side. After one look at her, he made up his mind and picked up the cell phone.

"Brad?" he said. "Colleen and I are skipping Bramson. We'll meet you there tomorrow night."

"Is Colleen okay?"

A little late to be concerned, Nick thought, but didn't say it. "She's fine." He glanced at her. She was watching him, some of the fire back in her eyes. "Tell the gas station guy I'll bring his truck back then and that he should take another hour or so fixing Steele's tire."

"What happened to Steele's tire?" Colleen asked once he broke the connection.

"I don't have any idea. He rolled into the station with a flat."

"Oh." Colleen made a face. "I was hoping you'd slashed it."

"Nope. I slugged him, though, if that counts for anything."

"You did?" Her voice sounded altogether too pleased. "I wish I had seen it."

"I'm sure you'll get your chance. Every camera on the media bus was aimed at me."

"Your own media moment," she said with a sigh. "How cool."

He ought to be concerned about the publicity, but his thoughts right now were far from such worries. No, he was more interested in how close Colleen's long bare legs were to him and how the rain was closing them off in their own little world. He could just lean over—

He started the motor with an abrupt turn of the key. What she needed right now was a shower and some dry clothes, not his amorous attentions. So he should stop steaming up the windows with his mental meanderings and get going.

"So what are we doing until tomorrow night?" she asked.

He turned on the windshield wipers, checked the road for other cars, then pulled onto the blacktop. "We're going to drive along these little roads to the first town we come to. Then we're going to find some dry clothes, a place to eat some dinner and some rooms for the night."

"Sounds good."

"And you're going to tell me what's going on with Steele."

She gave him a look but said nothing. He supposed he could have pressed for an agreement but didn't think he needed to. She had to know by now she could trust him.

"So do you know where we're headed?" she asked after a few minutes of silence.

"Not a clue. I figure whatever town we come to is our destiny."

"Our destiny? Isn't that a—" She leaned forward as if peering through the rain and the gloom. "Oh, look, our destiny approaches."

He could see the sign, too, at the edge of the road with buildings just beyond. But the rain on the windshield left it a blur until they got closer, and then he could see what it said.

Romance, Missouri.

Population 245.

Colleen stared at the sign, not knowing whether to laugh or cry. She turned a narrowed eye toward Neal. "You knew where we were going, didn't you?"

"Are you kidding?" He was peering into the rain-drenched streets ahead of them. "This doesn't look like any lover's paradise, regardless of the name."

She looked out the window, too. He was right. The place looked like any other small town they'd driven through. A row of stores along Main Street. Side streets of stately looking older houses. Bars and churches in about equal numbers. Everything looking drenched and deserted.

Still, it seemed just too cutesy. She glanced at Neal, frowning in concentration as he drove slowly past the stores. He wasn't Steele, though, she had to remind herself. This would have been Steele's idea of a great joke. Neal was too honest to do things that way. Honest enough to believe whatever story she made up about Steele.

Still, there were some things that couldn't go unchallenged. "I don't believe in destiny," she told him.

"No?"

"Hard work gets you where you want to go. Not some invisible hand of fate."

"Well, I'm not sure whose hard work got us here. I'm not taking credit. Or blame." He pulled to the curb and stopped the truck.

"Blame?" She followed his gaze out the window but saw nothing. Nothing but closed up stores, that is. "So why are we stopping? I don't see anything open here."

"Neither do I."

She turned to face him. He was frowning into the early evening gloom.

"It's Sunday night, small town mid-America. Nothing's open."

"Nothing?" She looked out at downtown Romance again as if to prove him wrong. But she couldn't. There wasn't even a light on in any of the buildings. Suddenly she began to laugh. "We've come looking for Romance only to find it closed for the day."

"Talk about destiny," he said with a grin. "It's got a cruel streak. I can see the headlines. Love Strikes Out in Romance."

"Or No Romance for Love."

Neal put the car in gear. "So now what? Want to try our luck at the next town?"

But she was feeling good sitting in the truck with Neal. Stronger than she'd felt in ages. And happier, too. For the moment, she wasn't alone. She wasn't sure why she was feeling that way, and knew it wouldn't last, but she did know

Neal had not concocted this trip to Romance with some secret plan.

"We can't leave," she said. "We'd forever be haunted by our lost chance in Romance."

He groaned.

"There's got to be someplace open," she said.

"Only place I saw was the gas station we passed coming into town."

"So let's go there. They'll direct us to a great little country restaurant with home-cooked meals and a quaint little inn with windows that open instead of rattling air conditioners."

"Okay," he said and made a U-turn in the deserted street. "But you must be seeing a different side to Romance than I am."

"Women always do," she said, and set them both laughing.

He drove to the other end of town and pulled into the parking lot at the combination service station and convenience store. "I'll just run in," he said and turned off the motor. "Maybe they can tell us where the nearest hotel would be."

"As long as it's in Romance," she called after him.

Once the door was shut, she leaned her head against the seat back. The rain and murkiness outside made it all the more cozy inside. This was so weird she didn't know what to think. She'd gone from being so scared of Steele that she was hiding from him to being so furious with him that she wanted to cry to having a surprisingly wonderful time with Neal.

But maybe it wasn't so surprising. She'd always had a good time with Neal. Even that night when he'd had his concussion was fun, in a way. And over the last two weeks, she'd come to see he was special. He wasn't the ordinary Hollywood jerk. He was a nice guy.

She turned at the sound of Neal tossing some stuff in the back of the truck and closing the cap. Before she had time to try to make out the lumpy objects, he was climbing into the front seat, his arms laden with bags.

"Well, there are no rooms for rent in town," he said.

"There isn't a single motel, hotel, inn or boardinghouse in Romance."

Shoot. It really didn't matter, but somehow the place had become special to her. "How far to the nearest motel?"

"About thirty miles. Assuming the road isn't washed out."

"And the nearest restaurant?"

"Same thing."

Colleen sighed, feeling her shoulders slump. Damn. They should have gone to Bramson with the rest of the crew. They wouldn't have this privacy, but at least they'd have modern accommodations.

"But you said you wanted to stay in Romance," Neal said. "And your wish is my command."

She looked at him, hope bringing back her smile. "And can we? How?"

"Maybe I should ask you first how you feel about roughing it."

"Roughing it?" What did that mean? "You mean no air-conditioning? No room service?"

"How about no beds?"

She stared at him. "We sleep standing up?"

"Sleeping bags. In the bed of the truck, parked in the campground around back."

"Do they have bathrooms?"

"With running water." He pulled open one of the bags and began to take out little packages. "And as a special treat, I even have a comb, shampoo, soap, toothbrush and paste and a towel, plus some first aid cream and a package of bandages for those scratches."

She looked at the last thing he handed her. They were bright adhesive bandages with red hearts on them. "How romantic," she teased.

"What do you expect in Romance?" He started the motor but stopped before he put it in gear. "You sure you're game for this?"

"Absolutely."

So he pulled around to the campground and parked next to

the bathroom building. She was enjoying herself. She'd never had an adventure like this.

"Here's some clean clothes," he said, and handed her another bag. "Just shorts, a T-shirt and scuffs. Apparently they don't make St. Louis Blues bras."

"I couldn't wear one anyway. I'm a Kings fan."

He gave her another bag that felt like—she peered inside. "Coins?"

"Quarters. For the hair dryer. Don't want you catching cold."

It somehow was the sweetest thing anybody had ever given her, and her stupid eyes got all watery. He'd thought of everything, from her scratches to her hair. No wonder women were always falling in love with him. He deserved it.

Before she started bawling like a baby, she clutched her bags tighter to her chest and raced to the bathroom. She had the room to herself and took her time. The shower washed away the mud and dried blood on her arms and legs, leaving them looking much better than she had expected. The shampoo was a brand that would make her hairdresser cringe, but it smelled good and clean and fresh.

The clothes Neal had bought were a St. Louis Blues hockey T-shirt, a matching pair of shorts and a pair of shower sandals. A little big and way too expensive, she saw from the tags. But they were dry and clean, and she loved them.

When she went outside, Neal was doing something in the back of the truck. He came out and hurried her into the front of the truck. It was still pouring, and darkness was coming with a vengeance.

"Okay, now we just have to find site number twelve, and we're set," he said.

"We're set?" she asked. "What about the restaurant with the good home cooking?"

"All at site number twelve," he assured her. "Ah, there it is."

The headlights showed a sign with the number twelve on it, and Neal pulled up, then backed the truck into the space.

"Okay," he said as he turned off the motor. "We make a mad dash for the back of the truck on the count of three. One, two—"

She was out of the truck and around back before he'd finished, beating him by a mile. Of course, that let her stand in the rain a couple of seconds longer.

"Competitive, aren't we?" he murmured.

"And you aren't?"

She couldn't believe the back of the truck. He'd made it almost homey. The two sleeping bags—with air mattresses underneath—were stretched out side by side. And on a small box in the middle sat two citronella candles in glass jars, which Neal lit once they were inside. The flickering light cast soft shadows, matching the gentle sound of a light rain falling on the cap roof.

"Cozy," she said.

"We aim to please." He opened one of the bags sitting on his sleeping bag. "Skipping right to the main course of our delectable dinner, we have chili dogs."

He handed her one and took another out for himself. She could feel the warmth through the paper wrapping.

"Home cooked, I feel," she said.

"Right here in Ready-Set-Go's home."

She took a bite, too hungry to give him any more of a hard time. It tasted so good. "What else did you get?" she asked as she chewed.

"Potato chips, corn chips and frozen fudge."

"Great," she muttered. "Salt, fat, food dye and chocolate. It looks like you've covered all the major food groups."

"And to accompany the meal." He held up two glasses. "Two chocolate mushees."

"This is heaven," she said with a laugh.

Nick wasn't sure he agreed with Colleen after another few hours in the truck. Was this heaven or was it hell? Being alone with her in this tiny space was torture, that was for sure.

After they finished eating, he brought out the deck of cards he'd bought and they played war, and rummy, and old maid, and every other card game they could think of. By the time she won her tenth game of crazy eights, it was getting late and the candles were ready to flicker out.

"I'm tired," he said. "What do you say we turn in?"

"You're just tired of losing," she teased as she helped pick up the cards.

But once the makeshift table was moved to one side, the lights were out and they were stretched on their sleeping bags, he wondered how he was going to get to sleep with Colleen lying just a few feet away.

"This is cozy," she said and turned to face him. "Much better than Bramson."

He couldn't see her features in the darkness, but he could sure sense her nearness. Feel the warmth of her presence wash over him. Know the sudden rush of hunger.

"Oh, I don't know about that," he said. "Bramson has its advantages, too." Like separate rooms. Like breathing space.

"I can't think of many," she said, and inched closer. "Too many people. No privacy." Her fingers brushed his arm, sending sparks shooting out into the night.

"Those can be good or bad." His hand reached out to touch her, to see if her skin was as soft as it seemed. To see if he could touch her, breathe in her sweetness and still stay sane.

"I'm sure glad it was you that came after me," she said into the night.

The sound of the rain outside was a lullaby, washing away the rest of the world and leaving them safe in their little cave. "I'm glad, too."

They moved as if one. Their lips touched. A soft and gentle touch. A questioning touch. Then it seemed as if the rain grew harder, or maybe it was just the pounding of his heart, for their kiss changed. It was hard and demanding. Hungry with the heat of desire. Mind-numbing as it drove all else away.

His arms slid around her, pulling her closer. Their bodies sang to each other. Their hands played the music. It was all it should be or could be or ever would be. Even as his heart raced and pounded and was ready to burst, his body cried out to know her softness, to bury itself in her arms and know true peace and joy.

Then their lips parted and the cry of his heart went unanswered, but she didn't move away, just lay in his arms as the darkness and rain sang love songs.

"Did you ever wish you had somebody?" she asked him softly. He could feel the words against his cheek, then in his heart.

"Somebody?" Something trembled in his soul. Something that felt like fear, but he tried to push it away. Tried to deny it. "Do we ever really have somebody?"

But she didn't seem interested in a philosophical discussion. "Sometimes I feel so alone. I just really wish I had someone that understood."

But understanding could be a burden, too. "I think we're thinking too much," he said and rolled over so she lay beneath him. "I can think of much better ways to spend the time."

He kissed her again, taking her lips in the wild hope that they would once again drive all thought away. That somehow her touch could keep the ghosts from pouring in and taking possession of him. Her sweetness was a lure, and her willing softness beneath him promised forgetfulness.

She moved then. Not much, but enough. The spell was broken, even though her arms still held him. "You've had someone, haven't you?" she asked. "That's what the cream soda stuff is about, isn't it?"

All the ghosts came rushing back. The past swallowed him up, gloating that he had never really been free.

It had been two years ago today. How could he have passed through the whole day without giving it a single thought? What kind of husband did that make him?

He'd helped with a birthing at Meadow Ridge Farm, but when he was ready to leave, his truck wouldn't start. Jerry had two other calls to make before he could come take a look, so Nick had called Donna to say he'd be late. It had been her idea to come get him, and he'd been tired enough to agree. It was a ten-minute drive. There was no risk. Or none that they'd seen.

"Neal?"

He came out of his black hole of memories to find Colleen touching his cheek gently.

"What's the matter?" she asked.

"Nothing," he said and tried to force a laugh. What a slip. He had to get back to being Neal on the outside, never mind who he was on the inside. He let go of her and rolled onto his back. The rain washed over them with desolation. "Maybe it's the chili dog. I haven't eaten them in ages."

She moved to her sleeping bag, taking the warmth and softness with her. "Maybe you aren't into confiding any more than I am." Her voice was hard.

"What's that mean?" he asked. The pain hovering too close made his voice sharp. "I don't have a Steele in my past, stalking me."

"No, you've got cream soda," she said. "And from the sound of it, it's about ten times worse than Steele Blazes."

He wanted to tell her lay off, to butt out of his life and leave him alone. He wanted to make some joke and start her laughing so she forgot all about cream soda and moods. He wanted to tell her everything—about Donna and their love and how he had promised to love her forever and then almost forgot it was the anniversary of her death.

Instead he closed his eyes and lay still. "You have an active imagination," he said. "Must be why you're such a good actress."

"You're just as bad as I am about trust."

"Hey, I'm not the one being stalked."

"Oh, no?" Her voice was almost soft. Almost. "Had me fooled."

"Wait a minute." She was blowing this all out of proportion. "I'm not being threatened. I'm not being kidnapped. I'm not having to hide behind some security guards."

"No? Then those are happy memories you're reliving?"

Nick was glad it was dark. "Why does it have to be anything I'm reliving?" he snapped.

"Because I know the signs."

He lay there for the longest time. The rain was picking up again and the drumming on the fiberglass cap became louder. A breeze—fresh with dampness—came in through the side vents. It was a night for romance. Even a place for it, in its own cozy way. Yet never had his heart felt farther from love.

"It's just the anniversary of a sad day," he said. "I almost forgot about it."

"Time does that," she said gently. "No matter how much we hurt, time eases it. Other friends, loves, memories get in the way."

"But they shouldn't," he said as the past came racing over him in the darkness. "It was two years ago today that my...brother's wife died."

He felt like a traitor saying it that way. Like he hadn't loved Donna enough to remember the anniversary of her death and not even enough to claim her.

"What happened?" Colleen asked softly.

"An accident. Deer ran in front of her car. She tried to swerve but there wasn't time."

"How terrible!"

He barely heard her, lost in the memories. "One minute she was full of life, planning a dinner, and the next she was gone. Her laughter. Her smile. Her calming presence. Nothing's been the same since."

"It must have been very hard for your brother."

That brought him out of his shadows. Now was the time to admit the truth, to claim Donna as his along with his identity—but he couldn't. Not without possibly hurting Neal. He had agreed to this stupid masquerade and had to see it through.

"It was hard on us all," he said. "But worse for Nick, of course. She was everything to him."

"But still, he needs to let go. He's too young to spend his whole life grieving."

"He's not," Nick said, then feared his words had come out too sharply. "He's getting along just fine."

"If he was, you wouldn't be still grieving yourself," Colleen pointed out. "You aren't just grieving for the loss of your sister-in-law, you're grieving for the loss of your brother too. For the person he was before his wife died."

"He's not that different." Was that true though? It had to have changed him. "Well, he's changed some, but he's happy with his life."

"He's found someone else then?"

"Someone else?" The idea astounded him. Hurt. Ached. Tugged at his heart until it wanted to bleed. "No, of course not."

But that was it, he saw suddenly. Colleen had gotten in the way. For all his brave pronouncements that he was going to be Neal, the king of the three-week romance, he'd let Colleen slip up close to him. He had gotten caught up in her life and her needs, and hadn't noticed how helping her had pushed other things out of the way. He'd only meant to escape the memories for a time; he hadn't wanted to replace them. How could he have failed Donna like that? She deserved better than a husband like him.

He rolled over on his side. He could see Colleen's form on her sleeping bag and something stirred inside him. He ought to look away, but he didn't want to. That was the real trouble—he wasn't a husband anymore.

Colleen did a lot of thinking after Neal went to sleep. No matter what he insisted, something was very wrong. This was a man who was haunted by his past. Was it the death of his sister-in-law that had made him so afraid of attachments? Had it given him his cream soda look? It was possible, she guessed, but there had to be more to the story.

He had been so kind to her, so thoughtful and honest, that she was determined to repay him by freeing him from this past hurt, if she could. But to do that, she had to find out. And the best way to get him to open up more, she decided, was if she told him all about Steele. Well, not *all*. She would make up some story, but confidentiality would breed confidentiality. It was just a matter of finding the right time and place.

The little restaurant they found for breakfast might have been the right place, but it wasn't the right time. "I'm not much of a morning person," she was forced to tell him after the third yawn.

"I bet you aren't usually up before eight back in Los Angeles."

She frowned, wondering if that made her seem like a party-mad wild woman, but that was her reputation, so it would seem silly to deny it. "When I was a kid, I did terribly when we had math as the first class."

"Well, I won't ask you to figure the tip then," he said and went back to studying the menu.

After a breakfast of wonderful pecan pancakes, she felt much more alive and alert. But by that time they were walking through the small shopping district of Romance where anyone could overhear them. It didn't feel like the right place.

Neal stopped to read the real estate listings posted in a window. "Imagine living in a sixteen-bedroom house," he said. "Here's one in Bramson that's got tennis courts, two built-in pools—one indoor, one outdoor—and a three-mile jogging trail."

"Sounds like something Steele would like," she said, and waited for the look of curiosity. None came.

"I think half the fun of jogging is meeting people along the way."

"Don't you get mobbed for autographs?"

He looked like she'd caught him with his hand in the cookie jar. "Well, yeah. Sometimes. I wear sunglasses a lot. Hey, is that an antique store across the street?"

So much for whetting his curiosity about Steele. She was just going to have to tell him and not wait for him to show interest. But she couldn't do it at the antique store, or at the used book store next door. No one was that interested in empty old stamp collecting albums. He had to be avoiding her because of the confidences last night.

"Let's go on a picnic lunch," she suggested when they finally left the used bookstore. "We can get stuff at the Ready-Set-Go and find a quiet little place to eat it."

"What if it rains?"

"It won't."

And for once it didn't. They got sandwiches and lemonade at the convenience store and packed them with the chips and fudge left from last night's dinner. They found the perfect spot after only a half hour of driving down back roads. A little stream meandered through some trees down the hill from a pasture of grazing horses. She and Neal sat on the bank and ate, half in the sun and half in shade, letting their bare feet dangle in the water.

"I like it here," he said. "I like the quiet."

She made a face and looked around her. "Doesn't it seem too quiet? I bet the bugs are all planning some kind of uprising."

He laughed, almost with relief. "I never figured you for a country girl. Bet you don't believe in happily ever after, either."

"Well, the king of the three-week romances sure doesn't, I know."

"No, I sure don't."

But then they were through with their sandwiches. It was time to start her story, and she was finding herself sidetracked. It was remarkably cozy here. Almost frighteningly so. His hand on the ground so close to hers. His leg almost brushing hers. His arms just waiting to go around her.

Colleen looked away and took a deep breath. "I want to tell you about Steele," she said briskly "I think I owe you the story."

"If you want." His voice was hesitant, as if he didn't want to push.

Now all she had to do was think of a version to tell. "Steele and I came up in the business together," she said.

"So he's a friend of yours?"

Colleen laughed and kicked at a leaf floating by her foot. Friend? What did the word mean? She had no—

She stopped. Lisa was her friend, of course, but so was Neal. He was someone she could trust. Someone who put her safety and well-being up close to his own. Someone who wasn't out to use her for his own ends. She hadn't thought about it before, but he'd become a friend in the past few weeks, and she liked the idea. It made telling him about Steele easier, more right.

"No, Steele and I were not friends," she said. "But we did make a few movies together."

"Then why is he following you?"

Colleen shook her head. It was the moment of truth. Or rather the moment of lie. This was where she wove some story that Neal would believe. But it was harder than she'd expected. Though every cell in her brain shouted for her to concoct a story, every bit of her heart said to tell him the truth. To let one person see the real her.

"He wanted my help," she said in a rush. "He wanted us to pretend we were lovers."

Neal stared at her. "What would that help?"

His question surprised her. "For someone who's been in this business as long as you have, you're sure naive at times."

He laughed away her slight criticism. "I meant, specifically what did he want from it?"

"PR," she said. "He's got a new part on a soap opera and he figured, with a little bit of exposure, he could make it a long-term thing. Something where he'd work and get paid regular."

"Why did he come to you?" Nick asked.

"Like I said, we were never friends, but Steele helped me out when I needed it." She took a deep breath and reached over to trace her fingers lightly over the back of his hand. "A couple of years ago, just before I tried out for the Sassy Mirabel part, I had the same problem Steele has now. Low exposure."

"And he helped you?"

She shrugged and looked away, as if the horses grazing in the sunshine would give her strength. "My agent arranged a PR campaign and Steele pretended to be my lover."

"So that story that kid told about you and—" Neal stopped.

"Was a fake," Colleen finished for him. "All publicity. Steele and I were never a real couple. Everybody thought we were, but that was the whole point of the PR campaign."

"And you didn't want to do that again," Nick said. His voice was soft and reassuring, yet there was a hint of anger in it, too. "I don't blame you."

"Steele said I owed him."

"Like hell you do," Nick snapped.

She smiled at him and realized that he was holding her hand. When had that happened? She ought to let go. She ought not be needing to lean on him. But she ignored her inner scoldings.

"If I didn't help him," she went on, "he was going to expose me. He was going to sell an interview to *Worldwide News,* telling everybody that I really hadn't been his lover."

"So?" The air around Neal fairly rippled with indignation.

"He was going to get others to say that I've never been anybody's lover." She held her breath, then plunged ahead. "And then people would know Sassy Mirabel was a big fake. That she doesn't really know how to handle men."

It was out. It had been said. Now he knew that she wasn't what she pretended to be. But did he understand just how far she was from a great, experienced lover?

"Sassy Mirabel is a fictitious character," Nick pointed out.

"She's a television character," Colleen replied. "For a lot of people, that makes her more real than you and me. And if they think she's a fake, they may not watch her anymore."

"I guess that would bother our sponsor."

"It wouldn't do my bank account any good, either," she replied, her voice suddenly filled with fear and vulnerability.

He tugged on her hand until she moved into his arms. They were around her in a flash, holding her so gently, yet like they would never let her go. His embrace told her to relax, to trust, to stop seeing demons where there were none. She let her breath out with a weary sigh and laid her head on his shoulder.

"You have to let people know the real you," he said softly. "Let them see who you really are so they can make up their own minds. My father always used to tell me, the people you have to lie to to impress aren't worth impressing in the first place."

"It's not as simple as you make it sound."

"It's not as hard as you think it is."

He looked at her then, and the world stopped. Ever so slowly his lips came down to meet hers, and she felt her heart sigh. His touch was magic, as soft as silk, as potent as aged brandy. She moved slightly to deepen the touch, to meet his soft passion with her sudden needs. The tightening of his arms around her echoed the ache in her heart.

She slipped her arms around him to pull him closer to her. The crush of her breasts against him, the taste of his lips on hers, the thunder in the air—

She pulled away from him suddenly. The sky had clouded over, big, dark, heavy clouds, and it was thundering. A few drops spattered on the ground around them.

"We better run for it," he said, grabbing the remains of their lunch even as he pushed his feet into his shoes.

She slipped on her shower scuffs and picked up the old blanket they'd sat on, then raced with him to the truck. It started to pour just as they slammed their doors shut, coming down in solid sheets that made visibility impossible. They were stuck here awhile.

"Now where were we?" Neal asked after he tossed the bags of food behind the seat.

Her heart knew exactly where they'd been, but it was warning her to be careful. The rain had drenched the fire that had been smoldering inside her. At least for now.

"I was surprised to hear you quote your father," she said. "I thought you said you hardly knew him."

He said nothing for a long moment, then laughed lightly.

"You caught me there. I do that all the time. You know, quote this wise old father of mine. It's sort of a homey touch, even if it's all made up."

"Oh."

"I guess it was my personal fake PR campaign," he went on.

"You do it well," she said. "It sounded so real."

He started the motor, peering at the rain. "It looks like it's starting to slow. Guess we should be on our way to Bramson."

She nodded, though she felt inexplicably lonely outside of his smile. "Talk about a summer romance."

"This one wasn't even three weeks," he said with a smile.

It wasn't until they were on their way that she realized she'd never got him to tell her about cream soda. Not that it mattered. There were lots of long nights on the tour ahead of them.

## Chapter Ten

It was scary how fast they fell into the routine of the tour. Mount Vernon. Carthage. Stockton. The days rolled into each other just as the towns became indistinguishable from one another. Yet there was one thing that had changed—she and Neal.

They'd become friends, and so it was natural to sit together on the bus. To eat together. To relax together. Cooper picked up on it, of course, and continued her harping about Colleen on the verge of wedlock, but Colleen was able to ignore it. She was enjoying Neal's company too much to let minor annoyances get in the way. Colleen found herself telling him things she'd never told anyone before. Never even wanted to tell anyone. Like about her mother.

"She just never seemed happy," Colleen told Neal one day late in the week. "I can remember watching her get ready for a date when I was really little. She was always so hopeful. This guy was going to be the one."

"And he wasn't," Neal finished for her.

"Oh, no, they all were. At least for a few days or a few weeks." Colleen stared out the bus window as endless farm fields stretched away to the horizon. "Then she'd be shut up in her room, crying her heart out, when he turned out to be just a regular guy."

"That must have been hard for you."

She shrugged as she felt the bus slow. They must be pulling into a town. "It was a great education in the ways of love," she said. "I learned really early not to trust my happiness to anyone but me. That love was a joke. A hormonal response designed to keep us propagating the species."

He shook his head, his eyes looking into the shadowy past. "It's not a joke," he said softly. "It's an addiction. A high when you have it. And real pain when you don't. Your mother sounds like she would have sold her soul to find it again."

Colleen watched him, watched the way the shadows danced in and out of his eyes. He had known love, too, but his reaction had been the opposite of her mother's. He would do anything to avoid it again. That must be how he got his reputation for three-week romances—things would be getting serious by that time, so he'd leave. It made her feel safe to be with him. Neither of them would let their hearts get involved.

They passed a large sign at the side of the road. "Welcome to Nevada," he read, then turned to her with a smile. "If it's Nevada, we must still be in Missouri."

She laughed and slipped her high-heeled sandals on. The moment was over, the sharing done. It was time to get on stage for yet another pet parade or 4-H meeting or county veterinarian association meeting.

It was almost a relief to have all these towns to stop in. The fire that had been smoldering in Romance hadn't been drenched, after all. And all too often, when Neal smiled just so or his voice was just the right tone, flames flickered up to lick at her heart. To try to melt it into fearlessness. To try to convince it to take a risk and care.

But then they'd roll into another town and sign hundreds of

autographs and talk about fleas and diets and ear mites and dental care, and she'd get her heart under control.

The constant barrage of small towns forced the sharing to be done in small doses, too. It almost felt as if she wasn't really telling anything or hearing anything, yet she was slowly seeing inside Neal Sheridan and getting a glimpse of the pain he carried in his soul. One day, he'd tell her all. And until that day, she was content to be given little pieces.

"So what have we got going in Nevada?" Neal asked.

"Some youth group."

"Oh, yeah. A little talk on the care of small animals."

"I hope that doesn't include snakes," she said.

Neal laughed. "You did quite well with the snake in Greenfield."

"Right. I avoided it." She'd dealt with enough men in her life to know how to handle a snake. No, that was wrong. Neal wasn't like her father or Steele or the others. Neal was different. Oops, there were those flames again, agreeing with the softening of her heart.

And so the days wore on. Osceola. Appleton City. Butler. Little by little, she found her natural instincts changing, weakening. She was still wary of men, but not of Neal. She had nothing to fear from being open and honest with him.

"Want to go for a run afterward?" he asked.

"I'd love to."

His arms were around her for a photo shoot. It was all fake, but it was all real, too. Independence, Missouri. Funny how these town names seemed to be fit so well. She'd always thought she was independent, but here in Independence, she felt freer than ever. The closer she got to Neal, the more alive she was. The more her desires burned in her soul, the stronger and more feminine she felt.

"I'll have Lila check out a route for us," Colleen said. Lila Dane was their female security guard and went running with them.

"She can pass the word to the others, too," Neal said.

A number of the younger media people ran with them. Colleen had been leery of their company at first, but they hadn't used the opportunity to pry into her or Neal's lives.

"Let's look a little cozier now," some photographer called out.

"Gladly," Neal said. Pulling Colleen closer into his arms, he gave her a quick peck on the cheek.

The cameras were all clicking and flashing, but Colleen's heart was disappointed. His embrace gave her a thrill, sent her temperature soaring, but his kiss was just enough to make her wish for more.

"Is that the best you can do?" she teased.

His eyes widened—deepened—in surprise, then he smiled in a way that tied her stomach in knots. "Lady, you haven't seen the best I can do," he said. "You don't want to see it. You'd be too miserable when the tour is over and we split."

She laughed. "I've noticed that the bigger the talk, the more pitiful the performance."

"Is that so?"

His lips came down on hers. She'd challenged him, her heart had egged him on purposely, and it wasn't disappointed. A rush of pleasure, a tingling that raced from her heart to her fingers and toes, a nagging need to be even closer that grew and grew with each touch and kiss and look.

She was playing with danger, she knew, but couldn't deny herself the thrill it brought. She'd never met someone she could trust so implicitly. Someone she wasn't afraid to let herself feel and explore and take risks with. It was delicious. Magic. A wonder to be marveled at.

Then it was over, and so was the embrace and the pretense and the moment. Back on the bus to another town and another photo session and another flash of glory. Yet something lingered. A dream, perhaps, a memory of the magic that his touch could bring her. Some hunger that awoke again at the slightest promise of passion.

Liberty. Plattsburg. Kingston. The next week started, and the days wore on, sending them to yet another presentation on animal care. Colleen gave a talk on the fun of having pets, then Neal spoke about the responsibilities of pet ownership. They worked so well together, Colleen thought. For the talks, the photo opportunities, each other.

Afterward, the kids formed a line and passed by the two of them, showing off their pets and generating more photo opportunities.

"His name is Fink," a young girl said, handing Colleen her pet white rat. "Actually that's his last name. His first name is Rat."

"I think I've met some cousins of his," Colleen joked, letting the animal rest on her forearm while she petted it.

"Hey, is that another insult to us guys?" Neal asked.

"Not to you, sweetie," she said and brushed his cheek with her lips. "Just to the ratty ones."

Colleen gave Fink to his young owner. "He's a great rat," Colleen said. "You take good care of him."

Neal leaned in close as the girl moved on. "Today rats," he whispered. "And tomorrow snakes."

"I can handle anything," Colleen said.

He smiled and took her hand. She'd come to believe that she could handle anything that came her way.


"You guys staying out here?" Lila asked.

"For a while," Nick said, his arm around Colleen's shoulders as they relaxed on a bench outside the motel's front door. He couldn't bear to let go of her just yet.

"Well, I need a shower after that run," the security woman said. "I'll tell Gus to watch you two."

"We'll be good," Colleen promised, but the woman grimaced as she went inside. Colleen sank into his arms. "I'm not sure you're trusted any more than I am."

Nick tightened his hold on Colleen. He wanted to pull her ever closer, to get as close as a man and a woman could. But he only let those thoughts dance in his dreams. "It must be your influence," he said. "Until I met you everyone trusted me. Kids. Dogs. Old ladies."

"Anyone you can bribe or con with a wink, huh?"

"That's cruel," he said.

She laughed and snuggled closer. They let the silence grow. It was both comfortable and uncomfortable, like the cool night air that couldn't quite extinguish the heat of the day. They'd passed the halfway mark a few days ago. The tour was more than half over. His foray into Neal's life was winding down. He was relieved and saddened by the thought. The tour hadn't been as straightforward as he'd expected it to be.

He'd come to a decision last night—yet another sleepless night—that he would treasure the time he had with Colleen. And though he died a little each time he touched her, he wouldn't let it go any farther. She was so beautiful, so perfect, so vulnerable that making love to her wouldn't be enough. He'd never get by with just a taste, never be satisfied to lose himself inside and then walk away. Yet neither could he give her what she deserved—himself, totally and unencumbered. So the decision had been easy—a friend and never a lover.

"A lot of fireflies out tonight," she said. "Did you ever catch them when you were a kid?"

He stopped. He had, certainly, but had Neal? He couldn't remember doing it when he'd visited Neal and their mother in Washington, D.C. Damn this stupid masquerade.

"Well, did you?" She pulled away from him, turning so she could see his face in the light coming from the motel. "You know, if I didn't know better, I'd think you had some deep, dark secrets you wanted to keep from me."

No, only one, really. "That run took a lot out of me tonight," Nick said. "The humidity's hell here in Savannah."

"It's Savannah, Missouri," she pointed out. "Besides, you grew up in Washington, D.C. That's one of the most humid areas in the country."

If he wasn't careful, she was going to catch him. Then where would he be? Without even her friendship. "You sound like one of those kids who always studied," he said. "Did you have any friends in school?"

"Lots of them," she informed him, then laughed. "Well, a few, anyway."

She sounded like she'd been lonely as a kid. Lonely and lost and probably a fair bit angry, too. "So who was your best friend growing up?" he asked.

"My best friend?" She sounded startled, uneasy.

He couldn't bear to hear that darting fear in her voice. "Sure. Mine was Tim Lawrence." It was a safe enough answer. Whenever Neal was in Three Oaks, he palled around with Tim, too. "He was the catcher on our baseball team. I was the pitcher."

"What's he doing now?"

"Ah." Tim was a dentist in Union Pier and still one of Nick's closest friends, but Neal could hardly say that. "He works for the government. Someplace in the Washington area."

Colleen laughed. "You guys certainly keep in close touch."

"Don't try to weasle out of answering my question," he said. "I'm waiting to hear all about your best friend."

It didn't seem like a hard question, but Colleen sure seemed to be struggling. Maybe he should just forget it. What difference did it make? He didn't need to know everything about her. All the information in the world wasn't going to make it easier not to make love to her.

"Why don't we—"

"Her name was Lisa," Colleen said suddenly. She sat forward, pulling away from him, almost in the shadows. "She was older than me by a few years, but we were really close. I met her when I was seven and just starting in the movies."

"Have you kept in touch with her?"

"Pretty much. Her family moved east when I was twelve. She runs her own business now and is looking to start a family."

He felt there was more to Lisa than Colleen was telling, but then wasn't there more to him than he was telling? And it wasn't as if she was talking about Lisa Hughes—

Hell. A sudden storm cloud descended on him, blocking out any sweetness the night might hold. What if it was Lisa Hughes? He had this sudden certain memory of a Colleen

Cassidy poster arriving at the clinic and Lisa saying she knew Colleen ages ago. What if his friend Lisa had been Colleen's best friend growing up?

And what if she was? he countered. What difference would it make? Lisa wasn't here to denounce him as a fake. And Colleen and Lisa weren't likely to compare personality traits later and discover the switch. And if they did, it was water under the bridge. Nothing at all to worry about. Except that she would hate him for sure then, and even though he knew they would part soon, he couldn't bear the thought of Colleen hating him.

Sleep became an illusion again.

It was late in the fourth week that the bus rumbled down the interstate and zipped by the sign that said Welcome To Iowa. It went by fast enough that Colleen's heart didn't have a chance to stop, though slow enough to awaken all her fears. To make her think of running back to L.A. right away.

But she couldn't do that. Her pride wouldn't allow her to run. She would stay and face her demons. She closed her eyes, took a deep breath and forced her nerves to settle down. It had been a hard four weeks, but it wasn't the tour that was bothering her. It was Iowa. The state held its own special horror for her.

"Neal?" He was in the aisle seat next to her, leaning back, the cowboy hat he'd bought in Omaha covering his face and the biography of Harry Truman he'd bought in Independence last weekend upside down in his lap. "Are you asleep?"

"Yes."

Colleen knew he was joking but still paused, taking time to stare at the scenery flashing by the bus window. Missouri, especially the southern part, had been wooded and hilly. The roads had had a lot of curves, almost as if promising a surprise just around the bend. Here the land was flat as a pool table, stretching out so far you could see the edge of the earth. Nothing could stay hidden here.

Why hadn't she told Neal about Lisa instead of playing

games with the truth? He probably barely knew her, and she him, since her reading of his personality had been so wrong. It was just that Colleen wasn't used to sharing these things. Habits were harder to break than she'd expected.

She turned to Neal, and her glance was caught by the picture of Harry Truman on the book cover. Good old plain-speaking, honest Harry.

"I wonder if Truman's family found him a hard act to follow," she said.

Neal pushed the hat from his eyes and grinned at her. "Because he was a natty dresser like me?"

She tried frowning at him but he brought her hand to his lips and kissed it. She quickly gave up her anger. No woman could get mad at Neal. Exasperated, yes, but never angry.

"No, silly," Colleen went on. "I'm talking about how honest he was. I wonder if he made the people around him be more honest."

Suddenly Neal's hand slipped away from hers. "I don't know," he mumbled. "Guess it depended on the person."

Colleen nodded. So what did her dishonesty with him say about her? She wanted to tell him everything—about Lisa and her father and Iowa—but the words wouldn't come out. Maybe she wasn't being dishonest, though—maybe she was just being private.

"I guess there's levels of honesty, too," she said. "Keeping something to yourself isn't the same as actually telling a lie. Not like deliberately trying to make someone believe something that's not the truth."

"I guess not."

He sounded distracted, like his mind was elsewhere. If she wasn't careful, she'd have him wondering what her sudden fascination with honesty was.

"So are you enjoying the tour?" she asked.

He gave her an odd look before flashing a crooked smile. "I guess. It's been a challenge, since I can't really get to know any of these people, yet they all want advice and help with their animals."

"Isn't that true of your job all the time?" she asked. "Whether you're on tour, broadcasting from a studio or doing a special on location?"

He nodded. "It's the nature of our business—address an issue quickly and then move on. It's just frustrating at times."

Colleen smiled at him. "Maybe you should trade places with your brother," she said. "You know, be a country vet for a while."

Neal gave her the strangest look. If she hadn't known better, she would have said horror filled his face. She made herself laugh.

"Don't worry. I was just joking." But her words didn't seem to calm him at all. "I know that you don't belong in Three Oaks any more than I do."

His expression seemed almost pained. "Why do you say that?"

"I don't know." Colleen shrugged. How had they gotten on this subject and how did they get off? "It's a small town. Has to be one of those places where everyone knows everyone else's business. The kind of place that would suffocate you if you're a private person like you or me."

"If we're so private, why'd we choose to be performers?"

"Because performing is all about pretend. It has nothing to do with who you really are inside."

Neal looked away, and Colleen turned to her window. Small towns. Somewhere out here was the small town her father was from, the place where the bastard had fled after he'd gotten her mother pregnant. Colleen didn't know the name of the place. Her mother probably hadn't even known. After all, if he'd told her where he was from, he could have been traced, could have been found again.

Colleen swallowed hard to get the bitter anger from her mouth. Or was it fear? They were to hit Harlan, Audobon and Guthrie Center today. What if one of those towns was the place? What if one of those old men who came to their show for dog food samples was her father?

The bitterness turned her stomach to churning, and she

leaned back in her seat, closing her eyes as she tried to settle her stomach. It didn't matter. She'd never know. He'd hardly come up to her wearing a name tag that said he was her father.

"You see *Worldwide News* yesterday?" Neal asked.

She opened her eyes. "It's not on my regular reading list," she said. "What lies are they spreading now?"

"Seems Steele's taken up with Mindy of 'Central High' and he's hot stuff again."

"Mindy?" Colleen was dumbfounded. "She's only eighteen. Of course, she's a lot older at eighteen than I was."

"I would guess he's given up on resurrecting his romance with you," Neal said. "I guess Cooper's going to have to find another line for her stories about you."

It would be a relief, if it had been a worry, but her mind was too occupied with thoughts of her father. And the fear of accidentally being nice to him. She was going to have to put him out of her mind. Neal had helped her see she could handle a lot. That included a father she had no interest in seeing.

"Sure would like to have your autograph, young lady," the old man said.

"We're done for the day," Colleen said stiffly.

Nick frowned at the pile of posters on the table before her. It would have taken her less time to sign one than to refuse to. "We've still got a few minutes," he said. "You can't refuse somebody who's come out in the rain just to see us."

"And who might need a boat to get home if I don't go soon," the man joked.

Colleen sighed and sat down. "Who shall I sign it to?"

"Bill Webster," the man said.

Colleen signed it quickly and handed it over with a tight smile. "There you go, Bill."

"I surely do thank you," he said, carefully rolling the poster up before wandering over to get his sample of dog food.

The meeting hall was almost empty. The heavy rains had kept the large crowds away. Or else there just weren't large

crowds in Guthrie Center, Iowa. Maybe Colleen had been upset by the small turnout.

Nick sat on the edge of the table, taking Colleen's hand in
his. Even the barest touch betrayed her tension.

"Tired?" he asked.

She smiled at him, but it was a poor acting job. "Dinner
was kind of heavy. It's been a long day."

"A long four weeks," he corrected her, and getting to his
feet, pulled her to hers. He couldn't do anything about the
dinner they'd had an hour or so ago, but he could do something about her weariness. "I think we can pull rank and head
out to the bus."

For once, Colleen didn't give him a hard time, but allowed
herself to be led outside. The rain had turned the world dark
and dreary and damp. Nick thought about suggesting a run for
the bus, or even carrying her again, but Colleen trudged into
the downpour before he could stop her.

"I wonder what time we'll get to Des Moines tonight?"
she muttered.

"Probably pretty quick if we get caught in the current of
this runoff."

He hurried her around the largest of the puddles and got her
into the bus, then suggested that she change into some dry,
comfortable clothes. She followed his suggestions without argument, which was in itself cause for concern.

It hadn't been just that one old man at the end of the day.
She'd been tense all day, jumping a dozen times an hour when
asked to pose with local citizens or meeting town dignitaries.
She'd been fine with the kids in Harlan and great with the
young mothers in Audubon who'd wanted her beauty secrets,
but other times, she'd turned pale and looked ready to pass
out.

There was only one explanation—she knew he was lying to
her. Oh, not the specifics, but she knew he wasn't being honest. That was what that whole Harry Truman discussion had
been about. It had been his chance to confess and clear the

decks. But he hadn't. He couldn't. And it had nothing to do with Neal and their stupid contest.

Once he told Colleen the truth, she'd hate him. He would confirm her assessment that men were liars and cheats. There would be nothing left between them. Not that there was anything long-term, anyway. But he wanted his last two weeks with her. His last two weeks of seeing the sun in her smile and the stars in her eyes. He'd tell her the truth then, but not until then.

It wasn't hard for him to keep his resolve not to confess all. When she sat in the seat next to him, she leaned back, closing her eyes and dozing—or pretending to—all the way to Des Moines. She didn't sit up until the bus had parked in the entryway of the hotel and Brad had come on with the room keys.

"Gracious, we're here already?" she asked with a yawn.

"Just in time to go back to sleep," Neal said.

"Sounds like a wonderful idea."

They went into the hotel together, but either it was too late for anyone to care they were there, or they looked so bedraggled from the day and the rain that they didn't look like celebrities. At any rate, for once, they were left alone. Colleen went up to her second-floor room undisturbed, and he went to his third-floor room.

He'd barely gotten his suitcase open when there was a knock at his door. Colleen was there.

"Haven't we done this before?" he asked as she came into the room.

She leaned against the closet door, smiling at him with just the slightest of smiles. "We have and we haven't," she said in a whisper that did strange things to the pit of his stomach.

He shut the door. She reached over to bolt it.

"I was lonesome," she said and took a step closer to him.

He frowned, uncertain what was going on, but certain that something was. "I thought you were sleepy," he said.

"My room was too big." Her fingers touched his cheek in the barest of caresses. "It was scary."

Her touch left streaks of fire across his soul. His heart felt ready to explode. But still he hesitated. This didn't seem like her. "Isn't my room the same size?"

"But you're here," she said. "It's not nearly so scary."

She went into his arms, and he had no choice but to hold her. Not that he didn't want to. It was just that this whole thing felt wrong. No, it felt wonderful, like the stuff of dreams. But it seemed wrong. Not even trying to figure out why she was here in his arms suddenly, he knew he shouldn't be holding her. He was a liar, a cheat. He couldn't make love to her, not when she didn't know who he was. Then he'd no longer be a liar and a cheat, but a thief, too.

But when she kissed him, he couldn't help but kiss her back. And when her touch lit flames in his heart, there was nothing he could do to stop the fire from burning. His hands had to touch her, and feel her softness. His lips had to taste her passion, had to feel the love songs in her heart.

What happened to sanity? To choice? To the ability to think and reason and be strong? There was just her softness pressed up against him, teasing his with desire, tempting him with the hunger for passion and the burning ache for her touch. He had to have her. More of her. All of her. Every thought and breath and gesture had to be his.

His hands roamed over her back, pulling her even closer to him. They slid over the gentle curve of her buttocks but the need to bury himself in her softness was too strong and hard to bear. It shot though him like wildfire racing over a prairie, consuming all coherence and logic in its path. He couldn't breathe. He wasn't sure he could even stand. All he knew suddenly was that he was Nick and that this was all a lie.

Finally, he got the strength to break away from her lips and held her against him. "I'm not sure we ought to be doing this," he said. His breath was raspy, his voice hoarse.

"Why not?" she asked.

Why not indeed? His mind had been burned to a crisp by the flames of his desire. There was nothing left to put up an argument.

"It's because I told you I didn't have much experience, isn't it?" she said and broke away from his arms. "You probably aren't interested in thirty-two year old virgins."

She was a virgin? Oh, Lordy, this made it even worse. Made it even more impossible. He'd thought from what she'd said that she was just not as experienced as she pretended, not that she had no experience. There was no way that her first time making love could be to such a scoundrel as he was.

But oh, did it hurt. How he wanted to be her first. Her only—

He took her back in his arms, as if torturing his body could somehow stop his treacherous thoughts from taking over. "It has nothing to do with what you told me," he said softly. "It's just that this isn't the right time or the right place."

"It could be," she said, her voice filled with a wistful tone. His heart wanted to break.

"You deserve so much more than me," he told her, his hands moving slowly over her back and shoulders. She felt so wonderful in his arms, so right. It was agony to hold her, knowing that was all he would do. "I don't have anything to give you."

"That's crazy." Her laugh was half humor, half tremble. "You're strong. You're kind. You make me feel safe."

*And you make me on fire,* he wanted to say, but didn't. It would be so easy to sweep her into his arms, to take her to his bed and spend the night teaching her the magic of love. It would be heaven. And it would turn to hell because he was a liar.

"I think you ought to go back to your room now," Nick said. Just saying the words tore his heart out.

She didn't move from his arms. "Can't I stay the night like I did before?"

Her voice pleaded with him. That faint thread of fear behind the teasing clawed at his soul, ripped out his honor and stomped his conscience into the dust. But he found an ounce of strength someplace.

"No," he said. "Not tonight. There's nothing to be afraid of here." Not once she left his room, that is.

"I hate Iowa," she said. "It's so flat, everyone can see you."

"Close your drapes and you'll be fine," he said and moved her from his arms. "Good night, Colleen."

She made a face and left. He closed the door, bolted it, then fell against it as if he didn't have the strength to move. He had to be the stupidest man alive for sending her away.

## Chapter Eleven

The weather got worse and the days got longer. Rather than the occasional showers that had followed them since they left Chicago, it poured all day, every day, and kept pouring all night. Still, they went on, leaving Des Moines for Newton, then on to Pella and Knoxville and Oskaloosa.

Colleen stayed on edge, and Nick stayed haunted by his lie. In a way, he could hardly wait to tell her the truth, to clear the air between them, but then she'd hate him and the tour would be over—two things he definitely was not looking forward to. He had ten more days with her, and he was not going to lose one of them.

He went down for breakfast, hoping Oskaloosa would offer something exciting, and joined Colleen in the coffee shop. She looked so beautiful, even with the shadows of worry in her green eyes. Whatever embarrassment she'd felt the other night in his room seemed finally to be gone. He ached looking at her, though, knowing the smile that came to her lips as he sat down would soon turn to anger. Why had he ever started this?

He gazed around the coffee shop. Anything to distract his thoughts. He focused on a television behind the counter.

"Rains continue over the entire Midwest, causing rivers to rise to dangerous levels," the newscaster announced. "The towns of Rome and Mount Pleasant along the Skunk River here in southeast Iowa are preparing for the worst." The male announcer—all blow-dried hair and perfect teeth—disappeared from the television screen, replaced with flickering images of people stacking sandbags along a riverbank.

"This whole state's gonna get washed down the Mississippi," John said as he took a seat next to Nick. He poured himself a cup of coffee from the pot on the table.

"I'm surprised the rivers didn't start flooding weeks ago," Colleen said. "It seems like it's done nothing but rain since we got out here."

"Those poor towns," Nick said, his eyes on the television set. "Floods are devastating, and most people don't have flood insurance."

Brad came in with Ashley. He stopped at the counter and motioned for them to turn down the volume on the TV, then looked at the group gathered for breakfast. Nick watched him with reluctance, his eyes flicking to the television. He'd learned weeks ago that he usually wasn't too fond of Brad's pronouncements.

"Listen up, people," Brad called over the murmur of conversation. "I just finished talking with St. Louis, and they've agreed we should call it quits."

That brought Nick's attention back in a flash. "Quit?" he cried. "What are you talking about?"

"I'm talking about the tour," Brad said. "We've only got ten days left, and it's just not worth the hassle of finishing. We're looking for a charter to fly us to Chicago. Then you're on your own until a week from Friday, when we'll expect you at McCormick Place."

"But there are people counting on us." Didn't anyone understand what a big deal these stops were to the little towns they were passing through? It was something that was planned for weeks, months, even.

"Who's counting on us?" Colleen asked, looking at him like he'd lost it. "There hasn't been anybody at the last few stops. The weather's too lousy to do anything but stay home."

"It's more than that," Brad said. "It's getting dangerous to keep going. Bridges are out. Roads are flooded. The bus driver was real unhappy about the route he had to take last night to get us here."

Nick stared at everyone sipping coffee and agreeing that the cancellation was for the best. Colleen turned away, and he followed her gaze to the silent television. More people sandbagging and fighting the rising floodwaters. Brad was right. The residents did have enough on their minds without celebrities coming to their town. Celebrities who—

It was so simple, he should have thought of it ages ago. He'd finally be doing something instead of talking, and it would keep him with Colleen a little longer.

"You know, Brad—" Nick stood so everyone could hear him better "—there'll be a lot of disappointed people if we cancel now. People who buy our sponsor's product."

"Neal," Brad said. "Get real. Those people wouldn't have time to see us anyway. They're busy sandbagging and pumping water and trying to keep their towns above water."

"Right. So we help them."

Everybody stared at him. "We what?" Brad repeated.

"We help them," Nick said with a smile. "We can fill sandbags. Serve food. Play with the kids. Help out like all the other volunteers."

"I think it's a great idea," Colleen said. The ever-present shadows in her eyes seemed to fade somewhat. "Think of how many good people we'd be helping."

Nick smiled at her. And think how all that hard work would distract him from her beauty while still keeping her near him. He could wear himself out each day so that maybe the sleep of exhaustion would finally come.

"This is fabulous." Brad's face lit up like the sun. "And

we'll be on every evening news broadcast in the world. Colleen and Neal. Our sponsor's name in bold letters. Love conquers all. Even a damn flood.''

Nick wanted to protest Brad's version, but stopped. Why bother? The towns would get help. He'd get to stay with Colleen a little longer, and Brad would get some great publicity. Everybody won.

"I presume you want us media people with you," a television cameraman asked.

"Unless you want the network news to get the big scoop." Laughing out loud, Brad turned to Nick. "You're a genius, baby. An absolute genius."

For once, Nick was inclined to agree with him. This was going to be perfect.

Not that Colleen was surprised, but the bus drivers didn't share Brad's enthusiasm. They flat-out refused to go any closer to the flooded areas. The roads were washed out in parts. Bridges were closed, and too many areas were in flash-flood watches. So Brad rented a couple of minivans and some cars, shipping most of their clothes and supplies on to Chicago.

After changing into shorts, a sweatshirt and running shoes, Colleen rode to a flooded area with Neal. "Where'd Brad finally decide we should go?" she asked.

"I think we're headed to Mount Pleasant," Neal said. "He was trying to decide which place would get us more coverage. I'm just following him and John and Ashley."

"Good old Brad. Always has things in perspective."

"Makes you wonder what things, though."

Colleen smiled and turned to watch the passing countryside through the steady rain. This whole idea was so typically Neal. Looking out for everybody else. So willing to give of himself. It would seem so churlish of her to hesitate because she was afraid of running into her father. And what were the chances, anyway? Iowa was filled with small towns. He could be any place here, assuming he was still living in the state, even.

"Looks like the roads may decide our destination for us,"

Neal said as the car ahead turned at a roadblock. A low-lying area was underwater. Neal followed along.

It didn't matter where they were going. Or where they ended up. This was all out of her control, so it wasn't worth worrying over.

"Do you believe in fate?" she asked. "Like things happen because they're meant to happen?"

Neal frowned with concentration as he drove through a shallow stretch of water that covered the road. The windshield wipers seemed to blur Colleen's vision more than help.

"I'm not sure," he said finally. "I guess if I did, there'd be no point in an awful lot that I do. If an animal is fated to live or die, then it doesn't matter how I treat it, does it?"

"I hadn't thought of it that way." She watched a farmer and his dog trying to herd some cows onto higher ground. "But suppose you did something totally out of character for you and because of it, you met someone you'd never have had a chance to meet any other way. Isn't that fate?"

"Uh, I guess." He sounded confused, suspicious. "You mean that we were fated to meet?"

She laughed and shook her head. "Well, that wasn't exactly what I was thinking of. I mean, giving all these performances wasn't exactly out of character for either of us, was it?"

"No, no. You're right," he said quickly. "I was thinking of something else."

"I was thinking about our going to this flood to help. It's certainly out of character for me."

"And while there, you're going to meet the man of your dreams?" he asked. His voice had a hint of bitterness in it. "Yep. I guess that would be fate, then."

She watched the rain streaming down the side window like so many tears. The man of her dreams? She guessed that was true, in a way, since she'd spent so much time thinking, dreaming, wondering about her father.

"I guess if it's meant to happen, it will," she said. "Nothing we can do to stop it."

"Except turn around."

"Which would be selfish."

He gave her an odd look but drove on in silence. It wasn't too long until they pulled into the outskirts of a small town. A state policeman stopped Brad's car and they talked a long time, then the cop waved Neal into a parking lot behind Brad.

"I hope we get to do something real instead of just posing for pictures," she said as Neal parked. She stuffed a handkerchief and some money into her pockets. "I'm tired of these fake photo opportunities."

"Hey, you're in charge," Neal said. "Make them what you want them to be."

It wasn't exactly a new idea, but in a way it was. She was in charge of herself, and if she wanted to help, not just pose and pretend to help, she would.

She and Neal followed the stream of workers heading into town and found a volunteer center in the downtown area. They went in out of the rain, but it seemed to follow them. The floor was muddy and wet, the air heavy with dampness. An older woman in bib overalls with a clipboard seemed to be in charge, and Brad rushed ahead of them to make sure she knew who was here to help. Colleen found it embarrassing.

"This is so wonderful of you." The woman looked too old and solid to gush, but gush she did as she shook their hands. "This will be such a thrill for the workers."

"But we're here to work, too," Neal said.

"Oh, we'll put you to work, no question," the woman said with a laugh, and turned to a teenager with his arm in a sling. "Joey, can you take Dr. Sheridan here over to Doc Myers? He can help with the strays that are wandering in. And Ms. Cassidy, how about if you go on over to the refreshment tent there and help pass out snacks?"

Pass out snacks? Neal got to work saving animals and she got to pass out cookies?

"I'll see you later then," Neal said to Colleen, squeezing her hand. His eyes were twinkling as he bent low to whisper in her ear. "Maybe you should tell them about your nursing skills."

"You'll pay for that remark," she said and caught him in a hug before he could get away.

Her lips took his in a brief kiss. A kiss to remind him that he wasn't free of her yet. That he couldn't get away with such remarks. But instead it almost knocked her shoes off. She knew it turned the dampness in the air to steam and stole all the oxygen from her lungs. Then he was gone and she was left to gasp as inconspicuously as possible.

The woman was smiling at her, a knowing look in her eyes. Everyone had that knowing look, Colleen thought, and there wasn't a damn thing for them to know. Maybe she was the only one feeling that knot in her stomach when they kissed. Maybe Neal didn't feel anything. Not a thought to dwell on.

"I want to do real work," Colleen told the woman briskly. "Fill sandbags or something. Not pass out refreshments."

But the woman shook her head and walked her to the door. "Honey, you can spend all afternoon filling about a dozen sandbags yourself, or you can pass lemonade and cookies out to all those people building the levee and give them the energy to make it another foot higher just from your smile."

Colleen sighed. "I don't think my smile can do that."

The woman looked at her. "Are you here to help us the way we need you or are you here for yourself?"

She said it too kindly to hurt, but Colleen felt taken aback. "To help you," she said slowly.

"The refreshment tent is a block west of here, just past the war memorial fountain," she said, then touched Colleen's arm to stop her. "We've got the Ottumwa football team out there, as well as our own squad. So if you get tired and need to dally a little bit, you do it around those boys in the green T-shirts, not the ones in red. We don't want our boys killing themselves trying to impress you."

Colleen laughed, echoing the glitter in the woman's eyes. "We want our team to win, I take it."

"Not that we aren't greatful to the Ottumwa boys for helping..."

Colleen laughed again and left, hurrying to the next block

and the refreshment tent. Some photographers were waiting outside and followed her to the tent, where she helped load a pickup truck with paper cups, huge coolers of lemonade and boxes and boxes of cookies. Only one photographer came along in the pickup to where the workers were reinforcing the levee, but Colleen didn't care. She wasn't here for publicity, but to work.

And work she did for the next zillion hours. She poured glass after glass of lemonade and passed them out to grinning, red-faced teenage boys, to giggling teenage girls, to moms and dads and all sorts of weary folk trying to save their town.

She'd started out wet but clean, but it was impossible to stay out of the mud so near the river. Her shoes and legs were soon splattered with it, then coated with it until it itched and ached. The bugs were pesty, and the rain was a constant. Someone gave her a John Deere cap to cover her hair, but it was soaked before too long. Yet, in spite of it all, she was having a wonderful time.

Every once in a while someone would come to take her picture, and whatever boys or girls or grandmothers were there at the time posed with her. Then, before the photographer could escape, they all had to find out who he was so they could get copies of the picture. Colleen began to see what the woman at the volunteer center meant—her presence was of value in itself. She could laugh and tease and play around with these people and give them a smile to take to the sandbagging. Maybe it wasn't saving animals, but it was good and worthwhile and a help. The river hadn't crested yet, so the town wasn't safe, but for today it was. And with her help.

By the time she went to the volunteer center at the end of the day, she felt better about herself than she had in ages. She had done something worthwhile that day. Something good.

Neal was waiting for her, and some of her bouyant good feelings fled when she saw his frown. "Brad and the others are leaving," he said.

"All of them?"

"Some of the media people are staying, but Brad wants us to go to Des Moines for the flight to Chicago."

Back to Chicago and what? Sitting around and feeling useless? "I'd rather stay," she said. "The river's supposed to crest the day after tomorrow. That's Friday. We'd still have a week before the convention."

He grinned. "Brad's going to have a fit."

And he did. "This is insane," Brad said. "I'm responsible for you two. I haven't gotten any hotel reservations anywhere near here. The security guards aren't staying."

"We'll be fine," Neal assured him.

"We don't need security guards here, anyway," Colleen said.

"Right," Neal agreed. "We're in Iowa. What's going to happen to us here?"


Colleen agreed to share a room with about a hundred other people that night. She and Neal would spend the night in the high school gym with the other nonlocal volunteers and the residents displaced by the floods. There wasn't an ounce of privacy, but it didn't bother her at all. She and Neal got their suitcases from the car and used the school locker rooms to shower and clean up. She felt fresh and alive.

She was amazed at the high spirits even among those whose homes had flooded. They would be sleeping on Red Cross cots and eating food other—luckier—local folks had brought, but they were embarrassingly grateful for all the help. And wanted her autograph.

"Makes you stop and think, doesn't it?"

Colleen looked up from signing the autograph and found Cooper at her side. "I thought you'd gone with the others," she said.

Cooper shook her head and reached into a pocket for a pack of cigarettes, then frowned. "I suppose smoking isn't allowed in here, is it?"

"Probably not." The other woman started toward the hallway, so Colleen fell in step beside her. Neal was playing bas-

ketball with some college kids from Illinois, and she felt at
loose ends. "So why are you still here?" she asked Cooper.

The woman shrugged. "Slow news week."

Colleen looked at the other woman's hand. Broken nails,
red skin. "You weren't filling sandbags, were you?"

Cooper shook her head as they passed some kids playing
tag down the long hallway, banging the metal locker doors as
they ran by. "Watching someone's brats while they were.
They screamed and cried and needed their diapers changed the
whole time. Now I know why I never married and had kids."

Colleen laughed. "I hope you didn't tell them about the
three-headed aliens."

"Nah, just about you and Steele. That put them right to
sleep."

"It ought to."

They went out the front door of the school and sat on the
steps. A wide overhang protected them from the rain, which
had slowed to a drizzle.

"Maybe it'll stop raining soon," Colleen said.

"It would help, but the crest'll come anyway." Cooper lit
a cigarette and leaned back on her elbows. "So what's with
you and the doc?"

Colleen stared into the darkness, waving aside something
with a persistent buzz. "Always out for the story, aren't you?"

"Actually, I'm not. It's bound to be too sweet to be interesting," the woman said. "You could do a lot worse, you
know."

"He's the king of the three-week romance."

"Is he?" Cooper took a long drag of her cigarette then
stubbed it out on the step next to her. "I have to give these
things up. It's been five weeks, you know. He ought to be
long gone, but he's not."

"We're under contract."

"He could still be here and be gone, you know. That look
in his eye hasn't changed. Gotten worse, if anything."

Colleen watched car headlights in the distance. "You're

dreaming. Trying to make your silly wedding prediction come true.''

"Am I?"

Something in Cooper's voice brought Colleen's gaze to her. "I'm not in the market, anyway," Colleen said. She swatted at a mosquito, then got to her feet. "I think I'll go in."

"Why not?" Cooper stood also, picking up her cigarette stub. "I could use a beer. You don't suppose they have any in here, do you?"

Colleen laughed. "No, I'm pretty sure that's forbidden in the school, too."

Cooper went in search of some other media people, and Colleen wandered to the gym where Neal had been playing basketball. They'd switched to soccer. He waved at her when she looked in, and she waved back, but didn't stay to watch. Cooper's words were bothering her. The reporter was wrong, of course. There was nothing in Neal's eyes. But what if there was?

"Ms. Cassidy? You wanna be on my team?" someone asked.

Colleen turned to find a handful of kids who looked like they were about ten to twelve years old. "What are you playing?"

"I betcha."

Colleen had never heard of the game, but it was better than stewing over Cooper's statement or the idea of love. The game turned out to be harmless. The other team bet you couldn't do some trick, and if you couldn't, your team lost a point. As long as they didn't bet her she couldn't fall in love, she was safe. Or should they bet her she could? It was too confusing.

"Betcha can't hop down the whole hall on one foot," someone challenged Colleen.

It almost killed her, but she did it, to her team's delight. "Betcha you can't tie your shoelaces blindfolded," she challenged.

They hopped and sang and recited the names of presidents,

did headstands and cartwheels and multiplication problems until they were exhausted—and tied.

"Betcha can't toss a penny into the drinking fountain from here," someone called.

The challenge went back and forth between the teams, with everyone missing until it was Colleen's turn. She stood straight, took aim and tossed the penny right into the water fountain for her team's victory.

But when she turned after exchanging high fives, she found Cooper in the doorway watching her. Smirking, was more like it.

"What?" Colleen asked with a frown.

"Tossing coins into fountains now?" she said.

"What are you—" Colleen stopped, something freezing in her heart. She looked at the girl next to her. Her T-shirt said Rome Elementary School. She looked at Cooper. "Don't tell me. This is Rome, right?"

"Two down and one to go," Cooper said with a laugh. "Better watch out for foggy nights in Casablanca." She turned to go.

"I'm not in love," Colleen called after her. "I'm not."

Cooper waved over her shoulder as she disappeared down the hallway.

"I'm not in love, either," one of the girls told her. "I think boys are stinky."

Colleen laughed, but she was worried. Terrified, was more like it.

# Chapter Twelve

"Sure you're up to this?" Neal asked. "You look beat."

Colleen pulled on the rubber boots someone had lent her as other volunteers stacked animal cages in a motorboat. They weren't going on the river itself, but rather over the lands already flooded, to rescue stranded pets.

"I had a little trouble sleeping last night," she admitted. "My roommate snored."

"Just one?"

"All right. About forty of them."

He smiled, and her soul lit up. Criminy, this was getting bad. Maybe she ought to stay and do refreshments again today instead of helping Neal with his animal rescue. But no, that would be running away and proving Cooper right. She was staying right here at Neal's side and not feeling a thing.

"You know how to run this motor?" one of the men asked Neal.

"It's like one I use each summer up at Eagle Lake."

"And you got your cellular phone?"

Neal held it in the air.

"You're set then," the man said and held the boat as Colleen and Neal climbed in.

It didn't rock as much as she feared. How long had it been since she was in a boat, anyway? She climbed over to sit on the seat just ahead of the middle of the boat, and looked back to see Neal start the motor. He looked weary and wet and slightly bedraggled and altogether perfectly wonderful. Like someone you could trust forever. That's why people were letting him go to their houses to try to find their pets. He wasn't a stranger to anyone, once he met them. He was a trusted friend in a matter of seconds. Cooper was right—she could do far worse. But that was if she was looking and if Neal was looking, which neither of them were.

A few little putt-putts gently rocked the boat, then Neal put it in gear, and they started over the flooded fields toward the first farmhouse. She turned to face the front. Much safer all around.

"Bet you're going to be glad to get back home to L.A.," he said. "This place is probably too small-town for you."

"I think it's nice," she said. "Very friendly."

"Very friendly can turn too friendly real fast."

She had liked it. There was something warm and reassuring about being here. "Good thing you don't live in a small town," she said. "If you feel that way."

Neal stopped talking after that, steering the boat over fairly still waters while she peered ahead for any submerged items that might cause them problems. They got to the first house with no trouble. There was no dry land around it, so Neal turned off the motor and let the boat drift close to the porch.

"What are we looking for here?" Neal asked.

But Colleen had already spotted the pooch, sitting atop a box on the corner of the porch. "Hey, sweetie, come on. Here, boy."

Before she had time to call him again, the dog came flying off the box, splashing through the few inches of water covering the porch floor and leaping into the boat with them. Neal helped her secure it in a large cage.

"Now if only they're all that easy," she said.

"You have the touch, it seems," he told her. "You call and men come racing."

"Oh, right," she said with a laugh, but his words set her heart wondering. If she called, would he come racing? Worse, would she want him to?

He started toward the next house. "I think I went to bed at ten o'clock last night," he said. "Can't remember the last time I turned in that early."

"The night before last, probably," she said.

"I meant before the tour started. It seems like I always had some party or dinner or something to go to. Ten o'clock seems like dinnertime, but then there's nothing much to do here, is there?"

"There's enough," she said. Why was he suddenly putting the place down? It had been his idea to come, and to stay. "I don't need a party every night, anyway. Pull around to the side yard. I think I see the dog up on the shed over there."

Sure enough, there was the dog on the shed roof. He was hard to coax down, but they managed and put him into a cage, then went to the third house. Neal stayed silent on the trip over, which was just as well. Colleen was having real trouble figuring out what his point had been.

He sounded almost like he was grumping, but he'd been the first one to pitch in and the last one to leave. Maybe he was hoping she'd see the downside of small towns and decide to go. Maybe he was getting to the end of his three-week romance with her and was tired of having her around. She felt a deadness in the pit of her stomach, like she had gone numb. Must be breakfast, because it couldn't have anything to do with Neal. His being tired of her would be distressing if Cooper had been even half right about Colleen's feelings—if Colleen had been in love with Neal. But Cooper was wrong. Colleen wasn't in love with anybody.

Colleen tucked her thoughts away and concentrated on their

job for the day. She wasn't out here to brood or to mope, but
to rescue pets, and that's all she was going to do.

The dog at the third house, a bedraggled-looking collie
named Daisy, was trapped on a tiny piece of land surrounded
by water. But fear made Daisy nervous, and that made her
snap. Somehow Neal's voice soothed her, though, until she
was brave enough to trust him. And trust was needed, for he
had to carry her from the patch of land to the boat. But Neal
had the knack of getting females to trust him, Colleen knew.
That was one way she would miss him.

"Have you ever been bitten?" Colleen asked as he got into
the boat.

"A few times, but nothing serious."

*Ever been bitten by the love bug?* she wanted to ask, but
knew enough to keep her mouth shut.

"What's next?" Neal asked.

"A cat," she replied. "At the next farmhouse."

While Neal steered the boat, Colleen filled the dish in
Daisy's cage with clean water. Not that the dog noticed. Her
eyes saw only Neal. No matter how the boat tilted or how he
moved, she watched him. Colleen sighed. She knew how that
felt, too, though she hoped she wasn't as obvious.

"The outbuildings are all underwater," Neal said as they
drew closer. "So the cat is either in the attic or—"

"—up in a tree," Colleen said, pointing at the cat as she
finished his sentence.

"Swell," Neal said. "Up where all the branches are thin."

"I'll go," Colleen said. She was not about to sit here with
Daisy the dog and watch him, all moony-eyed and entranced.
Sassy Mirabel was stronger than that.

"It's pretty tricky up there. You'd better let me—"

"No," she insisted. "I've climbed since I was a kid. When
I was eight years old, I played a jungle girl who'd been
brought up by chimpanzees. *Jungle Nursery.*"

"Ah, that old classic. You and your sidekick, Sammy."

She stopped, one leather glove half on. "You remember
it?"

"I said it was a classic."

"It had a two-week theater run."

"So theatergoers aren't very discriminating."

She wanted to ask him all sorts of questions, wanted to know how, why, when. All the things she knew better than to show an interest in. So he was an old movie fan. Or he had a good memory for trivia. It meant nothing except that she should be on his team if someone suggested playing board games. She pulled the gloves on with a decisive tug, then used an oar to position the boat better.

"Don't let us drift away," she warned, then pulled herself into the tree. She spotted the cat above her. "Come on, sweetie. We'll take you to your mommy."

"It's a boy," Neal called to her. "Orange tabbies are almost always male."

"So, can't I call a guy sweetie?"

"Only if you want to make me jealous."

Yeah, right. He was only trying to be nice. Pretending to flirt with her even though his heart wasn't in it anymore. She didn't bother to respond, just inched closer to the cat.

"Come on, boy," she said. "Come to Momma."

The cat had been making a lot of fierce noises, but once she got a hand on him he quieted and allowed himself to be taken down without the least bit of a fuss. Colleen put him in their last open cage, and Neal pointed the boat back to town.

"A full load for our first trip out," he said as they puttered along. "That's pretty good."

"We'll do better on our next trip."

"How can we do better than perfect?"

But better would be not being aware of him at all. Not getting chills down her spine every time he spoke. Not putting a "last time" label on everything they did.

Their next run was less than successful all the way around. They couldn't find the dogs at the first two houses, and they caught a cat only because he balked at going into the water. They did get a pygmy goat that wasn't on the list and two stray dogs that were trapped on the roof of an abandoned car, but she also got weak in the knees every time he spoke and ran a fever when he touched her helping her out of the boat.

"Maybe these dogs are the missing ones," Neal suggested.

"Maybe from somebody else's list." And what about her missing common sense? Would anybody have found that?

The last trip of the day was the worst. It wasn't the fact that each house they stopped at was deserted. Or that they got only one old dog, about ten million mosquito bites and almost overturned by a mailbox under the surface of the water. No, it was the worst because it was the last. They'd had a day together, and it was almost over. Just like the tour was almost over, and their friendship and the silly little jokes they shared. She sighed and checked her list.

"There's a cat missing at this last house," she said.

Neal grunted, steering the boat around a half-sunk log and up to the porch. It was under at least a foot of water. "I hope we find it before it gets too dark."

"Her, not it," Colleen said. "Her name is Sassy."

"I guess that means we're not leaving until we find her."

"You got that right. What if she's named after me?"

"I thought Sassy was your TV character, not you."

"Same thing."

She had started being Sassy more and more. Sassy was strong. Sassy didn't need anybody. Sassy relied only on herself. Oh, and on Love—Love Pet Foods, for their sponsorship. Never on the other love.

Neal tied the boat up and they got out. It was eerily still, just the gentle lapping of the water against the house. It might be a scene at a lake anywhere around the country, not a deserted house in a flood.

"I'll look upstairs," he said. The front door was partly open, and he pushed it open the rest of the way. "You take a quick look down here."

They waded through the water into the house. When Neal reached the stairs, he slogged up them while Colleen went into the family room. The television was half submerged, and the furniture was a total loss. Pillows floated on the surface along with letters and some newspapers. The far wall was covered with photos. Kids' school pictures. Old wedding portraits. Family portraits around the Christmas tree.

Colleen felt tears well up in her eyes. Which was so silly. She didn't have any of these things in her house and had told herself she didn't miss them. But now, seeing so many things ending, she was moved to tears. A houseful of memories lost. Her chance to make memories with Neal. They were all over.

Well, not necessarily all. Wiping her hand across her eyes, she hurried through the water and pulled all the photos off the wall. She could save a few things for someone. She shoved the paperback books on a high shelf against the back of the shelving unit, then piled the photos in front of them. They should be safe there.

"Any luck?" Neal called to her.

"I'm still looking."

She peeked into a bathroom, then went into the living room. Just a family Bible and somebody's well-loved teddy bear to rescue. A handmade quilt, some photo albums and an old baseball trophy. She stowed them all up high, then made her way to the kitchen. There wasn't much to rescue here. The food was spoiled, the dishes were washable and—

She turned, and there on top of the refrigerator was the cat. "You poor thing." Colleen climbed onto a stool. "How long—"

There wasn't one cat on top of the refrigerator—but four. A gray mama cat and three tiny, tiny gray and white babies. They had to be days old, at most. How long could the mother cat have kept them up there?

"It's a good thing we got here when we did," Colleen breathed. "Don't you worry. Big Sassy's going to take care of little Sassy."

She jumped off the stool and hurried into the hall—only to collide with Neal. His arms went around her to keep her from falling, and she grabbed at his shoulders to keep from slipping. For the longest moment, they stood there, staring at each other like they'd taken leave of their senses. Or just found them, for her senses were the only thing that seemed alive and alert. The smell of his aftershave. The sound of his breathing and the pounding of her heart. The feel of his hard muscles under her hands.

"Any luck?" he asked, his voice a whisper.

Or was it the rushing in her ears drowning his voice out? "Yeah, she's in the kitchen. But she's got three little babies. We need a box to carry her in."

Somehow they moved apart, but leaving his arms was like wrenching a piece of her off her body. She took a deep breath and got her emotions in line. Or tried to. Her heart kept making her see again that fire in Neal's eyes. Feel that electricity in his touch. Hear the way his breath caught and his voice stumbled. This wasn't a man at the end of his three weeks, was it?

But she didn't have any answers. Or none that she wanted to hear.

She followed Neal upstairs and found just the right box. Together, they loaded the cat and her babies into it and made it safely to town. While someone secured the boat, she and Neal handed over the rescued animals. Sassy's owner, an old lady in hip boots, was there waiting.

"Damn, that must be why Sassy was putting on so much weight all of a sudden," the old lady said as she peered into the box. Then grinned at Colleen. "Don't you get like me, so old I'm forgetting about love."

Colleen could hardly tell the woman she had vowed to stay away from love no matter what her age. "I'll try not to," she managed to say as the woman carried Sassy and her babies away.

"So Sassy was in love," Neal said as he helped Colleen from the boat.

Colleen tried not to notice the rush of fire where he touched her. The woman was wrong. The cat hadn't been in love, and neither was Colleen. "In heat, more likely," Colleen said. Both the cat and her. She just needed to get away from him and she'd cool down.

"You're so cynical," he said.

"A realist," she corrected, and slipped her rubber boots off. And someone who was determined to not follow in the love-struck footsteps of Daisy the dog or Sassy the cat.

Nick was up with the sun Friday morning and at the levee with the other workers taking their positions as the river crested. The day would be warm. Already the smell of the water and mud was getting stronger, but he didn't mind. It was good to be here doing something, even if it meant being alone with his thoughts. He wasn't avoiding Colleen, but he wasn't spending as much time with her, either—certainly not as much as he had yesterday, when they'd been out rescuing animals.

That had been a mistake. Or maybe this whole thing was a mistake. Every time he was close to her, every time he looked into her eyes, he had this terrible, terrible urge—to tell her the truth.

"Neal, there you are."

He turned. The sound of Colleen's voice tore at his soul. The sight of her walking along the muddy path next to the levee made his heart ready to explode. She was wearing shorts and a T-shirt. Her shoes were still flecked with yesterday's mud, but she looked so fresh and alive and sparkling. He felt like such a crud.

"Why'd you hurry out this morning?" she asked as she tucked her arm in his, stretching to give him a quick kiss.

A kiss he didn't deserve. "I couldn't sleep," he said. "Thought I'd come out and watch."

"Did you have breakfast?" she asked. "We've got coffee and sweet rolls at the refreshment tent."

"Uh, thanks," he said. "I ate." Actually, he couldn't remember if he had or not.

"Sure you did," she said, giving him a look. "Except that you were out here before breakfast was served. I'll get us both some."

He watched her walk away, knowing that one of these days

he'd be doing that for good. It made his gloom even darker. But it was the way it had to be. Once he got to Three Oaks, he'd be fine. Or as fine as he ever was.

He sat on a folding lawn chair that had been left at his watch position and stared at the wall of sandbags. It was a mess of mud and sand on this side, with water trickling through here and there, but the levee was holding. He had to do the same. Hold on to his plan until the end when they'd be parting and it wouldn't matter.

"I got cherry and apricot," Colleen said. "You can take your pick."

He jumped to his feet and took one of the cups from her. "Either is fine."

"You know, making a decision is quite gentlemanly at times," she said. "Sometimes a lady is tired of having that burden."

He smiled and reached for a sweet roll. "How about cherry?" he asked, looking at the red filling in the roll in his hand. "My favorite."

"Good." She took a bite of roll, a sip of coffee, then stared at the river. "They said it's cresting now."

"And holding so far."

"When will they know if it's safe?"

Safe? What was safe anymore? "Not really until the water goes down totally in a few weeks, but they'll have a good idea by this evening if it's likely to hold. Why don't you take this chair and I'll go get another one?"

He didn't wait for her agreement but hurried to the supply tent for another chair. He finished his coffee and roll, then found another chair. His heart was back to mere race speed by the time he got back, but that was normal around Colleen.

"I'm so glad most of the press is gone," she said. "I hated having our every move photographed. It was like the only reason we were here was for the publicity."

Her eyes were so trusting, so open and honest. All she was thinking about was the safety of the town and how she could be of help.

"Everybody's loved working with you," he said.

She laughed. "It's been an experience." She brushed aside some bugs. They were getting more active now that the sun was higher. "I've heard a number of people talk about how much you've done. I think they're surprised that you aren't just a pretty face. And that you don't seem that affected by your fame."

He took a deep breath, not able to hide from that clear vision anymore. "About that fame," he started, then stopped as her eyes watched him, waiting.

"Yes?" she prompted.

He took a deep breath. "There's some things about me you don't know."

That brought a laugh. The sound of a brook babbling over stones. The sound of tinsel being hung from Christmas trees. The sound of sun hitting a field of daffodils.

"There's lots you don't know about me," she said. "We could be here until winter, and I still would have things I hadn't told you."

"But this is important," he said.

She looked at him, smiling softly as she shook her head. "No," she said. "This is important." And she waved her hand at the levee. "What we've helped do here is important."

He wanted to go on. He wanted to tell her he was Nick, not Neal. That he wasn't famous or rich or king of the three-week romance. But he couldn't make the words come out.

So they sat and watched. They walked up and down the path. They talked to townsfolk, played cards with the woman watching the stretch next to them and posed for pictures for the local newspapers and TV stations. The day passed with agonizing slowness and only a few minor leaks. And no truth.

Nick grew more and more depressed as the sun traveled across the western sky. Another day closer to the end of the tour. Another day lived as a liar.

By evening, Nick was as depressed as he'd ever been, but everyone else seemed to be in a great mood.

"It's going to hold," someone cried.

"The water's gone down an inch," someone else shouted.

Whether any of it was true, the town was ready to celebrate. Nick tried to volunteer to take a turn watching the levee during the night, but they would have none of it. He and Colleen were celebrities, and along with the other volunteers from out of town, they were the guests of honor at the celebration. They were invited to the high school, where the cots had been moved into the classrooms and the gym hastily decorated for a party.

"I've been to lots of parties," Colleen said as she stood in the gym doorway. "But this has to be about the best."

Nick looked at the room, hung with streamers here and there, an occasional balloon bouquet tied to the back of a folding chair and a motley collection of local musicians trying to play something together. He knew just what she meant.

There air was charged with an excitement that couldn't be faked. The rows and rows of food covering the far tables had been prepared with love, and the people coming over to shake their hands meant every word of their thanks.

No matter what else happened on this tour, they had done something good. Something worthwhile. He began to relax, letting his overactive guilt recede for a time. No matter what happened later, he would have tonight with Colleen.

"Want a beer, Doc?" someone asked, and pressed one into his hand. "How 'bout you, Ms. Cassidy?"

"Thanks." He took a long drink and smiled at Colleen. "Well, it's been quite a trip, hasn't it?"

"One to remember," she agreed.

"With fondess, I hope," he said, and took another sip. "Hey, I think the band is finally getting it together. Want to try a dance?"

Colleen had no idea what time it was, but it sure seemed like the day had started a long time ago. She had to have danced with every man over the age of five, but it had been great fun. She watched as Neal made his way around the gym toward her. Her weariness began to slip away as a stronger feeling took its place. A tension, a hunger, a need to be close to him. To be wrapped in his arms and taken to paradise.

Gracious! She turned away to take a deep, steadying breath. She was getting moody because the tour was almost over. She hated change, that was all. Now, if she could hold on to that sensibleness, she thought, as Neal sank onto the lowest tier of the bleachers at her side.

"Getting tired?" she asked, resisting the temptation to run her fingers through his hair. She was not going to turn into one of those adoring animals they'd rescued.

"Not me," he said. "I'm just getting started." He watched the crowd partying for a few moments, then turned to her. "They moved our stuff into the chemistry lab. Not much room in it for the cots, they said, but you shouldn't be bugged by overzealous fans there."

Chemistry? That conversation ages ago with Brad came back to tease her, but she pushed it aside. She and Neal did have good chemistry, great chemistry, and nothing had blown up. That sweet tension in her stomach grew as she let her gaze slide over his arms so close to her, his legs so firm and tight. His lips just waiting to be kissed. At least their chemistry hadn't blown anything up yet.

"Everybody's been wonderful so far," she pointed out. "But I'm exhausted. Maybe you can point me in the right direction."

Instead of telling her where the room was, he took her there. The noise from the gym faded quickly as they moved away from it. Maybe sleep would be possible. But once Neal closed the door behind them, the room was unbelievably small.

She was suddenly aware of his height. Of the strength of his arms. Of the depth of his smile. Her stomach tightened, and she felt a delicious warmth spread through her. Maybe it was the beer she'd drunk, or the relief that the levee was holding. Or maybe it was just the way Neal had slid so unsuspectingly into her heart. Whatever, she had to keep her wayward thoughts in line.

She sat on a cot and kicked her shoes off. "I guess there's no reason to stay in Rome much longer," she said.

"I guess not." He was digging through his bag and stopped, looking around the room. "I've kind of enjoyed being here, though. It's been an experience."

"A new one for me," she said.

He looked at her, his eyes dark and mysterious yet filled with a fire she suddenly wanted to explore. "A new one?"

She waved at the room. "I've never slept in a chemistry lab."

Neal grinned. "Brad should be here," he said. "There's no end to the wonderful press releases he would think up."

"'The chemistry's right for Sassy and the vet.'"

"'Is it Love or is it just chemistry?'"

The words were funny, but somehow they seemed to burn rather than amuse. Time to change the subject. She got to her feet and started to unpack her bag, putting some toiletries on the nearest bench. It was a hard surface, scarred and chipped from years of use. A heart that was loved would be liked that, she thought. Scarred and chipped but still holding strong. Where had that thought come from?

"You take chemistry in school?" Neal asked. He had come up right behind her, and she felt his breath touch her neck.

She turned, almost facing him but not quite. Not quite daring to in her present mood. "I wasn't too good in it," she admitted. "Never could remember the elements and what was an acid and what was a base."

"Must have had a lot of surprises," he said.

"A few." She tried to breathe and found that his nearness seemed to make that harder. She tried to laugh and found it came out shaky and weak. "This tour has been fun," she said, hoping a change of subject would help. "I hadn't expected the time to go by as fast as it did."

"Me, neither."

He moved away then, but rather than relax, she felt a sense of loss. A disappointment that her heart was no longer dancing. The time had gone by fast. Too fast. They had less than a week left and then they would go their own ways.

She picked up some toiletries and the shorts and T-shirt she was going to sleep in and took them down the hall to the girls' washroom. One week, that was all. When the tour had started, it had seemed endless. Now it was almost over, and goodbyes were just around the corner.

She changed her clothes and brushed her teeth and did all the ordinary things she always did to get ready for bed, but the whole time the word *goodbye* kept echoing through her heart. What would she have when this was over but memories? And regrets?

She walked slowly down the hall, her bare feet making no sound on the cool tile floor. Faintly, in the distance, she could hear the sounds of the party, but it was like they were coming from another time, another world.

Memories were a part of everything she did, but regrets didn't have to be. She had found a special friend, a man she could trust, who wasn't using her for his own ends. Why not enjoy him the way a woman was supposed to enjoy a man?

She stopped in the doorway to the lab. Neal was stretched out on his cot, staring at the ceiling. Just looking at him set her blood on fire. She wanted to become a full woman in his arms. Tonight.

"Shall I turn the light off?" she asked.

"Sure, I'm ready."

"Are you now?" she asked with a laugh and flicked the switch.

The room was shadowed, but not completely dark. Not until she shut the door firmly behind her, holding in the button to lock it as she did so.

"Did I ever tell you I'm afraid of the dark?" she asked as she carefully made her way toward her cot.

"Does this mean we need to leave a light on?"

"No, I'll be brave."

She sat on the edge of her bed, uncertain how to bridge the gap of a few feet between them. Sassy would joke and tease while stripping her clothes off. Tanya would leap into bed with her man while holding the aliens at bay with her phaser. Lucinda would herd the man she wanted into a cave and then ride him until he was exhausted. Lola would—well, she wasn't doing anything Lola's way.

Maybe she should ask him. "Neal?"

"Yeah?"

But the darkness—as black as it was—wasn't thick enough to hide her uncertainty and worry. What if he refused? "Are you afraid of anything?" she asked in a rush.

She thought for a long moment he wasn't going to answer her, then he sighed. "I'm afraid that one morning I'll wake up and find myself leaning on someone."

She stared into the night. "You make it sound like love is something that creeps up on you unawares," she said. "I see it like an alien space monster. You keep your phaser at the ready, and it never comes close."

Neal laughed. "Okay, what's your fear? Your real one, I mean."

"Never knowing passion," she said.

"You seem pretty passionate to me," he said, though his voice had an odd quality.

"You know what I mean," she insisted. "I don't ever plan on falling in love, but that doesn't mean I don't want to feel passion."

"They don't go together for a lot of people," he said.

"And they don't have to for us," she said as she got to her feet. Those few steps seemed miles, but then she was sitting on the edge of his cot. "Make love to me, Neal."

"Make love?"

But even as he said the words, her hands had found his chest and were exploring that thick mat of hair. They were sliding over his shoulders, feeling the rock-hard muscles, finding that under all that strength he was trembling. And then she was lying at his side, her hands continuing their slow caress.

"Show me what passion is," she whispered. "Let's pretend just for tonight that love is more than just a pet food."

He grabbed her hand from its caress of his chest and brought it to his lips. "This is crazy," he said as he kissed each finger in turn. "Insane. We shouldn't be doing this."

"Why not?" His touch was magic. It made her heart race. Her voice was a breath in the darkness. "Who will it hurt?"

"You. Me. No one."

His voice was unsteady as he put his arms around her. His hands slid under her T-shirt slowly and tenderly, touching her breasts as if they might break—or disappear. But his stroke felt so wonderful,

"Why did you wait so long?" he murmured as he buried his face in her hair.

He rained down kisses along her neck, sending shivers all through her. She felt on fire yet so alive. She felt like she was flying. She felt like she was exploding. She felt her heart had never been so free.

"Maybe I was waiting for you," she said.

And she knew that in some way it was true. She had been waiting for him, for his honesty, his gentleness, his strength. She had somehow known that he would come someday, and that he would be worth the wait.

Their lips found each other, as if heart was talking to heart, soul to soul. They touched and pressed and breathed each other's air. She felt as if her body was on fire. Slow tongues of heat flicked at her, consuming her with an unhurried deliberateness.

His mouth grew harder, more demanding, and she answered in kind. She'd never known need like this. Never known that love could eat you alive and make you desire only to be touched and touched again.

His arms pulled her closer so that she was almost beneath him. She clung to him. She was drowning, and he was her only hope. Starving, and he was the only food. Lost, and he was the sun to guide her home.

She let her hands wander over his back, touching with wonder those muscles that held her so tightly yet so gently. And when she moved her caress to his shoulders, to his chest, she could feel his heart beneath his fingers. It was an echo of her own.

"This isn't right," Neal said with a gasp and tried to raise himself on his elbows. "There's things I should tell you."

"I don't want to talk," she said. She was able to slide under him, and laid feather-light kisses on his chest. Her lips could taste the salty flavor of him, could feel, too, the wild beating of his heart.

She let her hands roam lower, toward the hard and heavy shaft of his manhood. His breath was sharp as her hands went closer and closer. She pushed back his shorts, and she knew she was going to taste love.

"It seems to me you're overdressed," he said softly. His tongue touched her ear, tickling, teasing, stoking the fire.

"We can remedy that."

She slid off her shorts and pulled off her shirt with his help. Then it was as if a fuse had been lit. Neal's fever rose. His passion and hunger seemed insatiable. His hands seemed to touch every inch of her, his lips seemed to taste every memory, his heart seemed to call hers to join in its song.

She could not begin to tell where he began and left off. They were one in soul, one in heart and then, finally—with a gasp of wonder—one in body. He was part of her, part of her yesterday and today, part of her soul. She pulled him closer, farther, deeper and let the raging fire consume them both.

She wrapped her arms around him and moved with his rhythm, moved with his hunger as they searched for the light. Then suddenly the rhythm changed, the fire flared deeper, and the world exploded. She was with him as the stars spun around them, part of him as the heavens opened their arms and resting in his arms as they drifted to earth. Trusting with a newfound faith that there might be happiness in another.

"Some chemistry," she murmured into his shoulder.

"The best," he agreed.

* * *

There was a heavy pounding at the door, as if someone was trying to smash it in. Groggy with sleep, Colleen disentangled herself from Neal's embrace and pushed herself to a sitting position on the edge of the bed.

"Who's there?" she called.

"Is that you, Jenny Anne?" a voice answered. "Is that Jenny Anne Tutweiler?"

## Chapter Thirteen

"Damn it." Nick's mind was in a fog, and his head was throbbing from too much beer last night. He fumbled for his watch on the chair next to his cot, then gave up and squinted through the semidarkness at the clock on the wall. It was barely five-thirty.

"Open this door, Jenny Anne," someone was saying—it sounded like a young girl—in between pounding. "We need to talk to you."

"Just a minute, for crying out loud," Nick called, and grabbed his shorts. He turned on a small display light as he glanced at Colleen. "Somebody's got the wrong room—"

But the sweet and passionate lover of last night was gone, leaving a terrified woman in her place. Colleen was sitting on her cot. Her face was ghost white. She was deathly still.

"Colleen?" he said, fingers of fear clutching at his stomach. "It's okay, honey. Relax. It's just some kids screwing around."

But his words had no effect on her. Did he find out what

was wrong or get rid of the unwanted guests? Well, if he didn't get rid of them half the school would be in the room with them soon. He pulled on his shorts and hurried to the door. Did this kind of thing happen often to her? He should have insisted that Brad leave the security guards here. Damn, he'd never thought. More proof he never should have switched places with Neal. He jerked the door open.

"What the hell's going on out here?" he demanded in a harsh whisper.

Two people were in the hallway—a giant of a man and a young girl. The man was well over six feet tall with broad shoulders. His short black hair was streaked with gray, but his face wore a shy, childlike smile. The girl looked to be about ten, with green eyes and long red hair hanging in a single braid down her back. She looked Nick from top to bottom, her eyes almost sharp enough to draw blood before she turned to the darkness of the room.

"What's this, Jenny Anne?" she called. "One of them fancy-shmancy Hollywood guys?"

"Look, kid." Nick moved to fill the doorway more completely. He wished the townspeople hadn't been so considerate in putting Colleen and him by themselves. "I don't know who you're looking for, but she's not here. And if you don't leave, I'm calling the police."

The big man gasped. "Come on, Bobbie Anne." He tugged at the girl's sleeve. "We best be going."

"Don't worry, William," the girl said, her voice suddenly soft and soothing. "I'm handling this. Everything's cool."

"It would be a lot cooler if you and your friend would leave," Nick said.

Bobbie Anne spun on him. "I'm not leaving until I talk to Jenny Anne."

Nick stole a quick glance into the room. Colleen had put her clothes on, though there was an air of distractedness about her, a fear so strong he could almost smell it. What in the world was the matter?

"Look," Nick said, keeping his voice low. "You have the

wrong room. I don't know who you are looking for or why, but there's no Jenny Anne here. Now please—''

The girl pushed past him and charged into the room where Colleen sat so still and frightened. The girl was only a kid, but that didn't matter. She was in the wrong room, and the sooner he got her out, the sooner Colleen could relax.

Nick moved quickly. He wrapped his arms around Bobbie Anne and snatched her. "Now for the last time—''

Nick gasped. William had stepped forward and wrapped his thick arms around Nick and the girl, lifting them both into the air. The man had to be immensely strong—Nick was no lightweight.

Taking a deep breath, Nick tested his bonds. He could get free—if he dropped Bobbie Anne. Was it safe to do that? He looked at Colleen. She was on her feet, walking slowly toward them.

"Colleen," he said. "Run to the gym. Get help."

"You better not, Jenny Anne," the girl cried. "If you do, I'll tell everyone in the whole world who you really are. I'll tell them you ain't no princess and that you ain't nothin' but a hog farmer's daughter."

"Damn it," Nick snapped. "Her name's not Jenny Anne. So quit your nonsense and—''

"Yes, it is." Colleen's voice was low and soft, like the whisper of a dove, but it echoed in his ears like the bellow of a bull. "Jennifer Anne Tutweiler. That's my real name."

Nick sagged. All right. Lots of movie stars used fake names. It was no big deal. But it must be to Colleen, from the look on her face. This was not something she had expected. Not something she could talk about easily.

He didn't care about the bull of a man holding him or the loudmouthed girl. He suddenly wanted nothing more than to take Colleen in his arms and hold her until it was all right. Until the world went away and took her fears with it. All he wanted was to see that smile he loved so—

No, that wasn't right. That wasn't what he meant. It couldn't be love. He had vowed never again.

Noises from the hallway could be heard. People were approaching. Now, when he was more confused than he'd been in years and when Colleen looked like she'd rather die than have anyone else here.

"Hey, William," Nick called over his shoulder. "You know a good place to eat around here? I could really go for some pancakes."

"I can pour my own syrup, Bobbie Anne," William protested.

"Okay," the girl replied. "But don't put on too much."

Colleen watched in a daze, part of her sure this was all a dream and the other part hovering between shock and curiosity. She glanced at Neal, giving him a brief smile. This was not how she'd envisioned they'd spend the morning after they'd made such perfect love, but she was glad he was at her side. She felt stronger, more ready to find out what was going on.

The four of them were at a pancake house in Mount Pleasant—which was not where Bobbie Anne had wanted to go. But Nick had insisted. They were not going to Moms' Table in Trenton or the Country Kettle in Swedesburg, like Bobbie Anne had wanted. They were going to a larger town where they could be anonymous. Of course, he seemed to have forgotten that they couldn't be anonymous anywhere. They were getting their share of curious glances.

Or could it be Bobbie Anne and William were attracting the attention? William, who looked to be in his late forties, acted like a ten-year-old, while the ten-year-old girl acted like the adult. None of which mattered at the moment, though. Colleen wanted to know why they were looking for Jennifer Anne Tutweiler. And, more important, what they wanted from her.

Now that she was over her shock at being called by her old name, Colleen felt ready to tackle this strange pair of con artists. She took a sip of coffee and put the cup down.

"Anybody can start talking any time now," she said. When

that brought no response, she went on. "Maybe introductions are in order. We all seem to know who I am." She waved toward Neal. "He's Neal Sheridan."

"That TV doc?" Bobbie Anne asked, her mouth full of waffle. "Cool." She poked William. "Remember the show that taught you how to clean out Buster's ears? That's Neal here's show."

William looked at Neal. "Really? That was a good show. I keep Buster's ears real clean now."

"That's good," Colleen said, and made a pretense of eating some of her eggs. She wasn't letting some ten-year-old con artist get the better of her. "Now you two are..."

"Bobbie Anne and William," the girl said.

"Bobbie Anne and William what?" Nick prodded.

"Tutweiler," Bobbie Anne said.

"Tutweiler?" Colleen asked as she put her fork down. She had known it was a scam of some sort. "It couldn't be. That was my mother's name."

"Your daddy's, too." Bobbie Anne shoveled another load of food into her mouth. "We're sisters."

"No, we're not. My mother died twenty-five years ago."

The kid put a thoughtful expression on her face. "I guess we're half sisters. We had the same daddy."

Colleen fought the burst of bitterness that even a lying mention of the bastard brought forth. "Then we wouldn't have the same last name," she pointed out, her voice raw with anger at her father and this kid. She forced herself to nibble at her toast. "I have my mother's last name. My father never married her."

"Of course, he did," the girl said with a frown. "Your mom was Jane Higgins. They met in a park when Daddy was going to college in California."

Colleen stared at the girl, her anger refusing to die. This had to be some sort of scam because it couldn't be the truth. Oh, sure, her parents had met at a sit-in at a park in San Francisco, but they hadn't married. She would have known if they had.

"Where's your father now?" Neal asked Bobbie Anne. "It seems that he's the one to answer some of these questions."

Colleen put down her toast and held her breath, not wanting to hear the answer yet needing to. Maybe it was time to face up to the lying bastard once and for all.

"He died when I was seven," Bobbie Anne said.

Colleen let her breath out slowly. He was dead.

"He and Mommy were in a car accident in Des Moines," Bobbie Anne said.

"I miss him," William said. "He said I was a good hog farmer. As good as him."

All the hate and bitterness she'd stored up were useless. There was no one to spend it on. No one to turn her back on. She should dance for joy. She should laugh and sing and be glad. There was no reason to feel so cheated.

"You know, it might not be the same Tutweiler," Neal said as he reached over the corner of the table to take her hand. "It's not a real common name, but there have to be more of them around."

"We're the only ones in the county," Bobbie Anne said.

"There's more to the world than this county," Neal said.

"You think I'm lying but I'm not," the girl cried. "Amos Tutweiler was daddy to both of us. And Anne was his mommy's name. That's why the both of us have that as a middle name. Daddy gave it to us because he loved his momma."

Anne was her grandmother's name. She had her grandmother's name. Colleen felt a stinging in her eyes. Not that she believed any of this, of course. But the idea of having her grandmother's name was enough to rip something apart in her heart.

"Anne is a common name, too," Neal said. "Half of the women I know have Anne for a middle name."

"Not our Anne," Bobbie Anne said.

Our Anne. She was a part of someone. A part of something. Colleen blinked back the wetness and tried to stop the flow of tears that had come from nowhere. She was stronger than this.

Sassy never cried. Or Tanya. Or Lucinda. Of course, Lola had cried all the time. Neal sighed and handed her his handkerchief.

Bobbie Anne pushed her plate away, looking ready for a fight. "Our Anne is—"

"All right, already," Neal snapped. "That's enough for now."

"You're just all mad because Jenny Anne's crying," Bobbie Anne said, starting to cry herself. "But I don't care if she's sad. Daddy shed himself a ton of tears on account of her."

"Relax."

Colleen didn't know who Neal was talking to in those gentle tones, but her tears did slow and she was able to take a deep, steadying breath.

"Let's finish our breakfast," Neal said. "We'll talk about all this stuff later."

"She ain't a real princess, you know."

"Bobbie Anne, don't cry," William said, putting his arm awkwardly around the girl's shoulders. He sounded like he was ready to cry, too.

"How about if none of us cry anymore now?" Colleen said, her voice shaky but her smile determined. "If we're all done, we can go. This isn't the place to discuss any of this."

"We're going to Wayland." Bobbie Anne sounded grim. "The three of us."

Colleen was sure the girl wouldn't leave William behind, so it was obvious Neal was supposed to be the odd man out. Well, Colleen didn't know what the hell was going on with any of this, including their lovemaking last night, but she knew one thing.

"I'm not going anyplace without Neal," she said.

Bobbie Anne shrugged. "Fine with me. Miss Alma ain't never seen a Hollywood vet before."

Nick took one look at the semitrailer truck bearing down on them, braced himself against the dashboard, closed his eyes and almost welcomed the impact. The rush of air told him the truck had passed. He sighed.

He could not be in love. He would never be so stupid as to let that happen. There had to be some other explanation for the way his heart raced when he was near Colleen. For the way his every thought was of her. For the urge he had to pound senseless anyone who dared to make her cry.

Last night in her arms had been the purest, most wonderful night he'd ever had—but it didn't mean anything. Just that he was alive again. That he was a man with a man's desires. Love didn't come into it except as a pet food. He could come or go, stay or leave. Alone or together, none of it mattered. He was not in love.

A sudden jarring and a spray of gravel told him William had driven off the road again. With another jar, they were on the blacktop. Nick tried not to gasp. A nice, quick death that put him out of his misery would be preferred to slow and lingering.

They were shaking and rattling their way along a standard two-lane country road in a truck that belonged in a museum. William drove—if pointing the truck down the road could be called driving. Nick had offered to drive, as he had to the restaurant, but Bobbie Anne had refused. It was William's turn.

"We're almost there," William announced.

Nick looked ahead with something akin to resignation. Rising above the endless sea of corn was a cluster of buildings. A white farmhouse, a red barn and three or four smaller structures.

"My—" Bobbie Anne stopped. "*Our* great-grandpa George Tutweiler settled the farm in 1893."

"Really?" Colleen murmured.

Her hand found Nick's and squeezed tightly. And all of his brave declarations of independence blew out the window. Her touch left no doubt in his heart—this was more than some one-night stand. While he hadn't been watching, she'd laid siege to his heart and captured it. The only real question was what he could do about it.

Staying with her was out of the question. Loving meant losing. Maybe not today or tomorrow, but someday all too soon, and he was not going through that again. His feelings were an aberration. The sooner he was gone, the sooner his heart would heal. He would tell her the truth and end this. Oh, he wouldn't right now, not while she needed him. But soon.

As William drove closer, Nick could see the farmhouse better. It hadn't been all that white for a while now. In fact, all the buildings looked the worse for wear, badly needing repairs. A blind man could see they were desperate for money. That's what this all was leading to—they were going to hit Colleen up for money. Well, just let them try. She wasn't alone in all this.

William turned left onto a dirt lane and then left again, letting the truck roll to a stop in a yard filled with wildflowers.

"We're gonna see Miss Alma." Bobbie Anne squeezed out before them and jumped to the ground. "She's gonna be so surprised."

An elderly woman came onto the porch. No, she was more than elderly. She was bent like a gnarled old tree, with skin like cracked leather and fingers twisted by arthritis. Nick got out of the truck and helped Colleen down to the gravel driveway.

"Where you been off to, Bobbie Anne?" the woman scolded, then stopped her shuffling walk to stare at Colleen. "Lands sake, if it ain't Jenny Anne!"

"I told you I'd bring her, Miss Alma," Bobbie Anne said. She took Colleen's hand and pulled her toward the old woman. "Jenny Anne, this is Miss Alma. She's our cousin."

Nick walked to the porch behind Colleen and Bobbie Anne. From the rigid set of Colleen's shoulders, he knew she was tense. And when Miss Alma said nothing for the longest time, he was ready to bundle Colleen into the truck and tell William to take them back to Rome. But then he realized the old woman was crying. And so was Colleen.

"I never thought this day would come," the old woman finally said, wiping her eyes. "If only your daddy was here to see it."

Colleen's shoulders stiffened once more, and her tears stopped. "I would have liked that, too." Her voice had a touch of anger in it.

Bobbie Anne put Colleen's hand in Miss Alma's. "I'm going to take care of William," the girl said. "You set these two down in the parlor. I'll be in shortly."

Smiling, Miss Alma watched Bobbie Anne disappear into the house, dragging the giant man along. Then she turned toward them, her faded blue eyes sparkling.

"That child can be polite if she wants," she said. "But gracious didn't never come easy for a Tutweiler. Come on inside. Can I get you a glass of lemonade?"

"Not right now," Nick replied. "Thank you."

He was curious as to why William was led off before they all had a chance to talk. Were they afraid he wouldn't stick to the agreed-on story?

But he followed Colleen and Miss Alma into the parlor. The room had a worn look to it, but it was from age, not lack of care. Everything was shiny, with white handmade doilies on the arms and backs of the furniture. Colleen sat on the sofa, so he took a place next to her.

"I presume you know," Nick said, even before they were settled, "that Bobbie Anne and William came to our room this morning."

Miss Alma nodded. "She saw you on the TV last night. About how you helped save Rome from the flood. Weren't no stopping her once she saw Jenny Anne."

Nick settled on the sofa, trying to look relaxed. "I'm more concerned that Bobbie Anne inferred—"

"If that's another word for lying, you'd better start running right now, mister." Bobbie Anne dumped an old shoebox on the low table in front of the sofa before turning to Miss Alma. "I made William a sandwich and sent him out to work on the hay baler."

"You afraid he wouldn't remember his lines?" Nick asked. It was time somebody talked straight here.

Bobbie Anne came over to sit on the floor by the low table. "Talking about Daddy upsets William, and there ain't no need to," she said, and opened the shoe box. "I don't know if we can answer all your questions, Jenny Anne, but we can try. And you, Mr. Big Time Hollywood Vet, I'm going to make you eat your words."

Nick didn't know if he ate any words, but by the time the box was empty, all doubt seemed to have been washed from Colleen's mind. The box contained a marriage certificate for Jane Elizabeth Higgins and Amos Walter Tutweiler, and a birth certificate for Jenny Anne Tutweiler, as well as a few dozen photos.

"Amos and Jane met when he was a college student out in California," Miss Alma said. Bobbie Anne handed them a photo of two young people in a college setting. "Jane was needy right from the start, and Amos wanted nothing more than to take care of her. They fell in love, got married and soon discovered a baby was on the way."

Bobbie Anne gave them more photos. Same people, same look of love, different settings. Nick could feel Colleen reaching out to the people in the photos, wanting to see more than just their smiling faces.

"But then Grandpa had a stroke," the girl said. "Daddy came back here to see him. Your mom wouldn't come, Jenny Anne."

Miss Alma sighed. "Apparently, Jane grew up in Nebraska and hated it. She ran away to California the day after she graduated from high school and vowed she was never going back. She thought if she went with Amos, she'd be stuck here forever."

Bobbie Anne gave them some more photos. The happy couple with a tiny baby. "Daddy went to California after a few weeks, and he was there when you were born, but then Grandpa died."

Miss Alma took it from there. "Amos had to return home

for good this time.'' The old woman's voice was sad. "Molly, his mother, couldn't run the farm by herself, and then there was William. You've seen him. Sweet and gentle as can be, but needing someone to watch out for him. And that someone was Amos. He'd promised his father he would, and Amos wasn't one to break his promises.''

"Except for his marriage vows,'' Colleen said sharply, and put the photos down as if she couldn't bear to look at them. Nick took her hand.

"It wasn't Daddy's fault your mommy wouldn't come with him,'' Bobbie Anne snapped.

"They both were wrong,'' Miss Alma said, then sighed. "The young are so foolish. Jane had always known she wouldn't come back to the Midwest, and Amos always knew he would have to, but neither of them was really talking or listening. They both thought when the time came, they could change the other's mind. And even when Amos came back for good, he was certain Jane would follow.''

"But she divorced him and moved away and broke his heart,'' Bobbie Anne added.

Colleen said nothing. Her eyes were closed, and she was sitting ever so still. Her hold on Nick was strong, though.

"If Jane was telling it, this all might sound very different,'' Nick pointed out. He remembered all of Colleen's stories about her mother and her terrible need for love. "I would guess that they broke each other's hearts.''

"And both suffered,'' Miss Alma agreed.

"Along with Colleen,'' Nick reminded them.

"Why didn't he come for me after Mom died?'' Colleen asked suddenly.

Miss Alma shook her head. "He didn't know your mom died until years later. For a time, your mom would write to him, send him pictures and news of you. We all knew when you started in the movies. But the letters came so irregularly and never had a return address, he didn't know something had happened until three years after your mom had died. He went out then to get you, but you were living with some lady who had legal custody of you. Your mom had signed the papers and everything. There was nothing Amos could do.''

"He could have come see me," Colleen cried. "At least let me know he cared."

The old woman nodded. "By the time he knew that, he couldn't get close to you. He wrote to you a bunch of times, but I'm betting you never saw the letters."

Bobbie Anne had pulled some papers from the bottom of the box. "This is from some fan club, telling him how to be a member," she said, then handed Nick the letter. "This one's from some lawyer, telling him that his claims are being investigated. And this one's from a Trevor Madison. He says that it's always a pleasure to hear from your fans and that he will pass along Daddy's best wishes to you."

Nick took the papers and passed them to Colleen, but he was sure she wasn't reading them. Her hands were trembling, and tears were streaming down her cheeks. "If only I had known sooner," she said. "We might have had a chance to get to know each other."

"He would have liked that," Miss Alma agreed with a sigh.

Colleen's smile was dazzling in spite of her tears. "But I do have all of you now, and that's a miracle in itself."

Nick sat back, pulling himself away slowly. So this was her family. No matter what had happened in the past, they wanted her, and she appeared to want them. It seemed like a good time for him to pull out.

"There you are," Colleen said as she came into the barn. She'd been looking all over for Neal, and here he was, poking around in the engine of a tractor with William.

Neal looked up, wiping his hand on a rag. It was amazing how much at home he looked anyplace.

"You need me for something?"

It was a good question. But not one she wanted to answer yet. "Just wondering where you were," she said. "Miss Alma went to lie down. Bobbie Anne and I are going to start dinner soon, but I wanted to get out of the house for a bit."

She came over and tucked her arm around his, pulling him close as she stared into the engine. "What are you doing?"

"Fixing it," William said. "What are you making for dinner? Something fancy?"

She laughed. "Not me, I hardly ever cook. I live by myself and go out for meals when I want something special." The older man looked disappointed. "Hey, Neal here is the one who can cook. Wasn't there some special on different actors and sports figures who could cook?"

Neal looked uncomfortable as he shrugged. "I can make a great hot dog," he said.

"Hey, I like hot dogs," William said, then he frowned. "Did Bobbie Anne tell you about the taxes?"

"Yes, she did," Colleen said. "And you don't have to worry about them. I'll get it all straightened out."

While William looked relieved, Neal looked concerned. She smiled at him, took his arm and tugged him toward the door. "Want to go for a walk, handsome?"

"Watch out, Neal," William said with a laugh. "She's gonna start smooching."

"I'll be careful," Neal promised with a short laugh.

Arm in arm, they walked into the late afternoon sunshine. She didn't ever remember feeling so content. So at peace.

"So what are they hitting you up for?" Neal asked.

"Don't put it that way," she scolded. "You make it sound like highway robbery. They're family."

"Are you sure?" he asked, but his tone was less argumentative.

"Yes, I am." She stopped at the fence that enclosed the garden and leaned on the railings, looking at the vegetables. "There's tons of evidence. They aren't making anything up. And they didn't ask for anything, either."

Neal sighed, and she could read his skepticism.

"They didn't. I offered to help," she insisted. "Though I'm not sure how yet. Alma's son ran the farm until two years ago, when he died. Since then, they've done the best they can. They rented out most of the land to neighboring farmers and have tried to make do, but they're in danger of losing the place to back taxes."

"Even if you pay the taxes, I still don't see how they can keep going here," Neal pointed out. "There's only three of them, and it's not like any of them is equipped to be a full-time farmer. Maybe it's better to let it go and use the money to find them someplace else to live."

Colleen turned, leaning her back against the fence as she faced him. "That's what Cousin Otis wants. He's found a group home for William in Des Moines, a nursing home in Ottumwa for Alma, and he figures Bobbie Anne can go live with the Keokuk Tutweilers."

Neal sighed. "And why do I feel that they either have a ton of kids and don't need another one or have a baby and are looking for a built-in baby-sitter?"

She frowned. "Alma says that Myra and Wally are willing to come live here, but they're teachers, not farmers."

"So they turn the place into a group home for William, keep an eye on Alma and let Bobbie Anne go back to being a kid."

Colleen stared at him for a long moment. "You are a genius," she said, and threw her arms around him. "That is absolutely perfect."

She brought her lips to his—in celebration, excitement and wonder. It was the right way to express her happiness. The only way. Yet after the briefest of touches, he pulled away, leaving her empty and alone. Her heart hurt. She wanted to curl up in a ball and hide.

"Neal?" she said. "Is something wrong?"

"We need to talk," he said.

Something was. Fear ate a hole in her stomach, chilling her through and through. This was the best twenty-four hours in her whole life. She'd made love with Neal and then woke to find she had family. She wouldn't let him spoil it.

"We can't now," she said quickly. "I have to get back inside. Oh, and they want us to spend the night and I said okay. Could you drive to Rome and get our stuff after dinner? Unless you don't want to stay."

He looked at her, his eyes so sad and resigned. "No, that's fine. We'll stay. I'll be glad to get the stuff. Maybe when I get back we can talk."

"Sure," she said with a big smile. "When you get back." Or tomorrow. Or never.

Nick stared at the morning fog rolling over the yard and the road, covering everything in a fuzzy blanket of damp. Well, he had tried. He had tried hard, but Colleen was avoiding him. It was as if she knew what he wanted to say and didn't want to hear it.

He'd driven to Rome last night for their stuff, said their goodbyes to the townsfolk and given Cooper the slip. But when he got back, Colleen and William and Bobbie Anne had been in the middle of a game of cards. A long game of cards. A never-ending game of cards.

Then he'd suggested they go for a walk, but it turned out that Colleen was sleeping in Bobbie Anne's room and he was sleeping in William's—not that he minded that. One night of love was bad enough. Another and he'd never find the strength to leave. But Colleen had been determined that they all go to bed at the same time so no one got disturbed, which meant no walk and no talk. Which meant he spent another sleepless night as his guilt tossed him about.

Well, he wasn't waiting any longer. He couldn't. He had to get out of here. And if he had to blurt the truth in front Alma and the whole family, he would.

"You're up early," Colleen said, shutting the screen door softly behind her.

She walked to his side, her feet bare, her eyes still heavy with sleep. She looked so beautiful, it hurt. Leaning on the porch rail, she looked at the fog.

"Makes you feel like we're the only ones left in the world, doesn't it?"

He knew he should look at the yard, too, and make some

clever remark about the fog and the farm and the isolation, but he couldn't bear to take his eyes off her. In just a few short moments, all this would be lost to him. He had to savor it one last moment.

She turned to face him, half sitting on the railing. Her eyes were shadowed and serious. "What did you want to talk about?" she asked. "I didn't mean to put you off yesterday. It was just that it was such a special day. I couldn't bear to hear bad news."

He gazed into her eyes, looked so long and deep into them that he thought he was drowning in their depths, then he looked away. He could just make out the mailbox down by the road. A car drove by and someone put something in the newspaper tube under the mailbox.

"Paper's here," she said and started down the steps to the yard.

He followed her into the clammy dampness. "I'm not who you think I am," he said.

She laughed. "Are any of us?"

He took a deep breath and quickened his steps to catch up with her. He took her hand and turned her to face him. "No, I'm really not," he said. "I'm not Neal Sheridan. I'm his brother."

She stopped. The smile fled from her face, and she stared at him for half of forever. "His brother?" she repeated, then something came clear. The confusion in her face turned to anger. "His twin?"

He nodded. "I'm Nick."

"How long—" She stopped, swallowing what appeared to be growing anger, then looked away. "How long ago did you switch?"

He missed her eyes, her smile, the sight of her face, but that was for the best. Watching her soul shining in her eyes would only make his resolve weaken. "At the beginning of the tour," he said. "We switched so I could go on the tour instead of him."

"Why?" she asked. Her voice was tight. She was completely in control, not an emotion straying out.

Nick shrugged. It seemed so stupid now. So asinine. "For fun," he said, knowing how lame it sounded. He couldn't tell her about the ghosts in Three Oaks, or about Neal wanting the change, too. "Neal had such a glamorous life. I wanted to try it."

"You wanted to try it?" she said. Her voice was a whisper, but the tension had pulled it so tight, the words seemed shouted. "You were jealous of your brother's life and wanted to try it?"

He nodded, miserable. "I'm a vet, too," he said. "I've got a little practice in a small town. It's a good life. A good practice. But the kids that come to see the animal hospital all want to grow up to be Neal." He shrugged. "I did, too."

"Aren't you both a little old for these kinds of games?"

"I never meant to hurt you," he said. "I never meant to hurt anyone."

She laughed at that, though he heard no humor in the sound. "You didn't hurt me," she said. "I'm mad. I'm furious at myself for falling for your whole 'trust me' line."

He flinched as if she'd hit him.

"I'm annoyed that I forgot the truth about men and let one get the better of me," she went on. "But hurt? Not even close. Sassy Mirabel doesn't get hurt by men, and neither do I."

But he heard pain in her voice, and it tore him apart. "Colleen," he said and reached out. "You've got to believe me—"

She moved away as if his touch repelled her. "Believe you? I'm supposed to believe a lying, cheating bastard?"

He pulled back. "I'm...I'm sorry," he said, knowing it wasn't enough, but knowing it was for the best. For both of them. "I'll leave right away if you want, since things look good with your family here. But if you aren't sure about them, I'm willing to stay as long as you need me."

"As long as I need you?" she snapped. "You really take the prize. William can drive you into town when the fog clears."

She went to the road and pulled the newspaper from the box, then stopped as a car pulled up out of the mist. It was Cooper and her photographer.

Damn. What else could go wrong?

"Morning, all," Cooper called as the car slowed to a stop. "Lovely day, isn't it?"

"What are you doing here?" Colleen asked. She sounded tired, resigned to her fate.

"Just keeping tabs on my favorite people," Cooper said, and turned to look at Nick. "So, what's this I hear about you not being you?"

Nick couldn't move. He stared at the woman, unable to believe this was happening. She obviously had heard them talking, so what was the point of denying it? The story would be tomorrow's headlines. He had screwed up big-time. What would it do to Neal's reputation and his contract talks?

But Colleen was laughing. It was the sound of birds welcoming the dawn, of a gentle spring rain. There was no hint of her anger. "What are you talking about?" she asked. "How can Neal not be Neal?"

Cooper's eyes narrowed. "There's a rumor he's his twin brother," she said.

Colleen's smile brightened. "Oh, come on, Coop. You think a rookie could pass himself off as a celebrity and we wouldn't notice? I don't know about you, but I'm not that blind."

Cooper looked at Nick. "What do you have to say to all this?"

He looked from the reporter's hungry eyes to Colleen's wide-eyed innocent look. What did he do? Be honest and admit the truth and risk Neal's reputation? Or keep up the game and let Colleen continue thinking he was a lying, cheating crud? But did it matter what she thought of him? It was Neal's reputation that had to be safeguarded, not his.

"My mother raised me never to argue with a lady," he told Cooper.

"See?" Colleen said, her voice still light and laughing as she turned toward the old white house.

She disappeared into the fog, taking with him his ability to think or breathe or even exist. It was over. Done. Ended. Just like he wanted, and now he could relax.

"Want a ride to Chicago?" Cooper asked.

## Chapter Fourteen

"What a shame," Miss Alma said at breakfast. "He seemed like such a nice young man."

Colleen shrugged. Showed that she wasn't the only one fooled by the jerk. Good old Neal-Nick. She couldn't believe he went off with Cooper rather than have William drive him. Colleen could hardly wait to see the next issue of *Worldwide News*.

"He was just a Hollywood, Jenny Anne," Bobbie Anne assured her when they went to pick vegetables for the roadside stand out front. "You're better off without him."

No doubt about that. But still, as the numbness started to wear off she found an uncomfortable ache in her heart. How could he have lied like that? Saturday crawled by, and Sunday passed even slower. She needed to get busy; she had too much time on her hands.

"I'm going to call my lawyer first thing Monday morning," Colleen said during Sunday dinner. "I'll have him do some preliminary work for us. We need to get the taxes paid and then we'll go from there. I have to be in Chicago in a few days, but then I'll come back and we can get everything set.''

"You're such a saint," Miss Alma said. "I don't know what we'd be doing without you. You don't find many decent people anymore."

Colleen's smile froze at the word *decent*. Lisa! What if Lisa didn't know about the switch? Colleen got up from the table. "I need to make a call," she said. "I won't be long."

"Don't be calling the guy," Bobbie Anne called. "Tutweilers don't go crawling after nobody."

Neither did Sassy or Tanya or Lucinda. Lola crawled after everybody, but she was easy to overrule. Colleen used the phone in the parlor. Lisa answered on the first ring.

"Colleen," she cried. "I've been trying to reach you for weeks."

Her fear subsided into sympathy. "You know, then."

"They're scum."

"Vermin," Colleen agreed.

"Snakes, both of them."

"All of them," Colleen said. "They're no different than all men."

"That's for sure."

Silence came in and rode the line for a while, giving them both a breather. Colleen blinked back wetness in her eyes and went to stare out the window at the cornfields south of the house. Funny how empty everything seemed to be without the scum-vermin-snake around.

"You okay?" Lisa asked.

Colleen forced a smile into her voice and turned from the window. "Hey, I'm fine. So mad I could spit nails, but I'm fine."

"No emotional involvement?"

"Me? Emotionally involved? I know better than that." Colleen took a deep breath and chased away the mocking echoes in the air. "How about you? How are you doing?"

"Just great," Lisa said.

"No baby?"

"I'm rethinking that whole plan."

"Might be best," Colleen said. "Hey, I'm going to drop by one of these days. I have so much to tell you and I'd love to see—"

Damn. What was she thinking of? Neal-Nick lived in Three Oaks. There was no way in hell she was going anywhere near the place.

"Maybe we could meet in Chicago," Colleen said. "Or you could come out to L.A. for a vacation."

"Sounds great," Lisa said. "Men are jerks."

"Pond scum."

"We got a new batch of Love posters," Sara said as Nick came into the office. She put a package on the counter.

It was three weeks since he'd seen Colleen. Three weeks of misery. Three weeks of the familiar routine and friends. And a small sense of satisfaction that the whole town had guessed about the switch, but he'd fooled everyone on the road. Everyone but Colleen.

Did he dare look at the posters? Or should he give the whole lot to Sara for her kids? But Sara was watching, ready to report to his father, his grandmother and the whole town what his reaction was.

"Great," he said and picked up the package. "I can hardly wait to see them."

"Maybe you should give her a call," Sara said.

He tucked the package under his arm and trudged to his office. He couldn't win around here. If he didn't look at the posters, he was lovesick. If he did, he was lovesick. He was sick, that was true enough. Sick of everything.

He tossed the package onto his desk as Baron screeched his welcome from his cage in the corner. Nick barely heard the parrot as he sank into his chair. The trip had worked in one regard. The ghosts were gone. He could come into his office and see the reminders of Donna and think of her fondly, but she wasn't haunting him anymore. Maybe she had found some new guy up in heaven and was too busy to come back down here.

His eyes strayed to the Love package. Maybe he'd found somebody else and was letting Donna go.

Oh, what the hell. He picked up the package and ripped it open. There was a stack of posters rather than the usual one or two. He opened the first one. It was of him and Colleen in that park in St. Louis. She had the dogs, he had the cats. Love Is the Secret.

She had been so angry with him that day, and he'd been just as angry, feeling betrayed and used and plain stupid. She thought she had to be so strong always. She never seemed to understand that you could be strong and lean on someone, too.

The next poster was the one where she had a puppy and he had an older dog. She looked so beautiful, so fresh and alive and so ready to be kissed. He looked besotted with her. Love Can Make the Difference.

He pulled all the posters out and scattered them over the desk. She looked gorgeous and delectable and ever so vulnerable and needing care in every one of the posters. And he looked head over heels in love in every damned one.

All I Want Is Love.

Let's Live on Love.

Love Me Completely.

Love Puts the Wag in My Tail.

Was there a wag in his tail? Not since Colleen had walked away from him in that fog.

He got up and stalked to the window. He couldn't be in love. He'd vowed never to let that happen again. Sure, he'd grown to care for her, but love? He'd have to be an idiot to fall in love again. This hole in his heart was a reaction to the slower pace of life in Three Oaks. He couldn't sleep because he was so used to never sleeping. She was always in his thoughts because everybody and everything was always reminding him of her.

Guys in Cubs baseball hats. Ladies in sunglasses. Chicken for sale at the grocery store, for goodness sake. How was he supposed to forget her when there was a conspiracy to keep her in his mind?

Even if he did love her, he couldn't ask her to share his life here. Three Oaks was the Tyler kids riding their bikes down the street. Mo Richardson cutting his lawn. Heddy Gruber hanging clothes out on the line in her backyard. It was home, and being away had made him realize how much he missed it. He belonged in Three Oaks.

Not that they'd have to stay here all the time. Neal and Lisa were working things out. He and Colleen could, too. If there was something to work out.

"Wow, these are great," Sara said.

Nick turned. He hadn't heard her come in. "Yeah, they're pretty good."

"Pretty good?" Sara mocked. She picked one up. "They're great. Better than Neal's by a long shot."

"Well, having Colleen in the pictures does add something," Nick pointed out.

"It's not her and it's not you," she said. "It's the two of you together. Great chemistry."

"It exploded."

She looked at him. "It's supposed to. That's how love works."

"She doesn't love me, and that's not supposed to be how it works," he said.

"I don't think she knows what love is," Sara said. "You haven't read the *Worldwide News* articles I put in the scrapbook, have you?"

He shrugged. Why torture himself with the memories? "What am I going to find in them?" he asked. "That she loves me?"

She handed him the poster. Roughly, like she was losing patience with him. "You might be surprised."

He looked at the poster. Colleen with a woebegone looking dog and All I Need Is Love across the bottom. He pulled the scrapbook from a bottom shelf and opened it to the first story—Colleen at some Hollywood party talking about love.

* * *

"So who's the guest star for this show?" Colleen asked as she walked to the barn set.

"Wasn't it Tony Johnson?" the script girl said.

"I thought he got moved to next week's show."

The girl shook her head. "Beats me, then. All I know is somebody's playing Dr. Mitchell."

Colleen went into the barn and took her spot for the scene, standing on the straw-covered floor next to a steer—who was playing a bull—while the script girl took her place in the shadows. Colleen's costar, Jeff Donaldson, was already there, looking bored.

"Where's the guest star?" Colleen asked.

Jeff shrugged. "Getting his makeup checked. We're just supposed to start."

It didn't matter who else was in the show, anyway. Colleen didn't even care that some of these guests would pull in an even bigger audience for the show and help her get renewed for another year. The money was nice, especially since she was getting that group home started on the family farm and wanted to set up a trust fund for it. But her heart wasn't in the chase anymore.

It was just that she was still tired from the tour. Or that she picked up some bug in the Midwest.

The lights went on, flooding the barn with their intensity. "Places, everybody," the director called.

Colleen saw someone move behind one of the cameras and assumed it was the guest star. Everyone was there.

"Take one," the director called.

Colleen bent to look at the underbelly of the steer, carefully keeping her head turned to the camera. "I don't know, Zach. He looks fine. Maybe you need to play music to get him in the mood."

Jeff stepped closer to Colleen, reaching down to pull her to an upright position. "Enough of this nonsense, Sassy. What's going to get you in the mood?" He pulled her into his arms as a camera swung around to catch them from another angle.

Funny how his touch did nothing for her, Colleen thought.

Not that it ever had, but she'd never been so conscious of it before.

"Zach, not now," Colleen said. "You called me to check out your bull. I assumed you meant this animal."

He pulled her nearer as they both turned slightly for the close up. "I've missed you, Sassy," he said. "You've been avoiding me."

"That's all that this is about?" She pushed away from him, a look of distress on her face. "I called Frank Mitchell to come down here and consult on your case. What am I supposed to tell him?"

"Tell him you made a mistake. Tell him I made a mistake. Tell him you love me and can't be bothered with him." Jeff took a step toward her, then stopped.

Robby O'Neal came into the halo of lights. "Dr. Sassy," he said. "Doc Mitchell is here."

Colleen smiled toward the taped spot that represented the barn door. "Frank," she said as someone stepped into the lights. She stopped. It was Nick. Her smile died, and her heart skipped a beat. What was he doing here? "You aren't Frank."

"Cut," the director cried. "Colleen—"

"I'm Fred, his twin brother," Nick said, ignoring the stage directions. "We sometimes trade places."

"Cut! Come on, guys—"

Colleen's stupid heart leaped for joy at the sight of him. Part of her wanted to laugh and throw herself into his arms, but the rest of her knew better. "I hear a lot of jerks do that," she snapped. She had to ignore him. She had to pretend he didn't exist. "They think it's funny."

"No, they know it's pitiful, but sometimes it's the only way they can think of to escape."

His eyes pleaded with her for forgiveness, and for something else. An end to that weary look about him? She looked away, not about to let him anywhere close to her heart.

"Come on, Colleen," Jeff whined. "We've got to film this scene."

"They don't mean to hurt anybody," Nick went on.

She turned at that. "Who said they did?" Colleen asked, her voice as cold and distant as she could make it. "Somebody'd have to care in order to get hurt."

Figures scurried behind Nick. "Are the cameras still rolling?" a voice said. "*Worldwide*'ll pay a fortune for this."

Business as usual. They'd all go broke if she wasn't around to exploit.

"You care," Nick told her. "I know you do."

There was such a softness to his voice, such a pleading that she was almost tempted to let herself feel something. But that wasn't her. She looked at Nick and made a face. "Come off it, Doc. I'm Sassy Mirabel, and Sassy Mirabel doesn't care about anyone."

"No, you're Colleen Cassidy and Jenny Anne Tutweiler, and you're in love with me." He came a step closer.

"I'm what?" She felt a jolt of something race through her. Fear? Hope? Excitement?

"You heard me," he said. "It took me a long time to realize I was in love with you, but even longer to see that you loved me back."

She didn't care what she was feeling, she wasn't giving in. "You've been eating too much corn. I'm not in love with anybody."

"You said that love was dancing in the streets of Paris."

That's what he was basing his claim on? It was relief that washed over her, and maybe a touch of disappointment—not that she wanted him to be right about her feelings. Not really.

"Yeah, right," she said. "*An American in Paris.* We danced, not quite like Gene Kelly and Leslie Caron, but we danced."

"And throwing coins in a fountain in Rome."

"It was a penny in a drinking fountain, not *Three Coins in a Fountain,* but I'll give you that one, too."

"And—"

"And walking off in the fog in Casablanca," she finished for him. Triumphant that she'd won the argument. And suddenly so conscious of her loneliness. "Which I didn't do. We were never near a town named Casablanca."

He smiled and came a step closer. "You never said it had to be a town," he said. "You know what Casablanca means? White house. And you walked off into the fog toward an old white farmhouse after protecting my reputation."

What was he talking about? He wasn't allowed to twist things around like that. "That doesn't count," she cried.

"I never thought you were a coward," he said.

"I'm not, but you're cheating."

She stepped back from him, from the intensity of his smile and the knowledge in his eyes. From the love he wanted to offer her and she knew better than to take. So what if her heart was crying out for him? Her heart had never had any sense.

"Now, if you'll—" But she stepped back again as she started to speak, and hit the steer in the side.

It bellowed. It moaned. It turned and swung its head at her.

"Oh, damn," she muttered. It was all happening again. "Look out, Neal," she cried, then felt the shadows rush toward her and the floor rush up, then there was blackness.

It was quiet when she woke, and the bright lights were off. She was lying on a bale of hay to one side of the set. Sunlight streaming in the open door was the only light on the set. A few people were milling around, but Nick was the only one paying any attention to her. He was sitting on a folding chair next to her.

She sat up. The world wobbled, but not too badly. "Are you all right?"

He shook his head. "Another concussion," he said. "A bad one."

"Oh, no." Her eyes started to water. "I am so sorry. You should stay away from me. I only bring you trouble."

His smile was gentle as he took her hand in his. Little flickers of warmth eased through her from his touch, like he was bringing her back to life.

"The only concussion I have is from being hit over the head

by love," he said. "And the only way I can recover is to have you with me all the time, forever."

"It sounds like some kind of dementia to me."

"I do need nursing."

"Long-term?"

"Rest of my life," he said, and pulled her into his arms. "You will marry me, won't you?"

It felt so right, so much like being home. "We don't have to get married," she said. "We could just live together and see how it goes."

"No," he said. "Love doesn't see how it goes. Love is forever. I have to marry you because you're my heart, my soul. My reason for living. I tried life alone, and it was hell."

He bent and took her lips with his. It was heaven on earth. She felt like Sleeping Beauty, awakening from a sound sleep into beauty and wonder and life. A hunger ate at her, but it was a wonderful feeling, not something to worry about or deny. It was love.

"Why don't I feel scared?" she asked a moment later as she lay in his arms.

"Love makes it easy."

"Love is just a pet food," she reminded him.

"Don't kid yourself," he said. "Love is the food we all need for our souls."

# *Epilogue*

"This way, Colleen," a photographer shouted. "Look this way."

She turned, not to give them the full body pose they used to ask for, but so they could get Nick in the picture, too. Her Nick. Her Nick forever, she thought as she gazed at the ring so newly on her finger. The smell of her rose bouquet still sweetened the air around her.

"Dr. Sheridan, how about if you put your arm around your bride?" another photographer called.

Colleen looked at Lisa in her satin wedding dress, then at Nick and Neal in their tuxes.

"Which one?" they all asked together, then started to laugh.

The photographers laughed, too, and took pictures of Neal and Lisa in their wedding finery and one of Nick and Colleen before letting the couples wander among their wedding guests again.

Nick's grandmother hurried across the lawn. "You look

beautiful,'' she said before enveloping Colleen in yet another hug.

"Thanks."

"You're the best thing that's happened to Nick in a long time," his father said. "But you be sure to keep him in line."

Colleen laughed as Nick pulled her into his embrace. "I think we'll just move on along before someone fills your head with the wrong ideas."

Colleen smiled as he took her hand, leading her toward Lisa's shady front porch. She had never thought she could be so happy. The gardens were in spectacular late summer bloom and the weather was perfect—no hint of the rain that had been plaguing them on the tour. And Nick was at her side to stay. There was nothing else she could ever want. They climbed up on the porch and looked over the yard.

"This was the perfect place for the wedding," Colleen said with a sigh.

"You didn't mind sharing the spotlight?"

"Mind? Heavens, no, it was wonderful." She turned to smile at him. "I wouldn't have had it any other way."

He pulled her into his arms—a most delightful place to be—and kissed the tip of her nose. "Well, Mrs. Sheridan—"

"Jenny Anne." Bobbie Anne came bouncing up to join them. "You know what?"

Colleen loosened her hold on Nick a fraction to smile at her sister. "What?"

"Lisa said I could come stay on the farm for a visit when I'm on vacation."

"That's great. You'll have a wonderful time here."

The girl frowned as she climbed up to sit on the porch railing, obviously intending to stay awhile. "Yeah, but I don't know. I don't think I can leave William and Miss Alma."

"Then you should bring them along," Lisa said. "They're having a great time here now."

Colleen turned as her friend came up on the porch, arm in arm with Neal. Lisa looked as radiantly happy as Colleen felt.

And there was no doubt that was deep, deep love shining in Neal's eyes as he looked at her.

"You know what I just figured out?" Lisa asked, her eyes turning to Colleen. "We're sisters now."

"Hey, we are!" Colleen cried.

"Me, too?" Bobbie Anne asked.

"Yes, you, too," Lisa assured her. "Aren't we all the luckiest people around?"

Colleen pulled Nick's arms more tightly around her. "Haven't I always said, there's nothing like love?"

## Worldwide News Exclusive

July 4, Three Oaks, Michigan. Colleen Cassidy Sheridan and her sister-in-law, Lisa Hughes Sheridan, both gave birth to twins in a LaPorte, Indiana, hospital early this morning. Amanda Jane and Jessie Anne were born at 8:30 a.m. to Colleen and her husband, Dr. Nicholas Sheridan. Thomas James and Timothy John were born to Lisa and her husband, Dr. Neal Sheridan, ten minutes later, at 8:40 a.m. Both mothers and all babies are doing well and are expected to be released from the hospital by the end of the week.

Colleen Cassidy, the star of the hit TV show "Animal Life," has announced she will cut back her work schedule even farther to spend time with her family. Nicholas and Neal Sheridan, who divide duties on "Ask Your Vet," have announced that the filming of the show will move to a Chicago studio in the fall.

\* \* \* \* \*

# Take 2 bestselling love stories FREE

## Plus get a FREE surprise gift!

# HERE COME THE

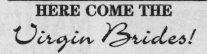

## *Virgin Brides!*

*Celebrate the joys of first love with more
unforgettable stories from Romance's
brightest stars:*

## SWEET BRIDE OF REVENGE
### by Suzanne Carey—June 1998 (SR #1300)

Reader favorite Suzanne Carey weaves a sensuously powerful
tale about a man who forces the daughter of his enemy to be
his bride of revenge. But what happens when this hard-
hearted husband falls head over heels…for his wife?

## THE BOUNTY HUNTER'S BRIDE
### by Sandra Steffen—July 1998 (SR #1306)

In this provocative page-turner by beloved author
Sandra Steffen, a shotgun wedding is only the beginning when
an injured bounty hunter and the sweet seductress who'd
nursed him to health are discovered in a remote mountain
cabin by her gun-toting dad and *four* brothers!

## SUDDENLY…MARRIAGE!
### by Marie Ferrarella—August 1998 (SR #1312)

RITA Award-winning author Marie Ferrarella weaves a
magical story set in sultry New Orleans about two people
determined to remain single who exchange vows in a mock
ceremony during Mardi Gras, only to learn their bogus
marriage is the real thing.…

*And look for more VIRGIN BRIDES in future months,
only in—*

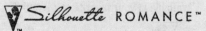

*Silhouette* ROMANCE™

Available at your favorite retail outlet.

# MARILYN PAPPANO

**Concludes the twelve-book series— 36 Hours—in June 1998 with the final installment**

# YOU MUST REMEMBER THIS

Who was "Martin Smith"? The sexy stranger had swept into town in the midst of catastrophe, with no name and no clue to his past. Shy, innocent Julie Crandall found herself fascinated—and willing to risk everything to be by his side. But as the shocking truth regarding his identity began to emerge, Julie couldn't help but wonder if the *real* man would prove simply too hot to handle.

For Martin and Julie and *all* the residents of Grand Springs, Colorado, the storm-induced blackout had been just the beginning of 36 Hours that changed *everything*—and guaranteed a lifetime forecast of happiness for twelve very special couples.

Available at your favorite retail outlet.

Silhouette

SPECIAL EDITION ®

™

*That's My Baby!*

Don't miss these heartwarming stories coming to
THAT'S MY BABY!—only from
Silhouette Special Edition®!

**June 1998     LITTLE DARLIN'**
**by Cheryl Reavis (SE# 1177)**
When cynical Sergeant Matt Beltran found an abandoned
baby girl that he might have fathered, he turned to compassionate foster mother Corey Madsen. Could the healing
touch of a tender family soothe his soul?

**August 1998   THE SURPRISE BABY**
**by Nikki Benjamin (SE# 1189)**
Aloof CEO Maxwell Hamilton married a smitten Jane Elliott
for the sake of convenience, but an impulsive night of
wedded bliss brought them a surprise bundle of joy—and a
new lease on love!

**October 1998 FATHER-TO-BE**
**by Laurie Paige (SE# 1201)**
Hunter McLean couldn't exactly recall fathering a glowing
Celia Campbell's unborn baby, but he insisted they marry
anyway. Would the impending arrival of their newborn
inspire this daddy-to-be to open his heart?

**THAT'S MY BABY!**
**Sometimes bringing up baby can bring surprises...**
**and showers of love.**

Available at your favorite retail outlet.

# MATERNITY LEAVE

## Coming September 1998

Three delightful stories about the blessings
and surprises of "Labor" Day.

### TABLOID BABY by Candace Camp

She was whisked to the hospital in the nick of time....

### THE NINE-MONTH KNIGHT
### by Cait London

A down-on-her-luck secretary is experiencing
odd little midnight cravings....

### THE PATERNITY TEST by Sherryl Woods

The stick turned blue before her
biological clock struck twelve....

*These three special women are very pregnant...and very
single, although they won't be either for too much longer,
because baby—and Daddy—are on their way!*

Available at your favorite retail outlet.

In **July 1998** comes

# ∽THE∾
# MACKENZIE
# FAMILY

by *New York Times* bestselling author

# LINDA
# HOWARD

## The dynasty continues with:

**Mackenzie's Pleasure:** Rescuing a pampered ambassador's
daughter from her terrorist kidnappers was a piece of cake for
navy SEAL Zane Mackenzie. It was only afterward, when they were
alone together, that the real danger began....

**Mackenzie's Magic:** Talented trainer Maris Mackenzie was
wanted for horse theft, but with no memory, she had little chance
of proving her innocence or eluding the real villains. Her only
hope for salvation? The stranger in her bed.

*Available this July for the first time ever in a two-in-one
trade-size edition. Fall in love with the Mackenzies for
the first time—or all over again!*

Available at your favorite retail outlet.

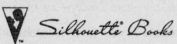

*Silhouette Books*